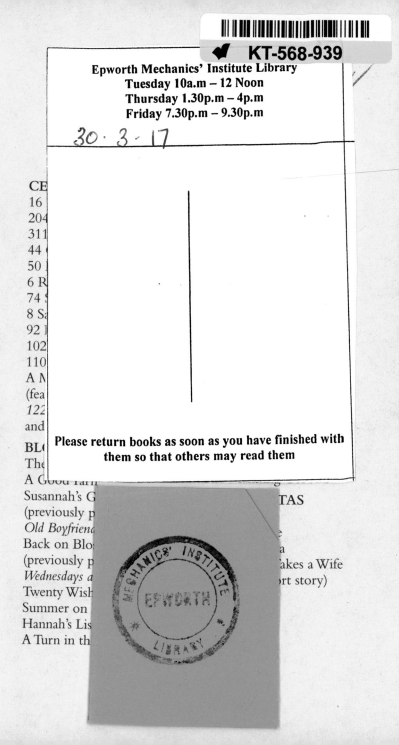

CE
16
204
311
44
50
6 R
74
8 S
92
102
110
A N
(fea
122
and

BL
The
A Good Far
Susannah's G   TAS
(previously p
Old Boyfriend
Back on Blo   a
(previously p   akes a Wife
Wednesdays a   rt story)
Twenty Wish
Summer on
Hannah's Lis
A Turn in th

Home for Christmas

DEBBIE MACOMBER

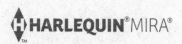

Published in Great Britain 2014
by Harlequin MIRA, an imprint of Harlequin (UK) Limited,
Eton House, 18-24 Paradise Road,
Richmond, Surrey, TW9 1SR

HOME FOR CHRISTMAS © 2014 Harlequin Books S.A.

The publisher acknowledges the copyright holder of the individual works as follows:

Return to Promise © 2000 Debbie Macomber
Can This Be Christmas? © 1998 Debbie Macomber

ISBN 978-1-848-45345-6

59-1014

Harlequin (UK) Limited's policy is to use papers that are natural, renewable and recyclable products and made from wood grown in sustainable forests. The logging and manufacturing processes conform to the legal environmental regulations of the country of origin.

Printed and bound by
CPI Group (UK) Ltd, Croydon, CR0 4YY

CONTENTS

Return to Promise

To
Ruthanne Devlin, Bookseller Extraordinaire,
for blessing my life with your friendship

One

Cal Patterson knew his wife would be furious. Competing in the annual Labor Day rodeo, however, was worth Jane's wrath—although little else was.

Bull riding had always enticed him, even more than bronc riding or roping or any of the other competitions. It was the thrill that got to him, the danger of riding a fifteen-hundred-pound bull, of staying on for eight seconds and sometimes longer. He craved the illusion that for those brief moments he was in control. Cal didn't do it for the trophy—if he was fortunate enough to take top prize—or to hear his name broadcast across the rodeo grounds. He was drawn by the challenge, pitting his will against the bull's savage strength, and yes, the risk. Jane would never understand that; she'd been raised a city girl and trained as a doctor, and she disapproved of what she called *unnecessary* risk. In her opinion, bull riding fell squarely into that category. He'd tried to explain his feelings about it, but clearly he'd failed. Jane still objected fervently whenever he mentioned his desire to enter rodeo competitions. Okay, okay, so he'd busted a rib a few years back and spent several pain-filled weeks recuperating. Jane had been angry with him then, too. She'd gotten over it, though, and she would again—but not without inducing a certain amount of guilt first.

He watched her out of the corner of his eye as she ushered their three-year-old son, Paul, into the bleachers. Cal dutifully followed behind, carrying eighteen-month-old Mary Ann, who was sound asleep in his arms. As soon as his family was settled, he'd be joining the other competitors near the arena. A few minutes later, Jane would open the program and see his name. Once she did, all hell would break loose. He sighed heavily. His brother and sister-in-law would be arriving shortly, and if he was lucky, that'd buy him a couple of minutes.

"Glen and Ellie are meeting us here, aren't they?" Jane asked, her voice lowered so as not to disturb the baby. His daughter rested her head of soft blond curls against his shoulder, thumb in her mouth. She looked peaceful, downright angelic—quite a contrast to her usual energetic behavior.

"They'll be here soon," Cal answered, handing Mary Ann to Jane.

With two children demanding her time and attention, plus the ranch house and everything else, Jane had cut back her hours at the medical clinic to one weekend a month. Cal knew she missed practicing medicine on a more frequent basis, but she never complained. He considered himself a lucky man to have married a woman so committed to family. When the kids were in school, she'd return to full-time practice, but for now, Paul and Mary Ann were the focus of her life.

Just then, Jane reached for the schedule of rodeo events and Cal tensed, anticipating her reaction.

"Cal Patterson, you *didn't!*" Her voice rose to something resembling a shriek as she turned and glared at him.

"Cal?" She waited, apparently hoping for an explanation.

However, he had nothing to say that he hadn't already said dozens of times. It wouldn't do any good to trot out his rationalizations yet again; one look told him she wouldn't be easily appeased. His only option was to throw himself on her good graces and pray she'd forgive him quickly.

"You signed up for the *bull ride?*"

"Honey, now listen—"

"Are you *crazy?* You got hurt before! What makes you think you won't get hurt this time, too?"

"If you'd give me a chance to—"

Jane stood, cradling Mary Ann against her. Paul stared up at his parents with a puzzled frown.

"Where are you going?" he asked, hoping he could mollify her without causing a scene.

"I refuse to watch."

"But, darling…"

She scowled at him. "Don't you darling me!"

Cal stood, too, and was given a reprieve when Glen and Ellie arrived, making their way down the long row of seats. His brother paused, glancing from one to the other, and seemed to realize what was happening. "I take it Jane found out?"

"You knew?" Jane asked coldly.

Ellie shook her head. "Not me! I just heard about it myself."

"Looks like Jane's leaving me," Cal joked, trying to inject some humor into the situation. His wife was overreacting. There wasn't a single reason she should walk out now, especially when she knew how excited their three-year-old son was about seeing his first rodeo.

"That's exactly what you deserve," she muttered, bending to pick up her purse and the diaper bag while holding Mary Ann tightly against her shoulder.

"Mommy?"

"Get your things," she told Paul. "We're going home."

Paul's lower lip started to quiver, and Cal could tell that his son was struggling not to cry. "I want to see the rodeo."

"Jane, let's talk about this," Cal murmured.

Paul looked expectantly from his father to his mother, and Jane hesitated.

"Honey, please," Cal said, hoping to talk her into forgiveness—or at least acceptance. True, he'd kept the fact that he'd signed up for bull riding a secret, but only because he'd been intent on delaying a fight. *This* fight.

"I don't want Paul to see you injured," she said.

"Have a little faith, would you?"

His wife frowned, her anger simmering.

"I rode bulls for years without a problem. Tell her, Glen," he said, nodding at his brother.

"Hey," Glen said, raising both hands in a gesture of surrender. "You're on your own with this one, big brother."

"I don't blame you for being mad," Ellie said, siding with Jane. "I'd be furious, too."

Women tended to stick together, but despite Ellie's support, Cal could see that Jane was weakening.

"Let Paul stay for the rodeo, okay?" he cajoled. "He's been looking forward to it all week. If you don't want him to see me compete, I understand. Just leave when the bull riding starts. I'll meet you at the chili cook-off when I'm done."

"Please, Mommy? I want to see the rodeo," Paul said again, eyes huge with longing. The boy pleaded his case far more eloquently than *he* could, and Cal wasn't fool enough to add anything more.

Jane nodded reluctantly, and with a scowl in his direction, she sat down. Cal vowed he'd make it up to her later.

"I'll be fine," he assured her, wanting Jane to know he loved and appreciated her. He slid his arm around her shoulders, hugging her close. But all the while, his heart thundered with excitement at the thought of getting on the back of that bull. He couldn't keep his gaze from wandering to the chute.

Jane might have been born and raised in the big city, but she was more than a little bit country now. Still, she'd probably never approve of certain rodeo events. Cal recognized her fears, and as a result, rarely competed anymore—hadn't in five years. But he expected Jane to recognize the impulses that drove him, too.

Compromise. Wasn't that what kept a marriage intact?

Jane had no intention of forgetting Cal's deceit, but now wasn't the time or place to have it out with her husband. He knew how she felt about his competing in the rodeo. She'd made her views completely clear, even before they were married.

Still, she'd acquiesced and held her tongue. She glanced at Cal's brother and sister-in-law and envied them. Their kids were with a baby-sitter, since they planned to attend the dance later that evening. Jane would've preferred to stay, too, but when she'd mentioned it to Cal, he'd balked. Dancing wasn't his favorite activity and he'd protested and complained until she dropped it.

Then he'd pulled *this* stunt. Men!

Partway through the rodeo, Paul fell asleep, leaning against her side. Cal had already left to wait down by the arena with the other amateur riders. As the time approached for him to compete, she considered leaving, but then decided to stay. Her stomach would be in knots whether she was there watching him or not. Out of sight wasn't going to put her risk-taking husband out of mind, and with Paul asleep, there was no reason to go now.

"Are you worried?" Ellie asked, casting her a sympathetic look.

She nodded. "Of course, I don't know what Cal was thinking."

"Who said he was thinking at all?" Ellie teased.

"Yeah—it's the testosterone," Jane muttered, wondering what her husband found so appealing about riding such dangerous beasts. Her nerves were shattered, and that wasn't going to change. Not until she knew he was safe.

"I was hoping you and Cal would come to the dance."

Ellie was obviously disappointed, but no more than Jane herself. She would've loved an evening out. Had she pressed the issue, Cal would eventually have given in, but it hadn't seemed worth the arguments and the guilt. Besides, getting a sitter would've been difficult, since nearly everyone in Promise attended the annual Labor Day rodeo—and Ellie had managed to snag the services of Emma Bishop, one of the few teenagers available for baby-sitting.

"Cal didn't want to leave the kids," she explained. There'd be other dances, other opportunities, Jane reassured herself.

"He's up next," Glen said.

"Go, Cal!" Ellie squealed. Despite her sister-in-law's effort to sound sympathetic, Jane could tell she was excited.

When Cal's name was announced, Jane didn't want to look but couldn't stop herself. Cal was inside the pen, sitting astride the bull, one end of a rope wrapped around the saddle horn and the other around his hand.

She held her sleeping child more tightly and bit her lower lip hard enough to draw blood. Suddenly the gate flew open and fifteen hundred pounds of angry bull charged into the arena.

Almost immediately, Glen and Ellie were on their feet, shouting. Jane remained seated, her arms around her children. "What's happening?" she asked Ellie in a tight, urgent voice.

"Cal's doing great!" she exclaimed. Jane could barely hear her over the noise of the crowd. Ellie clapped wildly when the buzzer went. "He stayed on!" she crowed. "So far, he's ahead!"

Jane nodded. How he'd managed to last all those seconds, she had no idea.

"Whew. Glad that's over." Ellie sank down next to Jane.

"My brother's got a real flair for this," Glen said to no one in particular. "He could've gone on the circuit if…" He let the rest fade.

"If he wasn't married," Jane said, completing his thought. Actually Glen's assessment wasn't really accurate. Her husband was a long-established rancher before she'd come on the scene. He'd competed in rodeos since he was in his teens, but if he'd been interested in turning professional, he would have done so when he was much younger. She had nothing to do with that decision.

"Glen," Ellie said, squeezing her husband's arm, "who's that woman over there?" Ellie was staring at a brunette standing near the fence.

"What woman?" Glen asked.

"The one talking to Cal."

Jane glanced over, and even from this distance she could see that the other woman was lovely. Tall and slender, she looked like a model from the pages of a Western-wear catalog in her tight jeans, red cowboy boots and brightly checked shirt. It was more than just her appearance, though. Jane noticed the confidence with which she held herself, the flirtatious way she flipped back her long brown hair. This was a woman who knew she looked good—especially to men.

"She seems familiar," Ellie said, nudging Glen. "Don't you think?"

"She does," he agreed, "but I can't place her."

"Apparently she's got a lot to say to Cal," Ellie added, then glanced apologetically toward Jane as though she regretted mentioning it.

Jane couldn't help being curious. The woman wasn't anyone she recognized. She wasn't the jealous type, but she found herself wondering how this Rodeo Princess knew her husband. It was clear that the woman was speaking animatedly to Cal, gesturing freely; for his part, Cal seemed more interested in what was happening with the rodeo than in listening to her.

Jane supposed she should be pleased by his lack of interest in another woman, and indeed she was. Then, as if aware of her scrutiny, her husband turned toward the bleachers and surveyed the crowd. His face broke into a wide grin when he caught her eye, and he waved. Earlier she'd been annoyed with him—in fact, she still was—but she'd never been able to resist one of Cal's smiles. She waved in return and blew him a kiss.

An hour later, after Cal had been awarded the trophy for the amateur bull-riding competition, they decided to leave. With Mary Ann in the stroller and Paul walking between them, they made one last circuit of the grounds before heading toward the parking lot. They passed the chili cook-off tent, where the winner's name was posted; for the first time in recent memory, it wasn't Nell Grant. But then, Jane understood that Nell had declined to enter this year.

It was near dusk and lights from the carnival rides sparkled, delighting both Paul and Mary Ann. Cal's arm was around Jane's shoulder as they skirted the area set aside for the dance. The fiddle players were entertaining the audience while the rest of the musicians set up their equipment. People had gathered around, tapping their feet in anticipation.

The lively music had Jane swaying to the beat. "I wish we were staying," she murmured, swallowing her disappointment.

"We'd better get home," Cal said, swinging his trophy at his side. "I didn't want to say anything before, but I'm about as sore as a man can get."

"Your rib?" she asked.

He grimaced, obviously in pain. "Are you going to lecture me?"

"I should," she told him. "But I won't. You knew the risks."

He leaned forward and kissed her cheek. "You're right. I did."

What really bothered her was that he'd known—and participated, anyway. He was fully aware that he could've been badly injured, or worse. And for what? She simply didn't understand why a man would do anything so foolish when he had so much to lose.

"I'm ready to go home," he said. "How about you?"

Jane nodded, but glanced longingly over her shoulder at the dance floor. Maybe next year.

The phone rang, shattering the night silence. Cal bolted upright and looked at the glowing digital numbers of the clock radio, then snatched the receiver from its cradle without bothering to check call display. It went without saying that anyone phoning at 3:23 a.m. was calling with bad news.

"Pattersons'," he barked gruffly.

"Cal? It's Stephanie."

Jane's mother. Something was very wrong; he could hear it in her voice. "What's happened?"

"It's…it's Harry," she stammered.

Jane awoke and leaned across the bed to turn on the bedside lamp. "Who is it?" she asked.

He raised one hand to defer her question. "Where are you?"

"At the hospital," Stephanie said, and rattled off the name of a medical facility in Southern California. "Harry's fallen—he got up the way he sometimes does in the middle of the night and…and he slipped."

"Is he all right?"

"No," his mother-in-law answered, her voice trembling. She took a moment to compose herself. "That's why I'm calling. His hip's broken—and it's a very bad break. He's sedated and scheduled for surgery first thing in the morning, but…but the doctors told me it's going to be weeks before he's back on his feet."

"Cal?" Jane was watching him, frowning, her hair disheveled, her face marked by sleep.

"It's your mother," he said, placing his hand over the mouthpiece.

"Is this about my dad?"

Cal nodded.

"Let me talk to her," Jane demanded, instantly alert.

"Stephanie, you'd better talk to Jane yourself," he said, and handed his wife the phone.

Cal was pretty much able to follow the conversation from that point. With her medical background, Jane was the best person to talk to in circumstances like this. She asked a number of questions concerning medication and tests that had been done, explained the kind of orthopedic surgery her dad would undergo and reassured her mother. She spoke with such confidence that Cal felt his own sense of foreboding diminish. And then she hesitated.

"I'll need to talk to Cal about that," she told her mother, voice dropping as though he wasn't supposed to hear.

"Talk to me about what?" he asked after she'd replaced the receiver.

Jane paused for a moment, then took a deep breath.

"Mom wants me and the kids to fly home."

"For how long?" The question was purely selfish; still, he needed to know. Being separated would be a hardship on all of them. He understood the situation and was willing to do whatever he could, but he didn't like the thought of being apart for any length of time.

"I don't know. A couple of weeks, maybe longer."

"Two *weeks?*" He hated the telltale irritation in his voice, but it was too late to take back the words.

Jane said nothing. Then, as though struck by some brilliant idea, she scrambled onto her knees and a slow smile spread across her face.

"Come with us," she said.

"To California? Now?" That was out of the question, but he hated to refuse his wife—especially after what he'd done at the rodeo. "Honey, I can't. Glen and I are getting ready for the bull sale this week. I'm sorry, but this just isn't a good time for me to be away."

"Glen could handle the sale."

What she said was true, but the prospect of spending two weeks at his in-laws' held little appeal. Cal got along with Jane's mother and he liked her father well enough, but Harry had a few annoying mannerisms. Plus, the two of them tended to become embroiled in ridiculous arguments that served no real purpose and usually went nowhere. Cal suspected it was more a matter of competing for Jane's attention. Jane was Harry's only daughter and he doted on her. Cal figured he'd be doing Harry a favor by staying away. Besides, what would he do with himself in a place like Los Angeles?

"Don't be so quick to say no," she said. "We could make this a family vacation. We always talk about going somewhere and it never happens." She knew he found it hard to leave the ranch for longer than a few days, but still…

"A vacation? I don't think so, not with your father laid up and your mother as worried as she is. Besides, Stephanie doesn't want *me* there."

"That's not true."

"It's not me she needs, it's you. Having the kids around will boost your father's spirits, and your mother's too. I'd just be in the way."

Jane's disappointment was obvious. "You're sure?"

He nodded. "You go. A visit with you and the kids will be the best thing for your parents, and you'll have a chance to connect with your friends, too. It'll do everyone good."

Still Jane showed reluctance. "You're *sure* you don't mind me being gone that long?"

"I'll hate it," he admitted, and reached for the lamp to turn off the light. Then he drew his wife into his arms.

Jane released a deep sigh. "I'm going to hate it, too."

Cal closed his eyes, already experiencing a sense of loss, and Jane and the children hadn't even left yet.

The next morning was hectic. The minute she got up, Jane arranged the flight to California and threw clothes, toiletries, toys and baby supplies into several suitcases. No sooner had she finished than Cal piled them all into the car, and drove his family to San Antonio. Paul was excited about riding in an airplane, and even Mary Ann seemed to realize there was adventure ahead.

As always, San Antonio International Airport was bustling with activity. Cal quickly ushered Jane and the kids to the airline's check-in counter, where they received their boarding passes.

Kneeling down to meet his son at eye level, Cal put both hands on Paul's shoulders. "You be good for Mommy, understand?"

His three-year-old nodded solemnly, then threw his small arms around Cal's neck, hugging him fiercely.

"I'm counting on you to be as much help to your grandma and grandpa as you can," Cal added. He felt a wrenching in his stomach. This would be the first time he'd been apart from his children.

"I will," Paul promised.

Cal noted that his son's "blankey" was tucked inside his backpack, but said nothing. The blanket was badly worn. It'd been a gift from Jane's friend Annie Porter, and a point of contention between him and Jane. Cal didn't like the idea of the boy dragging it around, and Jane felt that Paul would give it up when he was ready.

Cal stood and scooped Mary Ann into his arms. His

daughter squirmed, eager to break free and explore this wonderful new place.

"I'll phone often," Jane said when he'd kissed her.

"We'll talk every day."

Saying goodbye to his family was even more difficult than Cal had expected.

"I'm going to miss you," he murmured.

"Two weeks will go quickly."

"Right," Cal agreed, but at the moment those weeks loomed before him in all their emptiness.

Juggling two bags and clutching both children, Jane moved toward the security area. Cal left then, waving to the kids as he did. The feeling of emptiness stayed with him, and he knew he'd let his wife down. He should have gone with her; it was what she'd wanted, what she'd asked of him, but he'd refused. He shook his head miserably. This wasn't the first time he'd disappointed Jane.

As he made his way to the parking garage, Cal couldn't shake his reaction to seeing his wife leave. He didn't want to go to California, and yet he regretted not being on that plane with his family.

"You heard about Jane, didn't you?" Dovie Hennessey asked her husband. Frank had just come home from the golf course, where he'd played eighteen holes with Phil Patterson, Cal's father.

Frank, who'd retired three years earlier from his position as sheriff, nodded and walked straight to the refrigerator. "According to Phil, Cal drove Jane and the kids to the airport yesterday morning."

"I give him a week."

Frank turned around, a pitcher of iced tea in his hand. "A week before what?"

"Before Cal comes into town."

"Why?"

Exasperated, Dovie rolled her eyes. "Company. He's going to rattle around that house like a lost soul."

"Cal? No way!" Frank argued, pouring himself a glass of tea. "You seem to forget he was a confirmed bachelor before he met Jane. I was as surprised as anyone when he decided to marry her. Don't get me wrong. I think it was the smartest thing he ever did...."

"But?" Dovie said.

"Cal isn't any stranger to living alone," Frank continued, sitting down at the kitchen table with his tea and the newspaper. "He did it for years. Now, I know he loves Jane and the kids, but my guess is he's looking forward to two weeks of peace and quiet."

Dovie couldn't help herself. *Peace and quiet?* Frank made it sound as though Cal would welcome a vacation from his own family. Hands on her hips, she glared at her husband. "Frank Hennessey, what a rotten thing to say."

He glanced up from his paper, a puzzled expression on his face. "What was so terrible about that?"

"Jane and the children are *not* a nuisance in Cal's life," she said in a firm voice. "Don't you realize that?"

"Now, Dovie—"

"Furthermore, you seem to be implying that he's going to *enjoy* having them gone."

"I said no such thing," Frank insisted. "Cal's going to miss Jane—of course he is. The children, too. What I was *trying* to say is that spending a couple of weeks without his wife might not be all that bad." Flustered and avoiding her eyes, Frank rubbed his face. "That didn't come out right, either."

Dovie suppressed a smile. She knew what he meant, but she liked giving him a hard time once in a while— partly because he made it so easy. He'd remained a bachelor for the first sixty years of his life. Like Cal, he'd grown accustomed to his own company. He and Dovie had been involved for more than ten years, but Frank had resisted marriage until Pastor Wade Mc-Millen had offered a solution. They became husband and wife but kept their own residences. In the beginning, that had worked beautifully, but as time passed,

Frank ended up spending more and more nights with her, until it seemed wasteful to maintain two homes. Since he'd retired, Dovie, who owned an antique store, had reduced her hours. They were traveling frequently now, and with Frank taking a role in local politics and becoming active in the senior citizens' center, why, there just weren't enough hours in a day.

Patting her husband's arm as she passed, Dovie said, "I thought I'd make Cal one of my chicken pot pies and we could take it out to him later this week."

Frank nodded, apparently eager to leave the subject behind. "Good idea." Picking up his paper, he claimed the recliner and stretched out his legs. Almost immediately, Buttons, the black miniature poodle they'd recently acquired, leaped into Frank's lap and circled a couple of times before settling into a comfortable position.

"Nap time?" Dovie asked with a grin.

"Golf tires me out," Frank said.

Dovie laughed. "I meant the dog."

"I guess we're both tired...."

"You promised to drive me to the grocery store," she reminded him, although she was perfectly capable of making the trip on her own. It was the small things they did together that she enjoyed most. The ordinary domestic chores that were part of any marriage.

"In a while," Frank said sleepily, lowering the newspaper to the floor.

True to his word, an hour later Frank sought her out, obviously ready to tackle a trip to the supermarket. Once they got there, he found a convenient parking spot, accompanied her inside and grabbed a cart. Dovie marched toward the produce aisle, with Frank close behind.

"Do you have any idea what Cal would enjoy with his chicken pot pie?" she asked.

"I know what *I'd* enjoy," Frank teased and playfully swatted her backside.

"Frank Hennessey," Dovie protested, but not too loudly, since that would only encourage him. She didn't really mind, though. Frank was openly affectionate, unlike her first husband. Marvin had loved her, she'd never doubted that, but he'd displayed his feelings in less overt ways.

"Who's that?" Frank asked, his attention on a tall brunette who stood by the oranges, examining them closely.

It took Dovie a moment to remember. "Why, that's Nicole Nelson."

"Nicole Nelson," Frank repeated slowly, as though testing the name. "She's from Promise?"

"She lived here a few years back," Dovie said, taking

a plastic bag and choosing the freshest-looking bunch of celery.

"She seems familiar. How do I know her?" Frank asked, speaking into her ear.

Which told Dovie that Nicole had never crossed the law. Frank had perfect recall of everyone he'd encountered in his work as sheriff.

"She was a teller at the bank."

"When?"

"Oh, my." Dovie had to think about that one. "Quite a few years ago now…nine, maybe ten. She and Jennifer Healy were roommates."

"Healy. Healy. Why do I know that name."

Dovie whirled around, sighing loudly. "Frank, don't tell me you've forgotten Jennifer Healy!"

He stared back at her, his expression blank.

"She's the one who dumped Cal two days before their wedding. It nearly destroyed the poor boy. I still remember how upset Mary was, having to call everyone and tell them the wedding had been canceled." She shook her head. "Nicole was supposed to be Jennifer's maid of honor."

Frank's gaze followed the other woman as she pushed her cart toward the vegetables. "When Jennifer left town, did Nicole go with her?"

Dovie didn't know, but it seemed to her the two girls had moved at about the same time.

"Cal was pretty broken up when Jennifer dumped him," Frank said. "Good thing she left Promise. Wonder why this one came back…"

"Mary was worried sick about Cal," Dovie murmured, missing her dearest friend more than ever. Cal's mother had died almost three years ago, and not a day passed that Dovie didn't think of her.

"I know it was painful when it happened, but Jennifer's leaving was probably a lucky break for Cal."

Dovie agreed with him. "I'm sure Jane thinks so, too."

Frank generally didn't pay much attention to other women—unless they were potential or probable felons. His noticing Nicole was unusual enough, but it was the intensity of his focus that perturbed her.

She studied Nicole. Dovie had to admit that the years had been kind to Jennifer's friend. Nicole had been lovely before, but immature. Time had seasoned her beauty and given her an air of casual sophistication. Even the way she dressed had changed. Her hair, too.

Dovie saw that her husband wasn't the only man with his eye on this woman; half the men in the store had noticed her—and Nicole was well aware of it.

"I'll admit she looks attractive," Dovie said with a certain reluctance.

When Frank turned back to her, he was frowning. "What is it?" she asked.

"What she looks like to me," he said, ushering her down the aisle, "is trouble."

Two

Cal had lived in this ranch house his entire life, and the place had never seemed as big or as empty as it did now. Jane hadn't been gone a week but he couldn't stand the silence, wandering aimlessly from room to room. Exhausted from a day that had started before dawn, he'd come home and once again experienced a sharp pang of loneliness.

Normally when Cal got back to the house, Paul rushed outside to greet him. The little boy always launched himself off the porch steps into his father's arms as if he'd waited for this moment all day. Later, after Cal had showered and Jane got dinner on the table, he spent time with his daughter. As young as Mary Ann was, she had a dynamic personality and persuasive powers to match. Cal knew she was going to be a beauty when she grew up—and he'd be warding off the boys. Mary Ann was like her mother in her loveliness, her energy…and her stubborn nature.

Cal's life had changed forever the day he married Jane. Marriage wasn't just the smartest move of his life, it was the most comfortable. Being temporarily on his own made him appreciate what he had. He'd gotten used to a great many things, most of which he hadn't stopped to consider for quite a while: shared passion, the companionship of the woman he loved, a family that gave him a sense of purpose and belonging. In addition, Jane ran their household with efficiency and competence, and he'd grown used to the work she did for her family—meals, laundry, cleaning. He sighed. To say he missed Jane and the kids was an understatement.

He showered, changed clothes and dragged himself into the kitchen. His lunch had been skimpy and his stomach felt hollow, but he wasn't in the mood to cook. Had there been time before she left, Jane would have filled the freezer with precooked dinners he could pop into the microwave. When they heard he was a temporary bachelor, Frank and Dovie had dropped off a meal, but that was long gone. The cupboards were full, the refrigerator, too, but nothing seemed simple or appealing. Because he didn't want to bother with anything more complicated, he reached for a bag of microwave popcorn. That would take the edge off his hunger, he decided. Maybe later he'd feel like putting together a proper meal.

The scent of popped corn enticed him, but just as he was about to start eating it, the phone rang. Cal grabbed the receiver, thinking it might be Jane.

"Pattersons'," he said eagerly.

"Cal, it's Annie."

Annie. Cal couldn't squelch the letdown feeling that came over him. Annie Porter was his wife's best friend and a woman he liked very much. She'd moved to Promise a few years back and had quickly become part of the community. The town had needed a bookstore and Annie had needed Promise. It wasn't long before she'd married the local vet. Cal suddenly remembered that Jane had asked him to phone Annie. He'd forgotten.

"I just heard about Jane's dad. What happened? Dovie was in and said Jane went to stay with her parents—she assumed I knew. I wish someone had told me."

"That's my fault," Cal said. "I'm sorry, Annie. On the way to the airport, Jane asked me to call...." He let his words drift off.

"What happened?" Annie asked again, clearly upset. Cal knew she was close to Jane's parents and considered them a second family.

Cal told her everything he could and apologized a

second time for not contacting her earlier. He hoped Annie would see that the slight hadn't been intentional; the fact was, he hated making phone calls. Always had.

"I can't imagine why Jane hasn't called me herself," she said in a worried voice.

Cal had figured she would, too, which only went to show how hectic Jane's days must be with her parents and the children.

"Jane will be home in a week," Cal said, trying to sound hopeful and reassuring—although a week seemed like an eternity. He pushed the thought from his mind and forced himself to focus on their reunion. "Why don't you give her a call?" he suggested, knowing Annie was going to want more details. "I'm sure she'd love to hear from you."

"I'll do that."

"Great… Well, it's been good talking to you," he said, anxious to get off the phone.

"Before we hang up, I want to ask you about Nicole Nelson."

"Who?" Cal had no idea who she was talking about.

"You don't know Nicole? She came into the bookstore this afternoon and applied for a job. She put you and the bank down as references."

"Nicole Nelson." The name sounded vaguely familiar.

"I saw you talking to her at the rodeo," Annie said,

obviously surprised that he didn't remember the other woman.

"Oh, yeah—her," he said, finally recalling the incident. Then he realized how he knew Nicole. She'd been a good friend of Jennifer's. In fact, they'd been roommates when he and Jennifer were engaged. "She put my name down as a job reference?" He found that hard to believe.

"She said she's known you for quite a while," Annie added.

"Really?" To be fair, Cal's problem hadn't been with Nicole but with Jennifer, who'd played him for a fool. He'd been too blinded by his first encounter with love to recognize the kind of woman she was.

"Nicole said if I had any questions I should ask you."

"It's been years since I saw her—other than at the rodeo last week." He did remember talking to her briefly. She'd said something about how good it was to be back in Promise, how nice to see him, that sort of thing. At the time Cal had been distracted. He'd been more interested in watching the rodeo and cheering on his friends than in having a conversation with a woman he'd had trouble recognizing. Besides, Jane was upset with him, and appeasing her had been paramount. He'd barely noticed Nicole.

"Did she list any other personal references?" he asked.

"No, I told her you and the bank were the only ones I needed," Annie said. "So can you vouch for her?"

"I guess so. It's just that I haven't seen her in a long time. We—"

"You went out with her?"

Leave it to Annie to ask a question like that. "No, with her best friend. We almost got married." No need to go into details. Jennifer had taught him one of the most valuable lessons of his life. The worth of that experience could be measured in the pain and embarrassment that resulted when she'd callously canceled the wedding. He could've lived with her breaking their engagement—but why did she have to wait until they were practically at the altar?

"I talked with Janice over at Promise First National about her job history," Annie said, interrupting his thoughts. "She doesn't have anything negative to say about Nicole, but if you're uncomfortable giving her a recommendation…"

"Oh, I'm sure Nicole will do a great job for you."

The length of Annie's hesitation told him he hadn't been very convincing.

"Nicole's fine, really," he said. He didn't actually remember that much about her. She always seemed to be there whenever he picked up Jennifer, but he couldn't say he *knew* her. Years ago she'd been a sweet kid, but that was the extent of his recollection. He certainly couldn't dredge up anything that would prevent her from selling books. He'd never heard that she was dishonest or rude to customers, and those were things that would definitely have stuck in his mind. It was difficult enough to attract good employees; Cal didn't want to be responsible for Annie's turning someone down simply because he had negative feelings about that person's friends.

"I was thinking of hiring her for the bookstore."

"Do it," Cal said.

"She seems friendly and helpful."

"Yeah, she is," Cal said, and glanced longingly at the popcorn.

"Thanks, Cal, I appreciate the input."

"No problem." He didn't know what it was about women and the telephone. Even Jane, who had a sensible approach to everything and hated wasting time, could spend hours chatting with her friends. He sighed. Thinking about his wife produced a powerful yearning. Nothing seemed right without her.

"I'll call Jane tomorrow," Annie was saying.

"Good plan." He checked his watch, wondering how much longer this would take.

"Thanks again."

"Give Nicole my best," he said, thinking this was how to signal that he was ready to get off the phone.

"I will," Annie promised. "Bye, now."

Ah, success. Cal replaced the receiver, then frowned as he attempted to picture Nicole Nelson. Brown hair— or blond? He hadn't paid much attention to her at the rodeo. And he couldn't imagine what would bring her back to Promise. Not that she needed to justify the move, at least to him. His one hope was that Annie wouldn't regret hiring her.

Mary Ann's squeal of delight woke Jane from a deep sleep. She rolled over and looked bleary-eyed at the clock radio and gasped. Ten o'clock. She hadn't slept this late since she was in high school. Tossing back the covers, she grabbed her robe and headed out of the bedroom, yawning as she went.

"Mom!" she called.

"In here, sweetheart," her mother said from the kitchen.

Jane found the children and her mother busily playing on the tile floor. Mary Ann toddled gleefully, chasing a beach ball, intent on getting to it before her brother. Because he loved his little sister, Paul was letting her reach it first, then clapping and encouraging her to throw it to him.

"You should've woken me up," Jane said.

"Why? The children are fine."

"But, Mom, I'm supposed to be here to help you," she protested. The last week had been difficult. Taking Paul and Mary Ann away from home and the comfort of their normal routines had made both children irritable. The first night, Mary Ann hadn't slept more than a few hours, then whined all the next day. Paul had grown quiet and refused to talk to either grandparent. The children had required several days to adjust to the time change, and with the stress of her father's condition, Jane was completely exhausted.

"You needed the sleep," her mother said.

Jane couldn't argue with that. "But I didn't come all this way to spend the whole morning in bed."

"Stop fussing. Paul, Mary Ann and I are having a wonderful visit. If you intend to spoil it, then I suggest you go back to bed."

"Mother!"

"I'm the only grandma they have. Now, why don't you let us play and get yourself some breakfast?"

"But—"

"You heard me." Stephanie crawled over to the lower cupboards, then held on to the counter, using that as leverage to get up off the floor. "I'm not as limber as I once was," she joked.

"Oh, Mom…" Watching her, Jane felt guilty. She gathered Mary Ann into her arms, although the child immediately wanted to get down. Paul frowned up at her, disgruntled by the interruption.

"I called your father, and he's resting comfortably," her mother informed her. "He wants us to take the day for ourselves."

"Dad said that?" He'd been demanding and impatient ever since Jane had arrived.

"He did indeed, and I intend to take him up on his offer. I promised the kids lunch at McDonald's."

"Dad *must* be feeling better."

"He is," her mother said. "By the way, Annie phoned earlier."

"Annie?" Jane echoed. "Is everything all right at home?"

"Everything's just fine. She wanted to know how your father's doing. Apparently no one told her—"

"I asked Cal to tell her. I meant to phone her myself, but…you know how crazy it's been this week."

"I explained it all, so don't you worry. She'd already talked to Cal, who apologized profusely for not phoning her. She sounds well and has some news herself."

Jane paused, waiting, although she had her suspicions.

"Annie's pregnant again. She says they're all thrilled—Annie, Lucas and the children. She's reducing her hours at work, hiring extra help. It was great to chat with her."

"A baby. That's wonderful." Annie was such a good mother, patient and intuitive. And such a good friend. Her move to Texas had been a real blessing to Jane.

Thinking about Promise made Jane's heart hunger for home. A smile came as she recalled how out of place she'd once felt in the small Texas town. She'd accepted a job in the medical clinic soon after she'd qualified. It wasn't where she'd wanted to settle, and she'd only taken the assignment so she could pay off a portion of her huge college loans. The first few months had been dreadful—until she'd become friends with Dovie, who'd introduced her to Ellie.

This was networking at its finest. Soon afterward, Ellie and Glen had arranged Jane's first date with Cal. What a disaster that had been! Cal wasn't the least bit interested in a blind date. Things had changed, however, when Cal and his brother and Ellie had started to teach her how to act like a real Texan. When she'd decided to take riding lessons, Cal had volunteered to be her teacher.

Jane had never meant to fall in love with him. But they were a good match, bringing out the best in each other, and they'd both realized that. Because of Cal, she was a better person, even a better physician, and he reminded her often how her love had enriched his life. They were married within a year of meeting.

After the children were born, Jane felt it necessary to make her career less of a priority, but she didn't begrudge a moment of this new experience. In fact, she enjoyed being a full-time wife and mother—for a while—and managed to keep up her medical skills with a few weekend shifts.

Annie, too, had found love and happiness in their small town. The news of her latest pregnancy pleased Jane.

"Have you connected with Julie and Megan yet?" her mother asked.

Along with Annie, Julie and Megan had been Jane's best friends all through high school. Julie was married and lived ten minutes away. Megan was a divorced single mother. Jane hadn't seen either woman in three years—make that four. How quickly time got away from her.

"Not yet," Jane told her.

"I want you to have lunch with your friends while you're home."

"Mom, that isn't necessary. I'm not here to be entertained."

"I don't want you to argue with me, either."

Jane grinned, tempted to follow her mother's suggestion. Why not? She'd love to see her friends. "I'll try to set something up with Julie and Megan this week."

"Good." Her mother gently stroked Jane's cheek. "You're so pale and exhausted."

The comment brought tears to her eyes. *She* wasn't the one suffering pain and trauma, like her father, who'd broken his hip, or her mother who'd had to deal with the paramedics, the hospital, the surgeon and all the stress.

"I came here to help *you,*" Jane reiterated.

"You have, don't you see?" Her mother hugged Paul. "It's time with my precious grandbabies that's helping me cope with all this. I don't see nearly enough of them. Having the grandkids with me is such a treat, and I fully intend to take advantage of it."

Jane went to take a shower, looking forward to visiting with her friends. She missed Cal and Promise, but it was good to be in California, too.

The metallic whine of the can opener made Cal grit his teeth. This was the third night in a row that he'd eaten soup and crackers for dinner. The one night he'd fried himself a steak, he'd overcooked it. A few years back he'd been a pretty decent cook, but his skills had gotten rusty since his marriage. He dumped the ready-to-heat soup into the pan and stared at it, finding it utterly unappetizing.

Naturally he could always invite himself to his brother's house for dinner. Glen and Ellie would gladly set an extra plate at their table. He'd do that when he got desperate, but he wasn't, at least not yet. For that matter, he could call his father. Phil would appreciate the company, but by the time Cal was finished with his chores on the ranch, dinner had already been served at the retirement home.

Come to think of it, he was in the mood for Mexican food, and no place was better than Promise's own Mexican Lindo. His mouth had begun to water at the mere thought of his favorite enchiladas, dripping with melted cheese. He could practically taste them. Needing no other incentive, he set the pan of soup inside the refrigerator and grabbed his hat.

If he hurried, he'd be back in time for Jane's phone call. Her spirits had seemed better these past few days. Her father was improving, and today she'd met a couple of high-school friends for lunch.

Soon Harry would be released from the rehab center, and once his father-in-law was home, Jane and the children would return to Texas. Cal sincerely wished

Jane's father a speedy recovery—and his good wishes weren't entirely selfish, either. He liked Harry Dickinson, despite their long-winded arguments and despite his father-in-law's reservations about Jane's choice in a husband. He'd never actually said anything, but Cal knew. It was impossible not to. Still, Harry's attitude had gotten friendlier, especially after the children were born.

Promise was bustling when Cal drove up Main Street. All the activity surprised him, although it shouldn't have. It was a Thursday night, after all, and there'd been strong economic growth in the past few years. New businesses abounded, an area on the outskirts of town had been made into a golf course, and the city park had added a swimming pool and tennis courts. Ellie's feed store had been remodeled, but it remained the friendly place it'd always been. She'd kept the wooden rockers out front and his own father was among the retired men who met there to talk politics or play a game of chess. The tall white steeple of the church showed prominently in the distance. Cal reflected that it'd been a long time since he'd attended services. Life just seemed to get in the way. Too bad, because he genuinely enjoyed Wade McMillen's sermons.

The familiar tantalizing aroma of Texas barbecue from the Chili Pepper teased his nostrils, and for a moment Cal hesitated. He could go for a thick barbecue sandwich just as easily as his favorite enchiladas, but in the end he stuck with his original decision.

When he walked into the stucco-walled restaurant, he was immediately led to a booth. He'd barely had time to remove his hat before the waitress brought him a bowl of corn chips and a dish of extra-hot salsa. His mouth was full when Nicole Nelson stepped into the room, eyed him boldly and smiled. After only the slightest pause, she approached his table.

"Hello, Cal." Her voice was low and throaty.

Cal quickly swallowed the chip, almost choking as he did. The attractive woman standing there wasn't the kid he'd known all those years ago. Her jeans fit her like a second skin, and unless he missed his guess, her blouse was one of those designer numbers that cost more than he took to the bank in an average month. If her tastes ran to expensive clothes like that, Cal couldn't imagine how she was going to live on what Annie Porter could afford to pay her.

"Nicole," he managed. "Uh, hi. How're you doing?"

"Great, thanks." She peered over her shoulder as though expecting to meet someone. "Do you have a couple of minutes?"

"Uh...sure." He glanced around, grateful no one was watching.

Before he realized what she intended, Nicole slid into the booth opposite him. Her smile was bright enough to make him blink.

"I can't *tell* you how wonderful it is to see you again," she said.

"You, too," he muttered, although he wasn't sure he would've recognized her if he'd passed her in the street.

"I guess you're surprised I'm back in Promise."

"A little," he said. "What brings you to town?" He already knew she'd made the move without having a job lined up.

She reached for a chip, then shrugged. "A number of things. The year I lived in Promise was one of the best of my life. I really did grow to love this town. Jennifer and I got transferred here around the same time, but she never felt the way I did about it."

"Jennifer," he said aloud. "Are you still in touch with her?"

"Oh, sure. We've been friends for a lot of years."

"How is she?"

"Good," Nicole told him, offering no details.

"Did she ever marry?" He was a fool for asking, but he wanted to know.

Nicole dipped the chip in his salsa and laughed lightly. "She's been married—and divorced—twice."

"Twice?" Cal could believe it. "Someone told me

she was living with a computer salesman in Houston." He'd heard that from Glen, who'd heard it from Ellie, who'd heard it from Janice at the bank.

"She married him first, but they've been divorced longer than they were ever married."

"I'm sorry to hear that." He wasn't really, but it seemed like something he should say.

"Then she met Mick. He was from Australia."

"Oh," he said. "Australia, huh?"

"Jennifer thought Mick was pretty hot," Nicole continued. "They had a whirlwind courtship, got married in Vegas and divorced a year later."

"I'll bet she was upset about that," Cal said, mainly because he didn't know how else to comment.

"With Jennifer it's hard to tell," Nicole said.

The waitress approached the table and Nicole declined a menu, but asked for a margarita. "Actually I'm meeting someone later, but I saw you and thought this was a good opportunity to catch up on old times."

"Great." Not that they'd *had* any "old times." Then, because he wasn't sure she knew he was married, he added, "I could use the company. My wife and kids are in California with her family for the next week or so."

"Oh…"

He might've been wrong, but Cal thought he detected a note of disappointment in her voice. Surely she'd known he was married; surely Annie had told her. But then again, maybe not.

"My boy's three and my daughter's eighteen months."

"Congratulations."

"Thanks," Cal said, feeling a bit self-conscious about dragging Jane and the kids into this conversation. But it was the right thing to do—and it wouldn't hurt his ego if the information got back to Jennifer, either.

Nicole helped herself to another chip. "The last time Jennifer and I spoke, she said something that might interest you." Nicole loaded the chip with salsa and took a discreet nibble. Looking up, she widened her eyes. "Jen said she's always wondered what would've happened if she'd stayed in Promise and you two *had* gotten married."

Cal laughed. He knew the answer, even if Nicole and Jennifer didn't. "I would've been husband number one. Eventually she would have moved on." In retrospect, it was easy to see Jennifer's faults and appreciate anew the fact that they weren't married.

"I don't agree," Nicole said, shaking her head. "I think it might've been a different story if she'd stayed with you."

The waitress brought her drink and Nicole smiled. She took a sip, sliding her tongue along the salty edge of the glass. "Jennifer's my best friend," she went on, "but when it comes to men she's not very smart. Take you, for example. I couldn't *believe* it when she told me she was calling off the wedding. Turns out I was right, too."

Cal enjoyed hearing it, but wanted to know her reasoning. "Why's that?"

"Well, it's obvious. You were the only man strong enough to deal with her personality. I think the world of Jennifer, don't get me wrong, but she likes things her own way and that includes relationships. She was an idiot to break it off with you."

"Actually it was fortunate for both of us that she did."

"Fortunate for you, you mean," Nicole said with a deep sigh. "Like I said, Jennifer was a fool." After another sip, she leaned toward him, her tone confiding. "I doubt she'd admit it, but ever since she left Promise, Jennifer's been looking for a man just like you."

"You think so?" Her remark was a boost to his ego and superficial though that was, Cal couldn't restrain a smile.

The waitress returned with his order, and Nicole drank more of her margarita, then said, "I'll leave now and let you have your dinner."

She started to slip out of the booth, but Cal stopped her. "There's no need to rush off." He wasn't in any hurry and the truth was, he liked hearing what she had to say about Jennifer. If he missed Jane's call, he could always phone her back.

Nicole smiled. "I wanted to thank you, too," she murmured.

"For what?" He cut into an enchilada with his fork and glanced up.

"For giving me a recommendation at Tumbleweed Books."

"Hey," he said, grinning at her. "No problem."

"Annie called me this morning and said I have the job."

"I'm glad it worked out."

"Me, too. I've always loved books and I look forward to working with Annie."

He should probably mention that the bookstore owner was Jane's best friend, and would have, but he was too busy chewing and swallowing—and after that, it was too late.

Nicole checked her watch. "I'd better be going. Like I said, I'm meeting a…friend. If you don't mind, I'd like to buy your dinner."

Her words took him by surprise. He wondered what had prompted the offer.

"As a thank-you for the job reference," she explained.

"It was nothing—I was happy to do it. I'll get my own meal. But let me pay for your drink."

She agreed, they chatted a few more minutes, and then Nicole left. She hadn't said whom she was meeting, and although he was mildly curious, Cal didn't ask.

He sauntered out of the restaurant not long after Nicole. He'd been dragging when he arrived, but with his belly full and his spirits high, he felt almost cheerful as he walked toward his truck. He supposed he was sorry about Jennifer's marital troubles—but not *very* sorry.

As it happened, Cal did miss Jane's phone call, but was quick to reach her once he got home. In her message she'd sounded disappointed, anxious, emotionally drained.

"Where were you?" she asked curtly when he returned her call.

Cal cleared his throat. "I drove into town for dinner. Is everything okay?"

"Mexican Lindo, right?" she asked, answering one question and avoiding the other.

"Right."

"Did you eat alone?"

"Of course." There was Nicole Nelson, but she hadn't eaten with him, not exactly. He'd bought her a drink, that was all. But he didn't want to go into a lengthy explanation that could only lead to misunderstandings. Perhaps it was wrong not to say something about her being there, but he didn't want to waste these precious minutes answering irrelevant questions. Jane might feel slighted or suspicious, although she had no reason. At any rate, Annie would probably mention that she'd hired Nicole on his recommendation, but he could deal with that later. Right now, he wanted to know why she was upset.

"Tell me what's wrong," Cal urged softly, dismissing the thought of Nicole as easily as if he'd never seen her. Their twenty minutes together had been trivial, essentially meaningless. Not a man-woman thing at all but a pandering to his ego. Jane was his wife, the person who mattered to him.

"Dad didn't have a good day," Jane said after a moment. "He's in a lot of pain and he's cranky with me and Mom. A few tests came back and, well, it's too early to say, but I didn't like what I saw."

"He'll be home soon?"

"I don't know—I'd thought, no, I'd hoped…" She let the rest fade.

"Don't worry about it, sweetheart. Take as long as you need. I'll manage." That offer wasn't easy to make, but Cal could see she needed his support. These weeks apart were as hard on her as they were on him. This was the only way he could help.

"You *want* me to stay longer?" Jane demanded.

"No," he returned emphatically. "I thought I was being noble and wonderful."

The tension eased with her laugh. "You seem to be getting along far too well without me."

"That isn't true! I miss you something fierce."

"I miss you, too," Jane said with a deep sigh.

"How did lunch with your friends go?" he asked, thinking it might be a good idea to change the subject.

"All right," she said with no real enthusiasm.

"You didn't enjoy yourself?"

Jane didn't answer immediately. "Not really. We used to be close, but that seems so long ago now. We've grown apart. Julie's into this beauty-pageant thing for her daughter, and it was all she talked about. Every weekend she travels from one state to another, following the pageants."

"Does her daughter like it?"

"I don't know. It's certainly not something I'd ever impose on *my* daughter." She sighed again. "I don't mean to sound judgmental, but we have so little in common anymore."

"What about Megan?"

"She came with her twelve-year-old daughter. She's terribly bitter about her divorce. She dragged her husband's name into the conversation at every opportunity, calling him 'that jerk I was married to.'"

"In front of her kid?" Cal was shocked that any mother could be so insensitive.

"Repeatedly," Jane murmured. "I have to admit I felt depressed after seeing them." She paused, then took a deep breath. "I wonder what they thought of me."

"That concerns you?" Cal asked, thinking she was being ridiculous if it did.

"Not at all," Jane told him. "Today was a vivid reminder that my home's not in California anymore. It's in Promise with you."

Three

"I hate to trouble you," Nicole said to Annie. She sat in front of the computer in the bookstore office, feeling flustered and annoyed with herself. "But I can't seem to find this title under the author's name."

"Here, let me show you how it works," Annie said, sitting down next to Nicole.

Nicole was grateful for Annie Porter's patience. Working in a bookstore was a whole new experience for her. She was tired of banking, tired of working in a field dominated by women but managed by men. Her last job had left her with a bitter taste—not least because she'd had an ill-advised affair with her boss— and she was eager to move on to something completely new. Thus far, she liked the bookstore and the challenge of learning new systems and skills.

Annie carefully reviewed the instructions again.

It took Nicole a couple of tries to get it right. "This shouldn't be so difficult," she mumbled. "I mean, I've worked with lots of computer programs before."

"You're doing great," Annie said.

"I hope so."

"Hey, I can already see you're going to be an asset to the business," Annie said cheerfully, taking the packing slip out of a shipment of books. "Since you came on board, we've increased our business among young single men by two hundred percent."

Nicole laughed and wished that was true. She'd dated a handful of times since her return to Promise, but no one interested her as much as Cal Patterson. And he was married, she reminded herself. Married, married, married.

She should've known he wouldn't stay single long. She'd always found Cal attractive, even when he was engaged to Jennifer. However, the reason she'd given him for moving back to Promise was the truth. She had fallen in love with the town. She'd never found anywhere else that felt as comfortable. During her brief stint with the Promise bank, she'd made friends within the community. She loved the down-home feel of the feed store and the delights of Dovie's Antiques. The bowling alley had been a blast, with the midnight Rock-and-Bowl every Saturday night.

Jennifer Healy had never appreciated the town or the people. Her ex-roommate had once joked that Promise was like Mayberry RFD, the setting of that 60s TV show. Her comment had angered Nicole. These people were sincere, pleasant and kind. *She* preferred life in a town where people cared about each other, even if Jen didn't.

Only it wasn't just the town that had brought her back. She'd also returned because of Cal Patterson.

Almost ten years ago, she'd been infatuated with him, but since he was engaged to her best friend, she couldn't very well do anything about it. When Jennifer had dumped Cal, that would've been the perfect time to stick around and comfort him. Instead, she'd waited—and then she'd been transferred again, to a different branch in another town. Shortly after she'd left Promise, she'd had her first affair, and since then had drifted from one dead-end relationship to another. That was all about to change. This time she intended to claim the prize—Cal Patterson.

At the Mexican restaurant the other night, Nicole had told Cal that Jennifer compared every man she met to him, the one she'd deserted. Nicole hadn't a clue if that was the case or not. *She* was the one who'd done the comparing. In all these years she hadn't been able to get Cal Patterson out of her mind.

So he was married. She'd suspected as much when she made the decision to return to Promise, but dating a married man wasn't exactly unfamiliar to her. She would have preferred if he was single, although his being married wasn't a deterrent. It made things more... interesting. More of a challenge. Most of the time the married man ended up staying with his wife, and Nicole was the one who got hurt. This was something she knew far too well, but she'd also discovered that there were ways of undermining a marriage without having to do much of anything. And when a marriage was shaken, opportunities might present themselves....

"Nicole?"

Nicole realized Annie was staring at her. "Sorry, I got lost in my thoughts."

"It's time for a break." Annie led the way into the back room. Once inside, she reached for the coffee-pot and gestured toward one of two overstuffed chairs. "Sit down and relax. If Louise needs any help, she can call us."

Nicole didn't have to be asked twice. She'd been waiting for a chance to learn more about Cal, and she couldn't think of a better source than Annie Porter.

Annie handed her a coffee in a ceramic mug, and Nicole added a teaspoon of sugar, letting it slowly dissolve as she stirred. "How do you know Cal?" she asked, deciding this was the best place to start.

"His wife. You haven't met Jane, have you?"

Nicole shook her head. "Not yet," she said as though she was eager to make the other woman's acquaintance.

"We've been friends nearly our entire lives. Jane's the reason I moved to Promise."

Nicole took a cookie and nibbled daintily. "Cal said he has two children."

"Yes."

The perfect little family, a boy and a girl. Except that wifey seemed to be staying away far too long. If the marriage was as wonderful as everyone suggested, she would've expected Cal's wife to be home by now.

"This separation has been hard on them," Annie was saying.

"They're separated?" Nicole asked, trying to sound sympathetic.

She was forced to squelch a surge of hope when Annie explained, "Oh, no! Not that way. Just by distance. Jane's father has been ill."

"Yes, Cal mentioned that she was in California with her family." Nicole nodded earnestly. "She's a doctor, right?" She'd picked up that information without much difficulty at all. The people of Promise loved their Dr. Jane.

"A very capable one," Annie replied. "And the fact that she's with her parents seems to reassure them both."

"Oh, I'm sure she's a big help."

"I talked to her mom the other day, who's *so* glad she's there. I talked to Jane, too—I wanted to tell her about the baby and find out about her dad. She's looking forward to getting home."

"I know I'd want to be with my husband," Nicole said, thinking if she was married to Cal, she wouldn't be foolish enough to leave him for a day, let alone weeks at a time.

"The problem is, her father's not doing well," Annie said, then sipped her coffee. She, too, reached for a cookie.

"That's too bad."

Annie sighed. "I'm not sure how soon Jane will be able to come home." She shook her head. "Cal seems at loose ends without his family."

"Poor guy probably doesn't know what to do with himself." Nicole would love to show him, but she'd wait for the right moment.

"Do you like children?" Annie asked her.

"Very much. I hope to have a family one day." Nicole knew her employer was pregnant, so she said what she figured Annie would want to hear. In reality, she her-

"We'd better get back," Annie said, glancing at her watch.

Nicole set aside her mug and stood. Cal had been on his own for nearly two weeks now, if her calculations were correct. A man could get lonely after that much time without a woman.

He hadn't let her pay for his meal at the Mexican restaurant. Maybe she could come up with another way to demonstrate just how grateful she was for the job reference he'd provided.

"How long's Jane going to be away?" Glen asked Cal as they drove along the fence line. The bed of the pickup was filled with posts and wire and tools; they'd been examining their fencing, and doing necessary repairs all afternoon.

Cal didn't want to think about his wife or about their strained telephone conversations of the last few nights. Yesterday he'd hung up depressed and anxious when Jane told him she wouldn't be home as soon as she'd hoped. Apparently Harry Dickinson's broken hip had triggered a number of other medical concerns. Just when it seemed his hip was healing nicely, the doctors had discovered a spot on his lung, and in the weeks since, the spot had grown. All at once, the big *C* loomed over Jane's father. *Cancer.*

"I don't know when she'll be back," Cal muttered, preferring not to discuss the subject with his brother. Cal blamed himself for their uncomfortable conversations. He'd tried to be helpful, reassuring, but hadn't been able to prevent his disappointment from surfacing. He'd expected her home any day, and now it seemed she was going to be delayed yet again.

"Are you thinking of flying to California yourself?" his brother asked.

"No." Cal's response was flat.

"Why not?"

"I don't see that it'd do any good." He believed that her parents had become emotionally dependent on her, as though it was within Jane's power to take their problems away. She loved her parents and he knew she felt torn between their needs and his. And here he was, putting more pressure on her....

He didn't mean to add to her troubles, but he had.

"Do you think I'm an irrational jerk?"

"Yes," Glen said bluntly, "so what's your point?"

That made Cal smile. Leave it to his younger brother to say what he needed to hear. "You'd be a lot more sympathetic if it was *your* wife."

"Probably," Glen agreed.

Normally Cal kept his affairs to himself, but he wasn't sure about the current situation. After Jane had hung up, he'd battled the urge to call her back, settle matters. They hadn't fought, not really, but they were dissatisfied with each other. Cal understood how Jane felt, understood her intense desire to support her parents, guide them through this difficult time. But she wasn't an only child—she had a brother living nearby—and even if she had been, her uncle was a doctor, too. The Dickinsons didn't need to rely so heavily on Jane, in Cal's opinion—and he'd made that opinion all too clear.

"What would you do?" he asked his brother.

Glen met his look and shrugged. "Getting tired of your own cooking, are you?"

"It's more than that." Cal had hoped Jane would force her brother to take on some of the responsibility.

She hadn't.

Cal and Glen reached the top of the ridge that overlooked the ranch house. "Whose car is that?" Glen asked.

"Where?"

"Parked by the barn."

Cal squinted and shook his head. "Don't have a clue."

"We'd better find out, don't you think?"

Cal steered the pickup toward the house. As they neared the property, Cal recognized Nicole Nelson lounging on his porch. Her *again?* He groaned inwardly. Their meeting at the Mexican Lindo had been innocent enough, but he didn't want her mentioning it to his brother. Glen was sure to say something to Ellie, and his sister-in-law would inevitably have a few questions and would probably discuss it with Dovie, and... God only knew where this would all end.

"It's Nicole Nelson," Cal said in a low voice.

"The girl from the rodeo?"

"You met her before," he told his brother.

"I did?" Glen sounded doubtful. "When? She doesn't look like someone I'd forget that easily."

"It was a few years ago," Cal said as they approached the house. "She was Jennifer Healy's roommate. She looked different then. Younger."

He parked the truck, then climbed out of the cab.

"Hi," Nicole called, stepping down off the porch. "I was afraid I'd missed you."

"Hi," Cal returned gruffly, wanting her to know he was uncomfortable with her showing up at the ranch like this. "You remember my brother, Glen, don't you?"

"Hello, Glen."

Nicole sparkled with flirtatious warmth and friendliness, and it was hard not to react.

"Nicole." Glen touched the rim of his hat. "Good to see you again."

"I brought you dinner," Nicole told Cal as she strolled

casually back to her car. She seemed relaxed and non-chalant. The way she acted, anyone might assume she made a habit of stopping by unannounced.

Glen glanced at him and raised his eyebrows. He didn't need to say a word; Cal knew exactly what he was thinking.

"After everything you've done for me, it was the least I could do," Nicole said. "I really am grateful."

"For what?" Glen looked sharply at Cal, then Nicole.

Nicole opened the passenger door and straightened. "Cal was kind enough to give me a job recommendation for Tumbleweed Books."

"Annie phoned and asked if I knew her," Cal muttered under his breath, minimizing his role.

"I hope you like taco casserole," Nicole said, holding a glass dish with both hands. "I figured something Mexican would be a good bet, since you seem to enjoy it."

"How'd she know *that?*" Glen asked, glaring at his brother.

"We met at the Mexican Lindo a few nights ago," Cal supplied, figuring the news was better coming from him than Nicole.

"You did, did you?" Glen said, his eyes filled with meaning.

"I tried to buy his dinner," Nicole explained, "but Cal wouldn't let me."

Cal suspected his brother had misread the situation. "We didn't have dinner together if that's what you're thinking," he snapped. He was furious with Glen, as well as Nicole, for putting him in such an awkward position.

Holding the casserole, Nicole headed toward the house.

"I can take it from here," Cal said.

"Oh, it's no problem. I'll put it in the oven for you and get everything started so all you need to do is serve yourself."

She made it sound so reasonable. Unsure how to stop her, Cal stood in the doorway, arms loose at his sides. Dammit, he felt like a fool.

"There's plenty if Glen would like to stay for dinner," Nicole added, smiling at Cal's brother over her shoulder.

"No, thanks," Glen said pointedly, "I've got a wife and family to go home to."

"That's why I'm here," Nicole said, her expression sympathetic. "Cal's wife and children are away, so he has to fend for himself."

"I don't need anyone cooking meals for me," Cal said, wanting to set her straight. This hadn't been his idea. Bad enough that Nicole had brought him dinner;

even worse that she'd arrived when his brother was there to witness it.

"Of course you don't," Nicole murmured. "This is just my way of thanking you for welcoming me home to Promise."

"Are you actually going to let her do this?" Glen asked, following him onto the porch.

Cal hung back. "Dovie brought me dinner recently," he said, defending himself. "Savannah, too."

"That's a little different, don't you think?"

"No!" he said. "Nicole's just doing something thoughtful, the same as Dovie and Savannah."

"Yeah, right."

"I'm not going to stand out here and argue with you," Cal muttered, especially since he agreed with his brother and this entire setup made him uncomfortable. If she'd asked his preference, Cal would have told Nicole to forget it. He was perfectly capable of preparing his own meals, even if he had little interest in doing so. He missed Jane's dinners—but it was more than the food.

Cal was lonely. He'd lived by himself for several years and now he'd learned, somewhat to his dismay, that he no longer liked it. At first it'd been the little things he'd missed most—conversation over dinner, saying good-night to his children, sitting quietly with Jane in the evenings. Lately, though, it was *everything*.

"I'll be leaving," Glen said coldly, letting Cal know once again that he didn't approve of Nicole's being there.

"I'll give you a call later," Cal shouted as Glen got into his truck.

"What for?"

His brother could be mighty dense at times. "Never mind," Cal said, and stepped into the house.

Nicole was in the kitchen, bustling about, making herself at home. He found he resented that. "I've got the oven preheating to 350 degrees," she said, facing him.

He stood stiffly in the doorway, anxious to send her on her way.

"As soon as the oven's ready, bake the casserole for thirty minutes."

"Great. Thanks."

"Oh, I nearly forgot."

She hurried toward him and it took Cal an instant to realize she wanted out the door. He moved aside, but not quickly enough to avoid having her brush against him. The scent of her perfume reminded him of something Jane might wear. Roses, he guessed. Cal experienced a pang of longing. Not for Nicole, but for his wife. It wasn't right that another woman should walk into their home like this. *Jane* should be here, not Nicole—or anyone else.

"I left the sour cream and salsa in the car," Nicole said breathlessly when she returned. She placed both containers on the table, checked the oven and set the glass dish inside. "Okay." She rubbed her palms together. "I think that's everything."

Cal remained standing by the door, wanting nothing so much as to see her go.

She pointed to the oven. "Thirty minutes. Do you need me to write that down?"

He shook his head and didn't offer her an excuse to linger.

"I'll stay if you like and put together a salad."

He shook his head. "I'll be fine."

She smiled sweetly. "In that case, enjoy."

This time when she left, Cal knew to stand several feet away to avoid any physical contact. He watched her walk back to her car, aware of an overwhelming sense of relief.

Life at the retirement residence suited Phil Patterson. He had his own small apartment and didn't need to worry about cooking, since the monthly fee included three meals a day. He could choose to eat alone in his room or sit in the dining room if he wanted company.

Adjusting to life without Mary hadn't been easy—wasn't easy now—but he kept active and that helped. So did staying in touch with friends. Particularly Frank Hennessey. Gordon Pawling, too. The three men played golf every week.

Frank's wife, Dovie, and Mary had been close for many years, and in some ways Mary's death from Alzheimer's had been as hard on Dovie as it was on Phil. At the end, when Mary no longer recognized either of them, Phil had sat and wept with his wife's dear friend. He hadn't allowed himself to break down in front of his sons, but felt no such compunction when he was around Dovie. She'd cried with him, and their shared grief had meant more than any words she might have said.

Frank and Dovie had Phil to dinner at least once a month, usually on the first Monday. He found it a bit odd that Frank had issued an invitation that afternoon when they'd finished playing cards at the seniors' center.

"It's the middle of the month," Phil pointed out. "I was over at your place just two weeks ago."

"Do you want to come for dinner or not?" Frank said.

Only a fool would turn down one of Dovie's dinners. That woman could cook unlike anyone he knew. Even Mary, who was no slouch when it came to preparing a good meal, had envied Dovie's talent.

"I'll be there," Phil promised, and promptly at five-thirty, he arrived at Frank and Dovie's, a bouquet of autumn flowers in his hand.

"You didn't need to do that," Dovie said when she greeted him, lightly kissing his cheek.

As he entered the house, Phil caught a whiff of something delicious—a blend of delightful aromas. He smelled bread fresh from the oven and a cake of some sort, plus the spicy scent of one of her Cajun specialties.

Frank and Phil settled down in the living room and a few minutes later Dovie brought them an appetizer plate full of luscious little things. A man sure didn't eat this well at the retirement center, he thought. Good thing, too, or he'd be joining the women at their weekly weight-loss group.

Phil helped himself to a shrimp, dipping it in a spicy sauce. Frank opened a bottle of red wine and brought them each a glass.

They chatted amiably for a while, but Phil knew there was something on Dovie's mind. He had an inkling of what it was, too, and decided to break the ice and make it easier for his friends.

"It's times like this that I miss Mary the most," he murmured, choosing a brie-and-mushroom concoction next.

"You mean for social get-togethers and such?" Frank asked.

"Well, yes, those, too," Phil said. "The dinners with friends and all the things we'd planned to do…"

Dovie and Frank waited.

"I wish Mary was here to talk to Cal."

His friends exchanged a glance, and Phil realized he'd been right. They'd heard about Cal and Nicole Nelson.

"You know?" Frank asked.

Phil nodded. It wasn't as though he could *avoid* hearing. Promise, for all its prosperity and growth, remained a small town. The news that Nicole Nelson had delivered dinner to Cal had spread faster than last winter's flu bug. He didn't like it, but he wasn't about to discuss it with Cal, either. Mary could have had a gentle word with their son, and Cal wouldn't have taken offense. But Phil wasn't especially adroit at that kind of conversation. He knew Cal wouldn't appreciate the advice, nor did Phil think it was necessary. His son loved Jane, and that was all there was to it. Cal would never do anything to jeopardize his marriage.

"Apparently Nicole brought him dinner—supposedly to thank Cal for some help he recently gave her," Dovie said, her face pinched with disapproval.

"If you ask me, that young woman's trying to stir up trouble," Frank added.

"Maybe so," Phil agreed, but he knew his oldest son almost as well as he knew himself. Cal hadn't sought out this other woman; she was the one who'd come chasing after him. His son would handle the situation.

"No one's suggesting they're romantically involved," Frank said hastily.

"They aren't," Phil insisted, although he wished again that Mary could speak to Cal, warn him about the perceptions of others. That sort of conversation had been her specialty.

"Do you see Nicole Nelson as a troublemaker?" Phil directed the question to Dovie.

"I don't know... I don't *think* she is, but I do wish she'd shown a bit more discretion. She's still young—it's understandable."

Phil heard the reluctance in her response and noticed the way she eyed Frank, as though she expected him to leap in and express his opinion.

"Annie seems to like her," Dovie went on, "but with this new pregnancy, she's spending less and less time at the bookstore. Really, I hate to say anything...."

"I tell you, the woman's a homewrecker," Frank announced stiffly.

"Now, Frank." Dovie placed her hand on her husband's knee and shook her head.

"Dovie, give me some credit. I was in law enforcement for over thirty years. I recognized that hungry look of hers the minute I saw her."

Phil frowned, now starting to feel worried. "You think Nicole Nelson has her sights set on Cal?"

"I do," Frank stated firmly.

"What an unkind thing to say." Still, he sensed that Dovie was beginning to doubt her own assessment of Nicole.

"The minute I saw her, I said to Dovie, 'That woman's trouble,'" Frank told him.

"He did," Dovie confirmed, sighing.

"Mark my words."

"Frank, please," she said. "You're talking as though Cal wasn't a happily married man. We both know he isn't the type to get involved with another woman. He's a good husband and father."

"Yes," Frank agreed.

"How did you hear about her bringing dinner out to Cal?" Phil asked. It worried him that this trouble-maker was apparently dropping Cal's name into every conversation, stirring up speculation. Glen was the one who'd mentioned it to Phil—casually, but Phil wasn't fooled. This was his youngest son's way of letting him know he sensed trouble. Phil had weighed his options and decided his advice wasn't necessary. But it seemed that plenty of others had heard about Nicole's little trip to the ranch. Not from Glen and not from Ellie, which meant Nicole herself had been spreading the news. She had to be incredibly naive or just plain stupid or… Phil didn't want to think about what else would be going on in the woman's head. He didn't know her well enough to even guess. Whatever the reason for her actions, if Jane heard about this, there could be problems.

"Glen told Ellie," Dovie said, "and she was the one who told me. Not in any gossipy way, mind you, but because she's concerned. She asked what I knew about Nicole."

"Do you think anyone will tell Jane?"

Dovie immediately rejected that idea. "Not unless it's Nicole Nelson herself. To do so would be cruel and malicious. I can't think of a single person in Promise who'd purposely hurt Jane. This town loves Dr. Texas." Dr. Texas was what Jane had affectionately been called during her first few years at the clinic.

"The person in danger of getting hurt here is Cal," Frank said gruffly. "Man needs his head examined."

Phil had to grin at that. Frank could be right; perhaps it *was* time to step in, before things got out of hand. "Mary always was better at talking to the boys," he muttered. "But I suppose I could have a word with him…."

"You want me to do it?" Frank offered.

"Frank!" Dovie snapped.

"*Someone* has to warn him he's playing with fire," Frank blurted.

Phil shook his head. "Listen, if anyone says anything, it'll be me."

"You'll do it, won't you?" Frank pressed.

Reluctantly Phil nodded. He would, but he wasn't sure when. Sometimes a situation righted itself without anyone interfering. This might be one of those cases.

He sincerely hoped so.

Four

Jane stood at the foot of her father's hospital bed, reading his medical chart. Dr. Roth had allowed her to review his notes as a professional courtesy. She frowned as she studied them, then flipped through the test results, liking what they had to say even less.

"Janey? Is it that bad?" her father asked. She'd assumed he was asleep; his question took her by surprise.

Jane quickly set the chart aside. "Sorry if I woke you," she murmured.

He waved off her remark.

"It's bad news, isn't it?" he asked again. "You can tell me, Jane."

His persistence told her how worried he was. "Hmm. It says here you've been making a pest of yourself," she said, instead of answering his question.

He wore a sheepish grin. "How's a man supposed to

get any rest around here with people constantly waking him up for one thing or another? If I'd known how much blood they were going to take or how often, I swear I'd make them pay me." He paused. "Do you have any idea what they charge for all this—all these X-rays and CAT scans and tests?"

"Don't worry about that, Dad. You have health insurance." However, she was well aware that his real concern wasn't the expense but the other problems that had been discovered as a result of his broken hip.

"I want to know what's going on," he said, growing agitated.

"Dad." Jane placed one hand on his shoulder.

He reached for her fingers and squeezed them hard. For a long moment he said nothing. "Cal wants you home, doesn't he?"

She hesitated, not knowing what to say. Cal had become restive and even a bit demanding; he hadn't hidden his disappointment when she'd told him she couldn't return to Promise yet. Their last few conversations had been tense and had left Jane feeling impatient with her husband—and guilty for reacting that way.

"Your mother and I have come to rely on you far too much," her father murmured.

"It's all right," Jane said, uncomfortably aware that Cal had said essentially the same thing. "I'm not just your daughter, I'm a physician. It's only natural that you'd want me here. What's far more important is for you and Mom not to worry."

Her father sighed and closed his eyes. "This isn't fair to you."

"Dad," she said again, more emphatically. "It's all right, really. Cal understands." He might not like it, but he did understand.

"How much time do I have?" he shocked her by asking next. He was looking straight at her. "No one else will tell me the truth. You're the only one I can trust."

Her fingers curled around his and she met his look. "There are very effective treatments—"

"How much time?" he repeated, more loudly.

Jane shook her head.

"You won't tell me?" He sounded hurt, as if she'd somehow betrayed him.

"How do you expect me to answer a question like that?" she demanded. "Do I have a crystal ball or a direct line to God? For all we know, you could outlive me."

His smile was fleeting. "Okay, give me a ballpark figure."

Jane was uncomfortable doing even that. "Dad, you aren't listening to what I'm saying. You're only at the beginning stages of treatment."

"Apparently my heart isn't in great shape, either."

What he said was true, but the main concern right now was treating the cancer. He'd already had his first session of chemotherapy, and Jane hoped there'd be an immediate improvement. "Your heart is fine."

"Yeah, sure."

"Dad!"

He made an effort to smile. "It's a hard thing to face one's failing health—one's mortality."

When she nodded, he said quietly, "I worry about your mother without me."

Jane was worried about her mother, too, but she wasn't about to add to her father's burden. "Mom will do just fine."

Her father sighed and looked away. "You've made me very proud, Jane. I don't think I've ever told you that."

A lump formed in her throat and she couldn't speak.

"If anything happens to me, I want you to be there for your mother."

"Dad, please, of course I'll help Mom, but don't talk like that. Yes, you've got some medical problems, but they're all treatable. You trust me, don't you?"

He closed his eyes and nodded. "Love you, Janey."

"Love you, too, Dad." On impulse, she leaned forward and kissed his forehead.

"Tell your mother to take the kids to the beach again," he insisted. "Better yet, make that Disneyland."

"She wants to spend the time with you."

"Tell her not to visit me today. I need the rest." He opened his eyes and gave her an outrageous wink. "Now get out of here so I can sleep."

"Yes, Daddy," she said, reaching for her purse.

She might be a grown woman with children of her own, but the sick fragile man in that bed would always be the father she loved.

"Mommy, beach?" Paul asked as he walked into the kitchen a couple of mornings later, dragging his beloved blanket behind him. He automatically opened the cupboard door under the counter and checked out the selection of high-sugar breakfast cereals. Her mother had spoiled the children and it was going to take work to undo that once they got home.

Home. Jane felt so torn between her childhood home and her life in Promise, between her parents and her husband. She no longer belonged in California. Texas was in her blood now and she missed it—missed the ranch, her friends…and most of all, she missed Cal.

"Can we go to the beach?" Paul asked again, hugging the box of sugar-frosted cereal to his chest as he carried it to the table.

"Ah…" Her father's doctor was running another set of tests that afternoon.

"Go ahead," her mother urged, entering the kitchen, already dressed for the day. "Nothing's going to happen at the hospital until later."

"But, Mom…" Jane's sole reason for being in California was to help her parents. If she was going to be here, she wanted to feel she was making some contribution to her father's recovery. Since their conversation two days ago, he'd tried to rely on her less, insisting she spend more time with her children. But the fewer demands her father made on her, the more her mother seemed to cling. Any talk of returning to Texas was met with immediate resistance.

"I'll stay with your dad this morning while you go to the beach," her mother said. "Then we can meet at the hospital, and I'll take the children home for their naps."

Jane agreed and Paul gave a shout of glee. Mary Ann, who was sitting in the high chair, clapped her hands, although she couldn't possibly have known what her brother was celebrating.

"Mom, once we get the test results, I really need to think about going home. I'm needed back in Promise."

Stephanie Dickinson's smile faded. "I know you are," she said with a sigh. "It's been so wonderful having you here…."

"Yes, but—"

"I can't tell you how much my grandkids have helped me cope."

"I'm sure that's true." Her mother made it difficult to press the issue. Whenever Jane brought up the subject of leaving, Stephanie found an even stronger reason for her to remain "a few extra days." Jane had already spent far more time away than she'd intended.

"We'll find out about Dad's test results this afternoon, and if things look okay, I'm booking a flight home."

Her mother lifted Mary Ann from the high chair and held her close. "Don't worry, honey," she said tearfully. "Your father and I will be fine."

"Mother. Are you trying to make me feel guilty?"

Stephanie blinked as if she'd never heard anything more preposterous. "Why would you have any reason to feel guilty?" she asked.

Why, indeed. "I miss my life in Texas, Mom—anyway, Derek's here," she said, mentioning her younger brother, who to this point had left everything in Jane's hands. Five years younger, Derek was involved in his own life. He worked in the movie industry as an assistant casting director and had a different girlfriend every time Jane saw him. Derek came for brief visits, but it was clear that the emotional aspects of dealing with their parents' situation were beyond him.

"Of course you need to get back," her mother stated calmly as she reached for a bowl and set it on the table for Paul, along with a carton of milk.

The child opened the cereal box and filled his bowl, smiling proudly at accomplishing this feat by himself. Afraid of what would happen if he attempted to pour his own milk, Jane did it for him.

"I want you to brush your teeth as soon as you're finished your breakfast," she told him. Taking Mary Ann with her, she left the kitchen to get ready for a morning at the beach.

Just as she'd hoped, the tests that afternoon showed some improvement. Jane was thrilled for more reasons than the obvious. Without discussing it, she called the airline and booked a flight home, then informed her parents as matter-of-factly as possible.

Stephanie Dickinson went out that evening for a meeting with her church women's group—the first social event she'd attended since Harry's accident. A good sign, in her daughter's opinion. Jane welcomed the opportunity to pack her bags and prepare for their return. Paul moped around the bedroom while she waited for a phone call from Cal. She'd promised her son he could speak to his father, but wondered if that had been wise. Paul was already tired and cranky, and since Cal was attending a Cattlemen's Association meeting, he wouldn't be back until late.

"I want to go to the beach again," he said, pouting.

"We will soon," Jane promised. "Aren't you excited about seeing Daddy?"

Paul's lower lip quivered as he nodded. "Can Daddy go to the beach with us?"

"He will one day."

That seemed to appease her son, and Jane got him settled with crayons and a Disney coloring book.

When the phone finally rang, she leaped for it, expecting to hear her husband's voice. Eager to hear it.

"Hello," she said. "Cal?"

"It's me." He sounded reserved, as if he wasn't sure what kind of reception he'd get.

"Hello, you," she said warmly.

"You're coming home?"

"Tomorrow."

"Oh, honey, you don't know what good news that is!"

"I do know. I'll give you the details in a minute. Talk to Paul first, would you?"

"Paul's still up? It's after nine, your time."

"It's been a long day. I took the kids to the beach this morning, and then this afternoon I was at the hospital with my dad when we got the test results." She took a deep breath. "Anyway, I'll explain later. Here's Paul."

She handed her son the receiver and stepped back while he chatted with his father. The boy described their hours at the beach, then gave her the receiver again. "Daddy says he wants to talk to you now."

"All right," she said. "Give me a kiss good-night and go to bed, okay? We have to get up early tomorrow."

Paul stood on tiptoe and she bent down to receive a loud kiss. Not arguing, the boy trotted down the hallway to the bedroom he shared with Mary Ann. Jane waited long enough to make sure he went in.

"I've got the flight information, if you're ready to write it down," she said.

"Yup—pen in hand," Cal told her happily. Hearing the elation in his voice was just the balm she needed.

She read off the flight number and time of arrival, then felt obliged to add, "I know things have been strained between us lately and—"

"I'm sorry, Jane," he said simply. "It's my fault."

"I was about to apologize to you," she said, loving him, anticipating their reunion.

"It's just that I miss you so much."

"I've missed you, too." Jane sighed and closed her eyes. They spoke on the phone nearly every night, but lately their conversations had been tainted by the frustration they both felt with their predicament. She'd wanted sympathy and understanding; he'd been looking for the same. They tended to keep their phone calls brief.

"I have a sneaking suspicion your mother's been spoiling the kids."

"She sees them so seldom…" Jane started to offer an excuse, then decided they could deal with the subject of their children's routines later.

"Your dad's tests—how were they?" Cal asked.

"Well, put it this way. His doctors are cautiously optimistic. So Dad's feeling a lot more positive."

"Your mother, too?"

"Yes." Despite Stephanie's emotional dependence on her, Jane admired the courage her mother had shown in the past few weeks. Seeing her husband in the hospital, learning that he'd been diagnosed with cancer, was a terrifying experience. At least, the situation seemed more hopeful now.

"I'll be at the airport waiting for you," Cal promised. "Oh, honey, I can't tell you how good it's going to be to have you back."

"I imagine you're starved for a home-cooked meal," Jane teased.

"It isn't your cooking I miss as much as just having my wife at home," Cal said.

"So you're eating well, are you?"

"I'm eating." From the evasive way he said it, she knew that most of his dinners consisted of something thrown quickly together.

"I'll see you tomorrow," Jane whispered. "At five o'clock."

"Tomorrow at five," Cal echoed, "and that's none too soon."

Jane couldn't agree more.

Cal was in a good mood. By noon, he'd called it quits for the day; ten minutes later he was in the shower. He shaved, slapped on the aftershave Jane liked and donned a crisp clean shirt. He was ready to leave for San Antonio to pick up his family. His steps lightened as he passed the bedroom, and he realized he'd be sharing the bed with his wife that very night. He hesitated at the sight of the disheveled and twisted sheets. Jane had some kind of obsession with changing the bed linens every week. She'd been away almost three weeks now and he hadn't made the bed even once. She'd probably appreciate clean sheets.

He stripped the bed and piled the dirty sheets on top of the washer. The laundry-room floor was littered with numerous pairs of mud-caked jeans and everything else he'd dirtied in the time she'd been away. No need to run a load, he figured; Jane liked things done her own way. He'd never known that a woman could be so particular about laundry.

The kitchen wasn't in terrific shape, either, and Cal regretted not using the dishwasher more often. Until that very moment, he hadn't given the matter of house-cleaning a second thought. He hurriedly straightened the kitchen and wiped the countertops. Housework had never been his forte, and Jane was a real stickler about order and cleanliness. When he'd lived with his brother, they'd divided the tasks; Cal did most of the cooking and Glen was in charge of the dishes. During the weeks his wife was away, Cal hadn't done much of either.

Still, he hadn't been totally remiss. He'd washed Sa-vannah's and Dovie's dishes. Nicole Nelson's, too. He grabbed his good beige Stetson and started to leave yet again, but changed his mind.

He didn't have a thing to feel guilty about—but if Jane learned that Nicole had brought him a casserole, she'd be upset, particularly since he'd never mentioned it. That might look bad. He hadn't *meant* to keep it from her, but they'd been sidetracked by other concerns, and then they'd had their little spat. He'd decided just to let it go.

All Cal wanted was his wife and family home. That didn't strike him as unreasonable—especially when he heard about the way she seemed to be spending her days. How necessary was it to take the kids to Disneyland? Okay, once, maybe, but they'd gone three or four times. He'd lost count of their trips to the beach. This wasn't supposed to be a vacation. He immediately felt guilty about his lack of generosity. She'd had a lot of responsibility and he shouldn't begrudge her these excursions. Besides, she'd had to entertain the kids *somehow.*

Collecting the clean casserole dishes, Cal stuck them in the backseat of his car. He'd return them now, rather than risk having Jane find the dish that belonged to Nicole Nelson.

His first stop was at the home of Savannah and Laredo Smith. After a few minutes of searching, he found his neighbor in one of her rose gardens, winterizing the plants. They'd grown up next door to each other, and Savannah's brother, Grady Weston, had been Cal's closest friend his entire life.

Savannah, who'd been piling compost around the base of a rosebush, straightened when he pulled into the yard. She'd already started toward him by the time he climbed out of the car.

"Well, hello, Cal," she said, giving him a friendly hug.

"Thought I'd bring back your dish. I want you to know how much I appreciated the meal."

Savannah pressed her forearm against her moist brow. "I was glad to do it. I take it Jane'll be home soon?"

"This afternoon." He glanced at his watch and saw that he still had plenty of time.

"That's wonderful! How's her father doing?"

"Better," he said. He didn't want to go into all the complexities and details right now; he'd leave that for Jane.

"I should go," he told her. "I've got a couple of other stops to make before I head to the airport."

"Give Jane my best," Savannah said. "Ask her to call me when she's got a minute."

Cal nodded and set off again. His next stop was Dovie and Frank Hennessey's place. Besides a chicken pot pie, Dovie had baked him dessert—an apple pie. It was the best meal he'd eaten the whole time Jane was in California. Dovie had a special recipe she used for her crust that apparently included buttermilk. She'd passed it on to Jane, but despite several attempts, his wife's pie crust didn't compare with Dovie Hennessey's. But then, no one's did.

Frank answered the door and gave him a smile of welcome. "Hey, Cal! Good to see you." He held open the back door and Cal stepped inside.

"You, too, Frank." Cal passed him the ceramic pie

plate and casserole dish. "I'm on my way to the airport to pick up Jane and the kids."

"So that's why you're wearing a grin as wide as the Rio Grande."

"Wider," Cal said. "Can't wait to have 'em back."

"Did Phil catch up with you?" Frank asked.

"Dad's looking for me?"

Frank nodded. "Last I heard."

"I guess I should find out what he wants," Cal said. He had enough time, since it was just after two and Jane's flight wasn't due until five. Even if it took him a couple of hours hours to drive to the airport, he calculated, he should get there before the plane landed. Still, he'd have to keep their visit brief.

Frank nodded again; he seemed about to say something else, then apparently changed his mind.

"What?" Cal asked, standing on the porch.

Frank shook his head. "Nothing. This is a matter for you and your dad."

Cal frowned. He had to admit he was curious. If his father had something to talk over with him, Cal wondered why he hadn't just phoned. From Frank and Dovie's house, Cal drove down Elm Street to the seniors' residence. He found his father involved in a quiet game of chess with Bob Miller, a retired newspaperman.

"Hello, Cal," Phil murmured, raising his eyes from the board.

"Frank Hennessey said you wanted to see me," Cal said abruptly. "Hi, Bob," he added. He hadn't intended any rudeness, but this was all making him a bit nervous.

Phil stared at him. "Frank said that, did he?"

"I brought back Dovie's dishes, and Frank answered the door. If you want to talk to me, Dad, all you need to do is call."

"I know, I know." Phil stood and smiled apologetically at Bob. "I'll be back in a few minutes."

Bob was studying the arrangement of chess pieces. "Take all the time you need," he said without looking up.

Phil surveyed the lounge, but there was no privacy to be had there. Cal checked his watch again, thinking he should preface their conversation with the news that he was on his way to the airport. Before he had a chance to explain why he was in town—and why he couldn't stay long—his father shocked him by saying, "I want to know what's going on between you and Nicole Nelson."

"Nicole Nelson?" Cal echoed.

Phil peered over his shoulder. "Perhaps the best place to have this discussion is my apartment."

"There's nothing to discuss," Cal said, his jaw tightening.

Phil ignored him and marched toward the elevator. "You take back her dinner dishes yet?" he pried. "Or have you advanced to sharing candlelit meals?"

Cal nearly swallowed his tongue. His father knew Nicole had brought him dinner. How? Glen wasn't one to waste time on idle gossip. Nor was Ellie. He didn't like to think it was common knowledge or that the town was feasting on this tasty tidbit.

His father's apartment consisted of a small living area with his own television and a few bookcases. His mother's old piano took up one corner. Double glass doors led to the bedroom and an adjoining bath. Although he didn't play the piano, Phil hadn't sold it when Cal's mother died. Instead, he used the old upright to display family photographs.

He walked over to a photo of Cal with Jane and the two children, taken shortly after Mary Ann's birth. "You have a good-looking family, son."

Cal knew his father was using this conversation to lead into whatever nonsense was on his mind. Hard as it was, he kept his mouth shut.

"It'd be a shame to risk your marriage over a woman like Nicole Nelson."

"Dad, I'm *not* risking my marriage! There's nothing to this rumor. The whole thing's been blown out of proportion. Who told you she'd been out to the ranch?"

"Does it matter?" Phil challenged.

"Is this something folks are talking about?" That was Cal's biggest fear. He didn't want Jane returning to Promise and being subjected to a torrent of malicious gossip.

"I heard the two of you were seen together at the Mexican Lindo, too."

"Dad!" Cal cried, yanking off his hat to ram his fingers through his hair. "It wasn't *like* that. I was eating alone and Nicole happened to be there at the same time."

"She sat with you, didn't she?"

"For a while. She was meeting someone else."

Phil's frown darkened. "She didn't eat with you, but you bought her a drink, right?"

Reluctantly Cal nodded. He'd done nothing wrong; surely his father could see that.

"People saw you and Nicole in the Mexican Lindo. These things get around. Everyone in town knows she brought you a meal, but it wasn't Glen or Ellie who told them."

"Then who did?" Even as he asked the question, the answer dawned on Cal. He sank onto the sofa that had once stood in the library of his parents' bed-and-breakfast. "Nicole," he breathed, hardly able to believe she'd do something like that.

Phil nodded. "Must be. Frank thinks she's looking to make trouble." He paused, frowning slightly. "Dovie doesn't seem to agree. She thinks we're not being fair to Nicole."

"What do *you* think?" Cal asked his father. None of this made any sense to him.

Phil shrugged. "I don't know Nicole, but I don't like what I've heard. Be careful, son. You don't want to lose what's most important over nothing. Use your common sense."

"I didn't seek her out, if that's what you're thinking," Cal said angrily.

"Did I say you had?"

This entire situation was out of control. If he'd known that recommending Nicole for a job at the bookstore would lead to this, he wouldn't have said a word. It didn't help any that Jane's best friend, Annie Porter, owned Tumbleweed Books, although he assumed Annie would show some discretion. He could trust her to believe him—but even if she didn't, Annie would never say or do anything to hurt Jane.

"You plan on seeing Nicole again?"

"I didn't plan on seeing her the first time," Cal shot back. "I don't have any reason to see her."

"Good. Keep it that way."

Cal didn't need his father telling him something so obvious. Not until he reached the car did he remember the casserole dish. With his father's warning still ringing in his ears, he decided that returning it to Nicole could wait. When he had a chance, he'd tuck the dish in the cab of his pickup and drop it off at the bookstore. Besides, he no longer had the time. Because of this unexpected delay with his father, he'd have to hurry if he wanted to get to the airport before five.

Despite the likelihood that he'd now be facing rush-hour traffic, he had to smile.

His wife and family were coming home.

Exhausted, Jane stepped off the plane, balancing Mary Ann on her hip. The baby had fussed the entire flight, and Jane was pretty sure she had an ear infection. Her skin was flushed and she was running a fever and tugging persistently at her ear.

With Mary Ann crying during most of the flight, Paul hadn't taken his nap and whined for the last hour, wanting to know when he'd see his daddy again. Jane's own nerves were at the breaking point and she pitied her fellow passengers, although fortunately the plane had been half-empty.

"Where's Daddy?" Paul said as they exited the jetway.

"He'll be here," Jane assured her son. "He'll meet us

at the entrance." The diaper bag slipped off her shoulder and tangled with her purse strap, weighing down her arm.

"I don't see Daddy," Paul cried, more loudly this time.

"Just wait, okay?"

"I don't want to wait," Paul complained. He crossed his arms defiantly. "I'm *tired* of waiting. I want my daddy."

"Paul, please, I need you to be my helper."

Mary Ann started to cry, tugging at her ear again. Jane did what she could to comfort her daughter, but it was clear the child was in pain. She had Children's Tylenol with her, but it was packed in the luggage. The checked luggage, of course.

She made her way to the baggage area; she'd get their suitcases, then she could at least take out the medication for Mary Ann.

With the help of a friendly porter, she collected the bags and brought them over to the terminal entrance, looking around for her husband. No Cal anywhere. She opened the smaller bag to get the Tylenol. She found it just as she heard her name announced over the broadcast system.

"That must be your father," she told Paul.

"I want my daddy!" the boy shrieked again.

Jane wanted Cal, too—and when she saw him she intended to let him know she was not pleased. She located a house phone, dragged over her bags and, kids in tow, breathlessly picked up the receiver.

She was put through to Cal.

"Where the hell are you?" he snapped.

"Where the hell are *you?*" She was tempted to remind him that she had two suitcases and two children to worry about, plus assorted other bags. The only items he had to carry were his wallet and car keys. She'd appreciate a little help!

"I'm waiting for you at the entrance," he told her a little more calmly.

"So am I," she said, her voice puzzled.

"You aren't at Terminal 1."

"No, I'm at 2! That's where I'm supposed to be." She tried to restrain her frustration. "How on earth could you get that wrong?"

"Stay right there and I'll meet you," Cal promised, sounding anxious.

Ten minutes later Paul gave a loud cry. "Daddy! Daddy!"

There he was. Cal strolled toward them, a wide grin on his face as Paul raced in his direction. He looked wonderful, Jane had to admit. Tanned and relaxed, tall and lean. At the moment all she felt was exhausted. He reached down and scooped Paul into his arms, lifting him high. The boy wrapped his arms around Cal's neck and hugged him fiercely.

"Welcome home," Cal said. Still holding Paul, he pulled her and the baby into his arms and embraced them.

"What happened?" Jane asked. "Where were you?"

"Kiss me first," he said, lowering his head to hers. The kiss was long and potent, and it told Jane in no uncertain terms how happy he was to have her back.

"I'm so glad to be home," she whispered.

"I'm glad you are, too." He put his son back on the floor and Paul gripped his hand tightly. "I'm sorry about the mixup." Cal shook his head. "I gave myself plenty of time, but I stopped off to see my dad and got a later start than I wanted. And then traffic was bad. And *then* I obviously wasn't thinking straight and I went to the wrong terminal."

Jane sighed. Knowing she was going to have her hands full, he might've been a bit more thoughtful.

The hour and a half ride into Promise didn't go smoothly, either. Keyed up and refusing to sleep, Paul was on his worst behavior. Mary Ann's medication took almost an hour to kick in, and until then, she cried and whimpered incessantly. Jane's nerves were stretched to the limit. Cal tried to distract both children with his own renditions of country classics, but he had little success.

When he pulled into the driveway, Jane gazed at the house with a sense of homecoming that nearly brought tears to her eyes. It'd been an emotional day from the first. Her mother had broken down when she dropped Jane and the kids off at LAX; seeing their grandmother weep, both children had begun to cry, too. Then the flight and Mary Ann's fever and her difficulties at the airport. Instead of the loving reunion she'd longed for with Cal, there'd been one more disappointment.

"You and the kids go inside, and I'll get the luggage," Cal told her.

"All right." Jane unfastened her now-sleeping daughter from the car seat and held her against one shoulder.

Paul followed. "How come Daddy's going to his truck?" he asked.

Jane glanced over her shoulder. "I don't know." He seemed to be carrying something, but she couldn't see what and, frankly, she didn't care.

What Jane expected when she walked into the house was the same sense of welcome and familiar comfort. Instead, she walked into the kitchen—and found chaos. Dishes were stacked in the sink and three weeks' worth of mail was piled on the kitchen table. The garbage can was overflowing. Jane groaned and headed down the hallway. Dirty clothes littered the floor in front of the washer and dryer.

Attempting to take a positive view of the situation, Jane guessed this proved how much Cal needed her, how much she'd been missed.

She managed to keep her cool until she reached their bedroom. The bed was torn apart, the bedspread and blankets scattered across the floor, and that was her undoing. She proceeded to their daughter's room and gently set Mary Ann in her crib; fortunately she didn't wake up. Jane returned to the kitchen and met Cal just as he was walking in the back door with the last of her bags.

Hands on her hips, she glared at him. "You couldn't make the bed?"

"Ah…" He looked a bit sheepish. "I thought you'd want clean sheets."

"I do, but after three hours on a plane dealing with the kids, I didn't want to have to change them myself."

"Mommy! I'm hungry."

Jane had completely forgotten about dinner.

"The house is, uh, kind of a mess, isn't it?" Cal said guiltily. "I'm sorry, honey, my standards aren't as high as yours."

Rather than get involved in an argument, Jane went

to the linen closet for a clean set of sheets. "Could you fix Paul a sandwich?" she asked.

"Sure."

"I want tuna fish and pickles," Paul said.

"I suppose your mother let him eat anytime he wanted," Cal grumbled.

Stephanie had, but that was beside the point. "Let's not get into this now," she said.

"Fine."

By the time Jane finished unpacking, sorting through the mail and separating laundry, it was nearly midnight. Cal helped her make the bed. He glanced repeatedly in her direction, looking apologetic.

"I'm sorry, honey," he said again.

Jane didn't want to argue, but this homecoming had fallen far short of what she'd hoped. At least Mary Ann was sleeping soundly. But without a nap, Paul had been out of sorts. Cal had put him down and returned a few minutes later complaining that his son had turned into a spoiled brat.

Jane had had enough. "Don't even start," she warned him.

He raised both hands. "All right, all right."

They barely spoke afterward.

At last Cal undressed and slipped between the fresh sheets. "You ready for bed?"

Exhausted, Jane merely nodded; she didn't have the energy to speak.

He held out his arms, urging her to join him, and one look told her what he had in mind.

Jane hesitated. "I hope you're not thinking what I suspect you're thinking."

"Honey," he pleaded, "it's been nearly three weeks since we made love."

Jane sagged onto the side of the bed. "Not tonight."

Cal looked crestfallen. "Okay, I guess I asked for that. You're upset about the house being a mess, aren't you?"

"I'm not punishing you, if that's what you're saying." Couldn't he see she was nearly asleep on her feet?

"Sure, whatever," he muttered. Jerking the covers past his shoulder, he rolled over and presented her with a view of his back.

"Oh, Cal, stop it," she said, tempted to shake him. He was acting like a spoiled little boy—like their own son when he didn't get what he wanted. At this point, though, Jane didn't care. She undressed and turned off the light. Tired as she was, she assumed she'd be asleep the instant her head hit the pillow.

She wasn't.

Instead, she lay awake in the dark, wondering how their reunion could possibly have gone so wrong.

Five

To say that Jane's kitchen cupboards were bare would be an understatement. One of her first chores the next morning was to buy groceries. Cal kept Paul with him for the day, instead of taking him to preschool, and Jane buckled Mary Ann into her car seat and drove to town.

She was grateful to be home, grateful to wake up with her husband at her side and grateful that the unpleasantness of the night before seemed to be forgotten. With the washer and dryer humming and the children well rested, the day looked brighter all the way around. Even Mary Ann seemed to be feeling better, and a quick check of her ears revealed no infection.

Although she had a whole list of things to do, Jane took time to go and see Ellie. Later, when she'd finished with her errands, she planned to make a quick run over to Annie's.

"You look…" Ellie paused as she met Jane outside Frasier Feed.

"Exhausted," Jane filled in for her. "I'm telling you, Ellie, this time away was no vacation."

"I know," Ellie said, steering her toward the old-fashioned rockers positioned in front. "I remember what it was like. With my dad sick and my mother frantic, it was all I could do to keep myself sane."

Jane wished Cal understood how trying and difficult these weeks had been for her. He *should* know, seeing that his own mother had been so terribly ill, but then, Phil had protected his sons from the truth for far too long.

"I'm glad you're home." Ellie sank into one of the rockers.

"Me, too." Jane sat down beside her friend, balancing Mary Ann on her knee. She loved sitting right here with Ellie, looking out at the town park and at the street; she'd missed their chats. She could smell mesquite smoke from the Chili Pepper. California cuisine had nothing on good old Texas barbecue, she decided, her mouth watering at the thought of ribs dripping with tangy sauce. A bowl of Nell Grant's famous chili wouldn't go amiss, either.

"Everything will be better now," Ellie said.

Jane stared at her friend. "Better? How do you mean?"

Ellie's gaze instantly shot elsewhere. "Oh, nothing… I was thinking out loud. I'm just pleased you're back."

Jane was a little puzzled but let Ellie's odd remark slide. They talked about friends and family and planned a lunch date, then Jane left to get her groceries.

Buy-Right Foods had built a new supermarket on the outskirts of town, and it boasted one of the finest produce and seafood selections in the area. The day it opened, everyone in the county had shown up for the big event—not to mention the music, the clowns who painted kids' faces and, not least, the generous assortment of free samples. There hadn't been a parking space in the lot, which had occasioned plenty of complaints. People didn't understand that this kind of congestion was a way of life in California. Jane had forgotten what it was like to wait through two cycles at a traffic light just to make a left-turn lane. A traffic jam in Promise usually meant two cars at a stop sign.

Grabbing a cart at the Buy-Right, she fastened Mary Ann into the seat and headed down the first aisle. Everyone who saw Jane seemed to stop and chat, welcome her home. At this rate, it'd take all day to get everything on her list. Actually she didn't mind. If Cal had shown half the enthusiasm her friends and neighbors did, the unpleasantness the night before might have been averted.

"Jane Dickinson—I mean, Patterson! Aren't you a sight for sore eyes."

Jane recognized the voice immediately. Tammy Lee Kollenborn. The woman was a known flirt and trouble-maker. Jane tended to avoid her, remembering the grief Tammy had caused Dovie several years earlier. After a ten-year relationship, Dovie had wanted to get married and Frank hadn't. Then, for some ridiculous rea-son, Frank had asked Tammy Lee out. The night had been a disaster, and shortly afterward Frank had pro-posed to Dovie—although not before Tammy Lee had managed to upset Dovie with her lies and insinuations.

"Hello, Tammy Lee."

The older woman's gold heels made flip-flop sounds as she pushed her cart alongside Jane's. "My, your lit-tle one sure is a cutie-pie." She peered at Mary Ann through her rhinestone-rimmed glasses. "I swear I'd die for lashes that long," she said, winking up at Jane.

Trying to guess Tammy Lee's age was a fruitless ef-fort. She dressed in a style Jane privately called "Texas trash" and wore enough costume jewelry to qualify her for a weight-lifting award.

"From what I hear, it's a good thing you got home when you did," Tammy Lee said.

Jane frowned. "Why?"

Tammy Lee lowered her voice. "You mean to say no one's mentioned what's been going on with Cal and that other woman while you were away?"

Jane pinched her lips. If she was smart, she'd make a convenient excuse and leave without giving Tammy the pleasure of spreading her lies. They *had* to be lies. After five years of marriage, Jane knew her husband, and Cal was not the type of man to cheat on his wife.

"Her name's Nicole Nelson. Pretty little thing. Younger than you by, oh, six or seven years." Tammy Lee studied her critically. "Having children ages a woman. My first husband wanted kids, but I knew the minute I got pregnant I'd eat my way through the whole pregnancy. So I refused."

"Yes, well…listen, Tammy Lee, I've got a lot to do."

"I saw Cal with her myself."

"I really do need to be going—"

"They were having dinner together at the Mexican Lindo."

"Cal and Nicole Nelson?" Jane refused to believe it.

"They were *whispering.* This is a small town, Jane, and people notice these things. Like I said, I'm surprised no one's mentioned it. I probably shouldn't, either, but my fourth husband cheated on me and I would've given anything for someone to tell me sooner.

You've heard the saying? The wife is always the last to know."

"I'm sure there's a very logical reason Cal was with Nicole," Jane insisted, not allowing herself to feel jealous. Even if she was, she wouldn't have said anything in front of Tammy Lee.

"When my dear friend finally broke down and told me about Mark seeing another woman, I said the very same thing," Tammy Lee went on. "Wives are simply too trusting. We assume our husbands would never betray us like that."

"I really have a lot to do," Jane said again.

"Now, you listen to me, Jane. Later on, I want you to remember that I'm here for you. I know what you're feeling."

Jane was sure that couldn't be true.

"If you need someone to talk to, come to me. Like I said, I've been down this road myself. If you need a good attorney, I can recommend one in San Antonio. When she's finished with Cal Patterson, he won't have a dime."

"Tammy Lee, I don't have time for this," Jane said, and forcefully pushed her cart forward.

"Call me, you hear?" Tammy Lee gently patted Jane's shoulder. Jane found it a patronizing gesture and had to grit her teeth.

By the time she'd finished paying for her groceries, she was furious. No one needed to tell her who Nicole Nelson was; Jane had no trouble figuring it out. The other woman had approached Cal the afternoon of the rodeo. Jane had sat in the grandstand with her two children while that woman flirted outrageously with her husband.

For now, Jane was willing to give Cal the benefit of the doubt. But as she loaded the groceries into the car, she remembered Ellie's strange comment about everything being "better" now. So *that* was what her sister-in-law had meant.

The one person she trusted to talk this out with was Dovie. Jane hurried to her friend's antique store, although she couldn't stay long.

Dovie greeted her with a hug. The store looked wonderful, thanks to Dovie's gift for display. Her assortment of antiques, jewelry, dried flowers, silk scarves and more was presented in appealing and imaginative ways.

They chatted a few minutes while Dovie inquired about Jane's parents.

"I ran into Tammy Lee Kollenborn at the grocery store," Jane announced suddenly, watching for Dovie's reaction. It didn't take her long to see one. "So it's true?"

"Now, Jane—"

"Cal's been seeing Nicole Nelson?"

"I wouldn't say that."

"According to Tammy Lee, they were together at the Mexican Lindo. Is that right?"

Hands clenched in front of her, Dovie hesitated, then nodded.

Jane couldn't believe her ears. She felt as though her legs were about to collapse out from under her.

"I'm sure there's a perfectly logical reason," Dovie murmured, and Jane realized she'd said the very same words herself not ten minutes earlier.

"If that's the case, then why didn't Cal mention it?" she demanded, although she didn't expect an answer from Dovie.

The older woman shrugged uncomfortably. "You'll have to ask him."

"Oh, I intend to," Jane muttered as she headed out the door. She'd visit Annie another day. Right now, she was more interested in hearing what Cal had to say for himself.

When she pulled off the highway and hurtled down the long drive to the ranch house, the first thing she noticed was that the screen door was open. Cal and Paul walked out to the back porch to greet her. She saw that

her husband's expression was slightly embarrassed, as
if he knew he'd done something wrong.

"Don't be mad," he said when she stepped out of the
car, "but Paul and I had a small accident."

"What kind of accident?" she asked.

"We decided to make lunch for you and...well, let
me just say that I think we can save the pan." A smile
started to quiver at the corners of his mouth. "Come
on, honey, it's only a pan. I'm sure the smoke will wash
off the walls."

"Tell me about Nicole Nelson," Jane said point-blank.

The amusement vanished from his eyes. He stiffened. "What's there to say?"

"Plenty, from what I hear."

"Come on, Jane! You know me better than that."

"Do I?" She glared at him.

"Jane, you're being ridiculous."

"Did you or did you not have dinner with Nicole
Nelson?"

Cal didn't answer.

"It's a simple question," she said, growing impatient.

"Yeah, but the answer's complicated."

"I'll bet it is!" Jane was angrier than she'd been in
years. If they'd had a wonderful reunion, she might
have found the whole matter forgettable. Instead, he
hadn't even bothered to show up on time or at the right

terminal. The house was a mess and all he could think about was getting her in the sack. She shifted Mary Ann on her hip, grabbed a bag full of groceries and stomped into the house.

"Jane!"

She stood in the doorway. "I have all the answers I need."

"Fine!" Cal shouted, angry now.

"Daddy, Daddy!" Paul cried, covering his ears. "Mommy's mad."

"Is this what you want our son to see?" Cal yelled after her.

"That's just perfect," Jane yelled back. "You're running around town with another woman, you don't offer a word of explanation and then you blame *me* because our son sees us fighting." Hurt, angry and outraged, she stormed into the bedroom.

It was obvious to Glen that things weren't going well between his brother and Jane. He saw evidence of the trouble in their marriage every morning when he drove to work at the Lonesome Coyote Ranch.

He and Cal were partners, had worked together for years, and if anyone knew that Cal could be unreasonable, it was Glen. More importantly, though, Glen was well aware that his older brother loved his wife and kids.

By late October the demands of raising cattle had peaked for the season, since the greater part of their herd had been sold off. Not that the hours Cal kept gave any indication of that. Most mornings when Glen arrived, Cal had already left the house.

"Are you going to talk about it?" Glen asked him one afternoon. Cal hadn't said more than two words to him all day. They sat side by side in the truck, driving back to the house.

"No," Cal barked.

"This has to do with Jane, right?" Glen asked.

Cal purposely hit a pothole, which made Glen bounce so high in his seat that his head hit the truck roof, squashing the crown of his Stetson.

"Dammit, Cal, there was no call for that," Glen complained, repairing his hat.

"Sorry," Cal returned, but his tone said he was anything but.

"If you can't talk to me, then who can you talk to?" Glen asked. It bothered him that his only brother refused to even acknowledge, let alone discuss, his problems. Over the years Glen had spilled his guts any number of times. More than once Cal had steered him away from trouble. Glen hoped to do him the same favor.

"If I *wanted* to talk, you mean," Cal said.

"In other words, you'd prefer to keep it all to yourself."

"Yup."

"Okay, then, if that's what you want."

They drove for several minutes in tense silence. Finally Glen couldn't stand it anymore. "This is your wife—your *family*. Doesn't that matter to you? What's going on?" He could feel his patience with Cal fading.

Cal grumbled something he couldn't hear. Then he said in a grudging voice, "Jane paid a visit to Tumbleweed Books the other day."

His brother didn't have to explain further. Nicole Nelson worked at the bookstore, and although Jane was a good friend of Annie Porter's, Glen suspected she hadn't casually dropped by to see her.

"She talk to Nicole?"

Cal spoke through clenched teeth. "I don't like my wife checking up on me."

Glen mulled this over and wondered if Cal had explained the situation. "Jane knows you didn't take Nicole to dinner, doesn't she?"

"Yes!" he shouted. "I *told* her what happened. The next thing I know, she's all bent out of shape, slamming pots and pans around the kitchen like I did something terrible."

"Make it up to her," Glen advised. If his brother hadn't learned that lesson by now, it was high time he did.

"I didn't do anything wrong," Cal snapped. "If she doesn't believe me, then…"

"Cal, get real! Do what you've got to do, man. You aren't the only one, you know. Ellie gets a bee in her bonnet every now and then. Darned if I know what I did, but after a while I don't care. I want things settled. I want peace in the valley. Learn from me—apologize and be done with it."

Cal frowned, shaking his head. "I'm not you."

"Pride can make a man pretty miserable," Glen said. "It's…it's like sitting on a barbed-wire fence naked." He nodded, pleased with his analogy.

Cal shook his head again, and Glen doubted his brother had really heard him. Changing the subject, Glen tried another approach. "How's Jane's father?"

"All right, I guess. She talks to her mother nearly every day."

The ranch house came into view. Glen recalled a time not so long ago when they'd reached this same spot and had seen Nicole Nelson's vehicle parked down below. A thought occurred to him, a rather unpleasant one.

"Are you still in love with Jane?" Glen asked.

Cal hit the brakes with enough force to throw them both forward. If not for the restraint of the seat belts, they might have hit their heads on the windshield.

"What kind of question is that?" Cal roared.

"Do you still love Jane?" Glen yelled right back.

"Of course I do!"

Glen relaxed.

"What I want is a wife who trusts me," Cal said. "I haven't so much as looked at another woman since the day we met, and she damn well knows it."

"Maybe she doesn't."

"Well, she should" was his brother's response.

To Glen's way of thinking, there was plenty a wife should know and often didn't. He figured it was the man's job to set things straight and to make sure his wife had no doubt whatsoever about his feelings.

In the days that followed it was clear that the situation between Jane and Cal hadn't improved. Feeling helpless, Glen decided to seek his father's advice. He found Phil at the bowling alley Friday afternoon, when the senior league was just finishing up. It didn't take much to talk Phil into coffee and a piece of pie. The bowling alley café served the best breakfast in town and was a popular place to eat.

As they slid into the booth, the waitress automatically brought over the coffeepot.

"We'll each have a slice of pecan pie, Denise," Phil told her.

"Coming right up," she said, filling the thick white mugs with an expert hand. "How you doin', Phil? Glen?"

"Good," Glen answered for both of them.

No more than a minute later they were both served generous slices of pie. "Enjoy," she said cheerily.

Phil reached for his fork. "No problem there."

Glen wasn't as quick to grab his own fork. He had a lot on his mind.

"You want to talk to me about something?" Phil asked, busy doctoring his coffee.

Glen left his own coffee black and raised the mug, sipping carefully.

"I didn't think you were willing to buy me a slice of pecan pie for nothing."

Glen chuckled. Of the two sons, he shared his father's temperament. Their mother had been a take-charge kind of woman and Cal got that from her, but she'd never held her hurts close to the chest, the way Cal did.

"I take it you're worried about your brother." Phil picked up his fork again and cut into his pie.

"Yeah." Glen stared down at his favorite dessert and

realized he didn't have much of an appetite. "What should I say to him?"

"Listen." Phil leaned forward to rest his elbows on the table. "When your mother was alive and we had the bed-and-breakfast, she was constantly trying new recipes."

Glen couldn't understand what his mother's cooking had to do with the current situation, but he knew better than to ask. Phil would get around to explaining sooner or later.

"No matter what time of day it was, she'd sit down and eat some of whatever new dish she'd just made. When I asked her why, she said it was important to try a little of it herself before she served it to anyone else."

"Okay," Glen said, still wondering about the connection between his mother's culinary experiments and Cal and Jane.

"Advice is like that. Take some yourself before you hand it to others."

"I haven't given Cal any advice." Not for lack of trying, however. Cal simply wasn't in the mood to listen.

"I realize that. The advice is going to come from me, and I'm giving it to you—free of charge."

Glen laughed, shaking his head.

"Let Cal and Jane settle this themselves."

"But, Dad…"

Phil waved his fork at him. "Every couple has problems at one time or another. You and Ellie will probably go through a difficult patch yourselves, and when you do, you won't appreciate other people sticking their noses in your business."

"Do you think Cal and Jane are going to be okay?"

"Of course they are. Cal loves Jane. He won't do anything to jeopardize his family. Now eat your pie, or I just might help myself to a second slice."

Glen picked up his fork. His father knew what he was talking about; Cal did love Jane, and whatever was wrong would eventually right itself.

Jane noticed a change in Cal the moment he came into the house. They'd been ignoring each other all week. The tension was taking its toll, not only on her but on the children.

Cal paused in the middle of the kitchen, where she was busy putting together Halloween costumes for the children. As usual the church was holding a combined harvest and Halloween party.

Jane didn't leave her place at the kitchen table, nor did she speak to Cal. Instead, she waited for him to make the first move, which he did. He walked over to the stove and poured himself a cup of coffee, then approached the table.

"What are you doing?" he asked in a friendly voice.

"Making Mary Ann a costume for the church party." She gestured at a piece of white fabric printed with spots. "She's going as a dalmatian," Jane said.

Cal grinned. "One of the hundred and one?" They'd recently watched the Disney animated feature on DVD.

Jane nodded and held up a black plastic dog nose, complete with elastic tie.

"What about Paul?"

"He's going as a pirate."

Cal cradled his mug in both hands. "Do you mind if I sit here?"

"Please."

He pulled out the chair and set his coffee on the table. For at least a minute, he didn't say another word. When he finally spoke, his voice was low, deliberate. "This whole thing about Nicole Nelson is totally out of control. If you need reassurances, then I'll give them to you. I swear to you not a thing happened."

Jane said nothing. It'd taken him nearly two weeks to tell her what she already knew. His unwillingness to do so earlier had hurt her deeply. In her heart she knew she could trust her husband, but his pride and stubbornness had shut her out.

This situation with Nicole was regrettable. Not wanting to put Annie in the middle—it was awkward with

Nicole working at Tumbleweed Books—Jane had asked general questions about the other woman. Annie had told her she liked Nicole. After their talk, Jane was convinced that the encounter between Nicole and Cal, whatever it was, had been completely innocent.

Because they lived in a small town, the story had spread quickly and the truth had gotten stretched out of all proportion; Jane understood that. What troubled her most was Cal's attitude. Instead of answering her questions or reiterating his love, he'd acted as if *she'd* somehow wronged him. Well, she hadn't been out there generating gossip! Still, Jane felt a sense of relief that their quarrel was ending.

She caught her husband staring at her intently.

"Can we put this behind us?" Cal asked.

Jane smiled. "I think it's time, don't you?"

Cal's shoulders relaxed, and he nodded. Seconds later, Jane was in her husband's arms and he was kissing her with familiar passion. "I'm crazy about you, Jane," he whispered, weaving his fingers into her thick hair.

"I don't like it when we fight," she confessed, clinging to him.

"You think I do?" he asked. "Especially over something as stupid as this."

"Oh, Cal," she breathed as he bent to kiss her again.

"Want to put the kids to bed early tonight?"

She nodded eagerly and brought her mouth to his. "Right after dinner."

Afterward, Jane felt worlds better about everything. They'd both been at fault and they both swore it wouldn't happen again.

For the next few days Cal was loving and attentive, and so was Jane, but it didn't take them long to slip back into the old patterns. The first time she became aware of it was the night of the church party.

Amy McMillen, the pastor's wife, had asked Jane to arrive early to assist her in setting up. She'd assumed Cal would be driving her into town. Instead, he announced that he intended to stay home and catch up on paperwork. Jane made sure Cal knew she wanted him to attend the function with her, that she needed his help. Supervising both children, plus assisting with the games, would be virtually impossible otherwise. But she decided not to complain; she'd done so much of that in the past couple of months.

When it came time for her to leave, Cal walked her and the children out to the car. Once she'd buckled the kids into their seats, she started the engine, but Cal stopped her.

"You've got a headlight out."

"I do? Oh, no…"

"I don't want you driving into town with only one headlight."

Jane glanced at her watch.

"Take the truck," he said. "I'll change the car seats."

"But—"

"Sweetheart, please, it'll just take a minute." Fortunately his truck had a large four-door cab with ample space for both seats.

"What's this?" Jane asked. In front, on the passenger side, was a cardboard box with a glass casserole dish.

Cal took one look at it and his eyes rushed to meet hers. "A dish," he muttered.

"Of course it's a dish. *Whose* dish?"

He shrugged as if it was no big deal. "I don't know if I mentioned it, but Dovie and Savannah brought me meals while you were away," he said, wrapping the safety belt around Mary Ann's car seat and snapping it in place.

"You mean to say half the town was feeding you and you still managed to nearly destroy my kitchen?"

Cal chuckled.

"I meant to return the dish." He kissed Jane and closed the passenger door. "I'll see to that headlight first thing tomorrow morning," he promised, and opened the door on the driver's side.

Jane climbed in behind the wheel. Normally she didn't like driving Cal's vehicle, which was high off the ground and had a stick shift. She agreed, however, that in the interests of safety, it was the better choice.

The church was aglow when Jane drove up. Pastor Wade McMillen stood outside, welcoming early arrivals, and when he saw Jane, he walked over and helped her extract Mary Ann from her seat.

"Glad to have you back, Jane," he said. "I hope everything went well with your father."

"He's doing fine," she said, although that wasn't entirely true. She was in daily communication with her mother. It seemed her father wasn't responding to the chemotherapy anymore and grew weaker with every treatment. Her mother was at a loss. Several times she'd broken into tears and asked Jane to talk Cal into letting her and the children come back for a visit over Christmas. Knowing how Cal would feel, she hadn't broached the subject yet.

"Would you like me to carry in that box for you?" Wade asked.

"Please." Both Dovie and Savannah would be at the church party, and there was no reason to keep the casserole dish in the truck.

"I'll put it in the kitchen," Wade told her, leading the way.

Paul saw the display of pumpkins and dried corn-stalks in the large meeting room and shouted with delight. Although it was early, the place was hopping with children running in every direction.

Jane followed the pastor into the kitchen, and sure enough, found Dovie there.

"I understand this is yours," Jane said when Wade set the box down on the counter.

Dovie shook her head.

"Didn't you send dinner out to Cal?"

"I did, but he already returned the dishes."

"It must belong to Savannah, then," she said absently.

Not until much later in the evening did Jane see Savannah and learn otherwise. "Well, for heaven's sake," she muttered to Ellie as they were busy with the cleanup. "I don't want to drag this dish back home. Do you know who it belongs to?"

Ellie went suspiciously quiet.

"Ellie?" Jane asked, not understanding at first.

"Ask Cal," her sister-in-law said.

"Cal?" Jane repeated and then it hit her. She knew *exactly* who owned that casserole dish. And asking Cal was what she intended to do. Clearly more had gone on while she was away than he'd admitted. How dared he do this to her!

Glen carried the box containing the dish back to the truck for her. Tired from the party, both Paul and Mary Ann fell asleep long before she turned off the highway onto the dirt road that led to the house.

No sooner had she parked the truck than the back door opened and Cal stepped out. Although it was difficult to contain herself, she waited until the children were in bed before she brought up the subject of the unclaimed dish.

"I ran into Dovie and Savannah," she said casually as they walked into the living room, where the television was on. Apparently her husband didn't have as much paperwork as he'd suggested.

"Oh? How was the party?"

Jane ignored the question. "Neither one of them owns that casserole dish."

Jane watched as Cal's shoulders tensed.

"Tell me, Cal, who does own it?"

Not answering, Cal strode to the far side of the room.

"Don't tell me you've forgotten," Jane said.

He shook his head.

A sick feeling was beginning to build in the pit of her stomach. "Cal?"

"Sweetheart, listen—"

"All I want is a name," she interrupted, folding her arms and letting her actions tell him she was in no mood to be cajoled.

Cal started to say something, then stopped.

"You don't need to worry," Jane said without emotion. "I figured it out. That dish belongs to Nicole Nelson."

Six

Cal couldn't believe this was happening. Okay, so his wife had cause to be upset. He should've mentioned that Nicole Nelson had brought him a meal. The only reason he hadn't was that he'd been hoping to avoid yet another argument. He knew how much their disagreements distressed her, and she'd been through so much lately. He was just trying to protect her!

Without a word to him, Jane had gone to bed. Cal gave her a few minutes to cool down before he ventured into the bedroom. The lights were off, but he knew she wasn't asleep.

"Jane," he said, sitting on the edge of the bed. She had her back to him and was so far over on her side it was a wonder she hadn't tumbled out. "Can we talk about this?" he asked, willing to take his punishment and be done with it.

"No."

"You're right, I should've told you Nicole came to the ranch, but I swear she wasn't here more than ten minutes. If that. She brought over the casserole and that was it."

Jane flopped over onto her back. "Are you sure, or is there something *else* you're conveniently forgetting?"

Cal could live without the sarcasm, but let it drop. "I thought we'd decided to put this behind us." He could always hope tonight's installment of their ongoing argument would be quickly settled. The constant tension between them had worn his patience thin.

Jane suddenly bolted upright in bed. She reached for the lamp beside her bed and flipped the switch, casting a warm light about the room. "You have a very bad habit of keeping things from me."

That was unfair! Cal took a deep calming breath before responding. "It's true I didn't tell you Nicole fixed me dinner, but—"

"You didn't so much as mention her name!"

"Okay…but when was I supposed to do that? You were in California, remember?"

"We talked on the phone nearly every night," Jane said, crossing her arms. "Now that I think about it, you kept the conversations short and sweet, didn't you? Was there a reason for that?"

Again, Cal resented the implication, but again he swallowed his annoyance and said, "You know I'm not much of a conversationalist." Chatting on the phone had always felt awkward to him. That certainly wasn't news to Jane.

"What else haven't you told me about Nicole Nelson? How many other times have you two met without my knowing? When she brought you dinner, did she make a point of joining you? Did you *accidentally* bump into each other in town?"

"No," he answered from between gritted teeth.

"You're sure?"

"You make it sound like I'm having an affair with her! I've done nothing wrong, not a damn thing!"

"Tell me why I should believe you, seeing how you habitually conceal things from me."

"You think I purposely hid the truth?" Their marriage was in sad shape if she made such assumptions. Jane was his partner in life; he'd shared every aspect of his business, his home and his ranch with her, fathered two children with her. It came as a shock that she didn't trust him.

"What about the rodeo?" she asked. "You signed up for the bull-riding competition and you deliberately didn't tell me."

"I knew you didn't want me participating in the rodeo and—"

"What I don't know won't hurt me, right?"

She had a way of twisting his words into knots no cowhand could untangle, himself included. "Okay, fine, you win. I'm a rotten husband. That's what you want to hear, isn't it?"

Her eyes flared and she shook her head. "What I want to hear is the truth."

"I tell you the truth!" he shouted, losing his temper.

"But not until you're backed into a corner."

"I've been as honest with you as I know how." Cal tried again, but he'd reached his limit. Glen had advised him to say what he had to say, do what he had to do— whatever it took to make up with Jane. He'd attempted that once already, but it hadn't been enough. Not only wasn't she satisfied, now she was looking to collect a piece of his soul along with that pound of flesh.

"Why didn't you attend the church party with me and the kids?" she asked.

He frowned. Jane knew the answer to that as well as he did. "I told you. I had paperwork to do."

"How long did it take you?"

Cal ran a hand down his face. "Is there a reason you're asking?"

"A very good one," she informed him coolly. "I'm

trying to find out if you slipped away to be with Nicole."

Cal couldn't have been more staggered if his wife had pulled out a gun and shot him. He jumped off the bed and stood there staring, dumbstruck that Jane would actually suggest such a thing.

"I noticed you had the television on," she continued. "So you finished with all that paperwork earlier than you expected. Did you stop to think about me coping with the children alone? Or did you just want an evening to yourself—while I managed the children, the party and everything else on my own."

"Would you listen to yourself?" he muttered.

"I *am* listening," she shouted. "You sent me off to California with the kids, then you're seen around town with another woman. If *that* isn't enough, you lie and mislead me into thinking I'm overreacting. All at once everything's beginning to add up, and frankly I don't like the total. You're interested in having an affair with her, aren't you, Cal? That's what I see."

Cal had no intention of commenting on anything so ludicrous.

"What's the matter? Am I too close to the truth?"

Shaking his head, Cal looked down at her, unable to hide his disgust. "Until this moment I've never regretted marrying you." He headed out the door, letting it slam behind him.

Almost immediately the bedroom door flew open again. "You think *I* don't have regrets about marrying *you?*" Jane railed. "You're not alone in that department, Cal Patterson." Once again the door slammed with such force that he was sure he'd have to nail the molding back in place.

Not knowing where to go or what else to say, Cal stood in the middle of the darkened living room. In five years of marriage he and Jane had disagreed before, but never like this. He glanced toward their bedroom and knew there'd be hell to pay if he tried to sleep there.

Cal sat in his recliner, raised the footrest and covered himself with the afghan he'd grabbed from the back of the sofa.

Everything would be better in the morning, he told himself.

Cal had left the house by the time Jane got up. It was what she'd expected. What she *wanted,* she told herself. Luckily the children had been asleep and hadn't heard them fighting. She removed her robe from the back of the door and slipped it on. Sick at heart, she felt as though she hadn't slept all night.

The coffee was already made when she wandered

into the kitchen. She was just pouring herself a cup when Paul appeared, dragging his favorite blanket.

"Where's Daddy?" he asked, rubbing his eyes.

"He's with Uncle Glen." Jane crouched down to give her son a hug.

Paul pulled away and met her look, his dark eyes sad. "Is Daddy mad at you?"

"No, darling, Daddy and Mommy love each other very much." She was certain Cal felt as sorry about the argument as she did. She reached for her son and hugged him again.

Their fight had solved nothing. They'd both said things that should never have been said. The sudden tears that rushed into Jane's eyes were unexpected, and she didn't immediately realize she was crying. The children *had* heard their argument. At least Paul must have, otherwise he wouldn't be asking these questions.

"Mommy?" Paul touched his fingers to her face, noticed her tears, then broke away and raced into the other room. He returned a moment later with a box of tissues, which made Jane weep all the more. How could her beautiful son be so thoughtful and sweet, and his father so insensitive, so unreasonable?

After making breakfast for Paul and Mary Ann and getting them dressed, Jane loaded the stroller and diaper bag into the car and prepared to drive her son to preschool. The truck was parked where she'd left it the night before. Apparently Cal had gone out on Fury, his favorite gelding. He often rode when he needed time to think.

Peering into the truck, Jane saw that the casserole dish was still there. She looked at it for a moment, then took it out and placed it in the car. While Paul was in his preschool class, she'd personally return it to Nicole Nelson. And when she did, Jane planned to let her know how happily married Cal Patterson was.

After dropping Paul off, Jane drove to Tumbleweed Books. Cal had indeed replaced her headlight, just as he'd promised, and for some reason that almost made her cry again.

"Hello," Nicole Nelson called out when Jane walked into the bookstore. Jane recognized her right away. The previous time she'd seen the other woman had been at the rodeo, and that was from a distance. On closer inspection, she had to admit that Nicole was beautiful. Jane, by contrast, felt dowdy and unkempt. She wished she'd made more of an effort with her hair and makeup, especially since she'd decided to meet Nicole face-to-face.

"Is there anything I can help you find?" Nicole asked, glancing at Mary Ann in her stroller.

"Is Annie available?" Jane asked, making a sudden

decision that when she did confront Nicole, she'd do it looking her best.

"I'm sorry, Annie had a doctor's appointment this morning. I'd be delighted to assist you if I can."

So polite and helpful. So insincere. Jane didn't even know Nicole Nelson, and already she disliked her.

"That's all right. I'll come back another time." Feeling foolish, Jane was eager to leave.

"I don't think we've met," Nicole said. "I'm Annie's new sales assistant, Nicole Nelson."

Jane had no option but to introduce herself. She straightened and looked directly at Nicole. "I'm Jane Patterson."

"Cal's wife," Nicole said, not missing a beat. A knowing smile appeared on her face as she boldly met Jane's eye.

Standing no more than two feet apart, Jane and Nicole stared hard at each other. In that moment Jane knew the awful truth. Nicole Nelson wanted her husband. Wanted him enough to destroy Jane and ruin her marriage. Wanted him enough to deny his children their father. Cal was a challenge to her, a prize to be won, no matter what the cost.

"I believe I have something of yours," Jane said.

Nicole's smile became a bit cocky. "I believe you do."

"Luckily I brought the casserole dish with me," Jane

returned just as pointedly. She bent down, retrieved it from the stroller and handed it to Nicole.

"Did Cal happen to mention if he liked my taco casserole?" Nicole asked, following Jane to the front of the bookstore.

"Oh," Jane murmured, ever so sweetly, "he said it was much too spicy for him."

"I don't think so," Nicole said, opening one of the doors. "I think Cal might just find he prefers a bit of spice compared to the bland taste he's used to."

Fuming, Jane pushed Mary Ann's stroller out the door and discovered, when she reached the car, that her hands were trembling. This was even worse than she'd thought it would be. Because now she had reason to wonder if her husband had fallen willingly into the other woman's schemes.

Jane had a knot in her stomach for the rest of the day. She was sliding a roast into the oven as Cal walked into the house at four-thirty—early for him. He paused when he saw her, then lowered his head and walked past, ignoring her.

"I…think we should talk," she said, closing the oven, then leaning weakly against it. She set the pot holders aside and forced herself to straighten.

"Now?" Cal asked, as though any discussion with her was an unpleasant prospect.

"Paul…heard us last night," she said. She glanced into the other room, where their son was watching a children's nature program. Mary Ann sat next to him, tugging at her shoes and socks.

"It's not surprising he heard us," Cal said evenly. "You nearly tore the door off the hinges when you slammed it."

Cal had slammed the door first, but now didn't seem to be the time to point that out. "He had his blankey this morning."

"I thought you threw that thing away," Cal said, making it sound like an accusation.

"He…found it. Obviously he felt he needed it."

Cal's eyes narrowed, and she knew he'd seen through her explanation.

"That isn't important. What *is* important, at least to me," she said, pressing her hand to her heart, "is that we not argue in front of the children."

"So you're saying we can go into the barn and shout at each other all we want? Should we arrange for a baby-sitter first?"

Jane reached behind her to grab hold of the oven door. The day had been bad enough, and she wanted only to repair the damage that had been done to their relationship. This ongoing dissatisfaction with each other seemed to be getting worse; Jane knew it had to stop.

"I don't think I slept five minutes last night," she whispered.

Cal said nothing.

"I…I don't know what's going on between you and Nicole Nelson, but—"

Cal started to walk away from her.

"Cal!" she cried, stopping him.

"Nothing, Jane. There's nothing going on between me and Nicole Nelson. I don't know how many times I have to say it, and frankly, I'm getting tired of it."

Jane swallowed hard but tried to remain outwardly calm. "She wants you."

Cal's response was a short disbelieving laugh. "That's crazy."

Jane shook her head. There'd been no mistaking what she'd read in the other woman's expression. Nicole had decided to pursue Cal and was determined to do whatever she could to get him. Jane had to give her credit. Nicole wasn't overtly trying to seduce him. That would have gotten her nowhere with Cal, and somehow she knew it. Instead, Nicole had attacked the foundation of their marriage. She must be pleased with her victory. At this point Jane and Cal were barely talking.

"Just a minute," Cal said, frowning darkly. "Did you purposely seek out Nicole?"

Jane's shoulders heaved as she expelled a deep sigh. "This is the first time I've met her."

"Where?"

"I went by the bookstore after I dropped Paul off at preschool."

"To see Annie?"

"No," she admitted reluctantly. "I thought since I was in town, I'd return the casserole dish."

Jane watched as Cal's gaze widened and his jaw went white with the effort to restrain his anger.

"That was wrong?" she blurted.

"Yes, dammit!"

"You wanted to bring it back yourself, is that it?"

He slapped the table so hard that the saltshaker toppled onto its side. "You went in search of Nicole Nelson. Did you ever stop to think that might embarrass me?"

Stunned, she felt her mouth open. "You're afraid I might have embarrassed *you? That's rich." Despite herself, Jane's control began to slip. "How dare you say such a thing?" she cried. "What about everything you've done to embarrass *me?* I'm the one who's been humiliated here. While I'm away dealing with a family crisis, my husband's seen with another woman. And everyone's talking about it."

"I'd hoped you'd be above listening to malicious gossip."

"Oh, Cal, how can you say that? I was thrust right into the middle of it, and you know what? I didn't enjoy the experience."

He shook his head, still frowning. "You had no business confronting Nicole."

"No business?" she echoed, outraged. "How can you be so callous about my feelings? Don't you see what she's doing? Don't you understand? She wants you, Cal, and she didn't hide the fact, either. Are you going to let her destroy us? Are you?"

"This isn't about Nicole!" he shouted. "It's about trust and commitment."

"*Are* you committed to me?" she asked.

The look on his face was cold, uncompromising. "If you have to ask, that says everything."

"It does, doesn't it?" Jane felt shaky, almost light-headed. "I never thought it would come to this," she said, swallowing the pain. "Not with us…" She felt dis-illusioned and broken. Sinking into a chair, she buried her face in her hands.

"Jane." Cal stood on the other side of the table.

She glanced up.

"Neither of us got much sleep last night."

"I don't think—"

The phone rang, and Cal sighed irritably as he walked over and snatched up the receiver. His voice sharp, he said, "Hello," then he went still and his face instantly sobered. His gaze shot to her.

"She's here," he said. "Yes, yes, I understand."

Jane didn't know what to make of this. "Cal?" she said getting to her feet. The call seemed to be for her. As she approached, she heard her husband say he'd tell her. *Tell her what?*

Slowly Cal replaced the receiver. He put his hands on her shoulders and his eyes searched hers. "That was your uncle Ken," he said quietly.

"Uncle Ken? Why didn't he talk to me?" Jane demanded, and then intuition took over and she knew without asking. "What's wrong with my dad?"

Cal looked away for a moment. "Your father suffered a massive heart attack this afternoon."

A chill raced through her, a chill of foreboding and fear. The numbness she felt was replaced by a sense of purpose. She thought of the cardiac specialists she knew in Southern California, doctors her family should contact. Surely her uncle Ken had already reached someone. He was an experienced physician; he'd know what to do, who to call.

"What did he say?"

"Jane—"

"You should've let me talk to him."

"Jane." His hands gripped her shoulders as he tried to get her attention. "It's too late. Your father's gone."

She froze. Gone? Her father was dead? No! It couldn't be true. Not her father, not her daddy. Her knees buckled and she was immediately overwhelmed by deep heart-wrenching sobs.

"Honey, I'm so sorry." Cal pulled her into his arms and held her as she sobbed.

Jane had never experienced pain at this level. She could barely think, barely function. Cal helped her make the necessary arrangements. First they planned to leave the children with Glen and Ellie; later Jane decided she wanted them with her. While Cal booked the flights, she packed suitcases for him and the kids. Only when he started to carry the luggage out to the car did she realize she hadn't included anything for herself. The thought of having to choose a dress to wear at her own father's funeral nearly undid her. Unable to make a decision, she ended up stuffing every decent thing she owned into a suitcase.

"We can leave as soon as Glen and Ellie get here," Cal said, coming into the house for her bag.

"The roast," she said, remembering it was still in the oven.

"Don't worry about it. Glen and Ellie are on their

way. They'll take care of everything—they'll look after the place until we're back."

"Paul and Mary Ann?" The deep pain refused to go away, and she was incapable of thinking or acting without being directed by someone else.

"They're fine, honey. I'll get them dressed and ready to go."

She looked at her husband, and to her surprise felt nothing. Only a few minutes earlier she'd been convinced she was about to lose him to another woman. Right now, it didn't matter. Right now, she couldn't dredge up a single shred of feeling for Cal. Everything, even the love she felt for her husband, had been overshadowed by the grief she felt at her father's death.

Cal did whatever he could to help Jane, her younger brother and her mother with the funeral arrangements. Jane was in a stupor most of the first day. Her mother was in even worse shape. The day of the funeral Stephanie Dickinson had to be given a sedative.

Paul was too young to remember Cal's mother, and Cal doubted Mary Ann would recall much of Grandpa Dickinson, either. All the children knew was that something had happened that made their mother and grandmother cry. They didn't understand what Cal meant when he explained that their grandfather had died.

The funeral was well attended, as was the reception that followed. Cal was glad to see that there'd been flowers from quite a few people in Promise—including, of course, Annie. Harry Dickinson had been liked and respected. Cal admired the way Jane stepped in and handled the social formalities. Her mother just couldn't do it, and her brother, Derek, seemed trapped in his own private pain.

Later, after everyone had left, he found his wife sitting in the darkened kitchen. Cal sat at the table beside her, but when he reached for her, she stiffened. Not wanting to upset her, he removed his hand from her arm.

"You must be exhausted," he said. "When's the last time you ate?"

"I just buried my father, Cal. I don't feel like eating."

"Honey—"

"I need a few minutes alone, please."

Cal nodded, then stood up and walked out of the room. The house was dark, the children asleep, but the thought of going to bed held no appeal. Sedated, his mother-in-law was in her room and his wife sat in the shadows.

The day he'd buried his own mother had been the worst of his life. Jane had been by his side, his anchor. He didn't know how he could have survived without her. Yet now, with her father's death, she'd sent him away, asked for time alone. It felt like a rejection of him and his love, and that hurt.

Everyone handled grief differently, he reminded himself. People don't know how they'll react until it happens to them, he reasoned. Sitting on the edge of the bed, he mulled over the events of the past few days. They were a blur in his mind.

His arms ached to hold Jane. He loved his wife, loved his children. Their marriage had been going through a rough time, but everything would work out; he was sure of it. Cal waited for Jane to come to bed, and when she didn't, he must have fallen asleep. He awoke around two in the morning and discovered he was alone. Still in his clothes, he got up and went in search of his wife.

She was sitting where he'd left her. "Jane?" he whispered, not wanting to startle her.

"What time is it?" she asked.

"It's ten after two. Come to bed."

She responded with a shake of her head. "No. I can't."

"You've haven't slept in days."

"I know how long it's been," she snapped, showing the first bit of life since that phone call with the terrible news.

"Honey, please! This is crazy, sitting out here like

this. You haven't changed your clothes. This has been a hard day for you...."

She looked away, and in the room's faint light, he saw tears glistening on her face.

"I want to help you," he said urgently.

"Do you, Cal? Do you really?"

Her question shocked him. "You're my wife! Of course I do."

She started to sob then, and Cal was actually glad to see it. She needed to acknowledge her grief, to somehow express it. Other than when she'd first received the news, Jane had remained dry-eyed and strong. Her mother and brother were emotional wrecks, and her uncle Ken had been badly shaken. It was Jane who'd held them all together, Jane who'd made the decisions and arrangements, Jane who'd seen to the guests and reassured family and friends. It was time for her to let go, time to grieve.

"Go ahead and cry, Jane. It'll do you good." He handed her a clean handkerchief.

She clutched it to her face and sobbed more loudly.

"May I hold you?"

"No. Just leave me alone."

Cal crouched in front of her. "I'm afraid I can't do that. I want to help you," he said again. "Let me do that, all right?"

She shook her head.

"At least come to bed," he pleaded. She didn't resist when he clasped her by the forearms and drew her to her feet. Her legs must have gone numb from sitting there so long because she leaned heavily against him as he led her into the bedroom.

While she undressed, Cal turned back the covers.

She seemed to have trouble unfastening the large buttons of her tailored jacket. Brushing her hands aside, Cal unbuttoned it and helped take it off. When she was naked, he pulled the nightgown over her head, then brought her arms through the sleeves. He lowered her onto the bed and covered her with the blankets.

She went to sleep immediately—or that was what he thought.

As soon as he climbed into bed himself and switched off the light, she spoke. "Cal, I'm not going back."

"Back? Where?"

"To Promise," she told him.

This made no sense. "Not going back to Promise?" he repeated.

"No."

"Why not?" he asked, his voice louder than he'd intended. He stretched out one arm to turn on the lamp again.

"I can't deal with all the stress in our marriage. Not after this."

"But, Jane, we'll settle everything...."

"She wants you."

At first he didn't understand that Jane was talking about Nicole Nelson. Even when he did, it took him a while to control the anger and frustration. "Are you saying she can have me?" he asked, figuring a light approach might work better.

"She's determined, you know—except you *don't* know. You don't believe me."

"Jane, please, think about what you're saying."

"I have thought about it. It's all I've thought about for days. You're more worried about me embarrassing you than what that woman's doing to us. I don't have the strength or the will to fight for you. Not after today."

Patience had never been his strong suit, but Cal knew he had to give her some time and distance, not force her to resume their normal life too quickly. "Let's talk about it later. Tomorrow morning."

"I won't feel any differently about this in the morning. I've already spoken to Uncle Ken."

For years her uncle had wanted Jane to join his medical practice and had been bitterly disappointed when she'd chosen to stay in Texas, instead. "You're going to work for your uncle?"

"Temporarily."

Jane had arranged all this behind his back? Unable to hide his anger now, Cal tossed aside the sheet and vaulted out of bed. "You might've said something to me first! What the hell were you thinking?"

"Thinking?" she repeated. "I'm thinking about a man who lied to me and misled me."

"I never lied to you," he declared. "Not once."

"It was a lie of omission. You thought that what I didn't know wouldn't hurt me, right? Well, guess what, Cal? It does hurt. I don't want to be in a marriage where my husband's more concerned about being embarrassed than he is about the gossip and ridicule he subjects me to."

He couldn't believe they were having this conversation. "You're not being logical."

"Oh, yes, I am."

Cal strode to one end of the bedroom and stood there, not knowing what to do.

"You'll notice that even now, even when you know how I feel, you haven't once asked me to reconsider. Not once have you said you love me."

"You haven't exactly been proclaiming your love for me, either."

His words appeared to hit their mark, and she grew noticeably paler.

"Do you want me to leave right now?" he asked.

"I...I..." She floundered.

"No need to put it off," he said, letting his anger talk for him.

"You're right."

Cal jerked his suitcase out of the closet and crammed into it whatever clothes he could find. That didn't take long, although he gave Jane ample opportunity to talk him out of leaving, to say she hadn't really meant it.

Apparently she did.

Cal went into the bedroom where the children slept and kissed his daughter's soft cheek. He rested his hand on his son's shoulder, then abruptly turned away. A heaviness settled over his heart, and before he could surrender to regret, he walked away.

Seven

"I know how hard this is on you," Jane's mother said. It was two weeks since the funeral. Two weeks since Jane had separated from her husband. Stephanie busied herself about the kitchen and avoided eye contact. "But, Jane, are you sure you did the right thing?" She pressed her lips together and concentrated on cleaning up the breakfast dishes. "Ken's delighted that you're going to work with him, and the children are adjusting well, but..."

"I'm getting my own apartment."

"I won't hear of it," her mother insisted. "If you're going through with this, I want you to stay here. I don't want you dealing with a move on top of everything else."

"Mother, it's very sweet of you, but you need your space, too."

"No…" Tears filled her eyes. "I don't want to live alone— I don't think I can. I never have, you know. Not in my entire life and…well, I realize I'm leaning on you, but I need you so desperately."

"Mother, I understand."

"It's not just that. I'm so worried about you and Cal."

"I know," Jane whispered. She tried not to think of him, or of the situation between them. There'd been no contact whatsoever. Cal had left in anger, and at the time she'd wanted him out of her life.

"Did you make an appointment with an attorney?" her mother asked.

Jane shook her head. It was just one more thing she'd delayed doing. One more thing she couldn't make a decision about. Most days she could barely get out of bed and see to the needs of her children. Uncle Ken was eager to have her join his practice. He'd already discussed financial arrangements and suggested a date for her to start—the first Monday in the new year. Jane had listened carefully to his plans; however, she'd felt numb and disoriented. This wasn't what she wanted, but everything had been set in motion and she didn't know how to stop it. Yet she had to support herself and the children. So far she hadn't needed money, but she would soon. Cal would send support if she asked for it.

She lacked the courage to call him, though. She hated the idea of their first conversation being about money.

"You haven't heard from Cal, have you?" Her mother broke into her thoughts.

"No." His silence wasn't something Jane could ignore. She'd envisioned her husband coming back for her, proclaiming his love and vowing never to allow any woman to stand between him and his family. Ignoring Jane was bad enough, but the fact that he hadn't seen fit to contact the children made everything so much worse. It was as though he'd wiped his family from his mind.

Two months ago Jane assumed she had a near-perfect marriage. Now she was separated and living with her mother. Still, she believed that, if not for the death of her father, she'd be back in Texas right now. Eventually they would've worked out this discord; they would have rediscovered their love. Instead, in her pain and grief over the loss of her father, she'd sent Cal away.

She reminded herself that she hadn't needed to ask him twice. He'd been just as eager to escape.

Nicole Nelson had won.

At any other time in her life Jane would have fought for her husband, but now she had neither the strength nor the emotional energy to do so. From all appearances, Cal had made his choice—and it wasn't her or the children.

"We should talk about Thanksgiving," her mother said. "It's next week...."

"Thanksgiving?" Jane hadn't realized the holiday was so close.

"Ken and Jean asked us all to dinner. What do you think?"

Jane had noticed that her mother was having a hard time making decisions, too. "Sounds nice," she said, not wanting to plan that far ahead. Even a week was too much. She couldn't bear to think about the holidays, especially Christmas.

The doorbell chimed and Jane answered it, grateful for the interruption. Facing the future, making plans— it was just too difficult. A deliveryman stood with a box and a form for her to sign. Not until Jane closed the door did she see the label addressed to Paul in Cal's distinctive handwriting.

She carried the package into the bedroom, where her son sat doing a jigsaw puzzle. He glanced up when she entered the room.

"It's from Daddy," she said, setting the box on the carpet.

Paul tore into the package with gusto and let out a squeal when he found his favorite blanket. He bunched it up and hugged it to his chest, grinning hugely. Jane looked inside the box and saw a short letter. She read it aloud.

Dear Paul,
I thought you might want to have your old friend with you. Give your little sister a hug from me.

Love,
Daddy

Jane swallowed around the lump in her throat. Cal's message in that letter was loud and clear. He'd asked Paul to hug Mary Ann, but not her.

Jane was on her own.

The post office fell silent when Cal stepped into the building. The Moorhouse sisters, Edwina and Lily, stood at the counter, visiting with Caroline Weston, who was the wife of his best friend, as well as the local postmistress. Caroline had taken a leave of absence from her duties for the past few years, but had recently returned to her position.

When the three women saw Cal, the two retired schoolteachers pinched their lips together and stiffly drew themselves up.

"Good day, ladies," Cal said, touching the brim of his hat.

"Cal Patterson," Edwina said briskly. "I only wish

you were in the fifth grade again so I could box your ears."

"How're you doing, Cal?" Caroline asked in a friendlier tone.

He didn't answer because anyone looking at him ought to be able to tell. He was miserable and getting more so every day. By now he'd fully expected his wife to come to her senses and return home. He missed her and he missed his kids. He barely ate, hadn't slept an entire night since he got back and was in a foul mood most of the time.

Inserting the key in his postal box, he opened the small door. He was about to collect his mail when he heard Caroline's voice from the post-office side of the box. "Cal?"

He reached for the stack of envelopes and flyers, then peered through. Sure enough, Caroline was looking straight at him.

"I just wanted to tell you how sorry Grady and I are."

He nodded, rather than comment.

"Is there anything we can do?"

"Not a thing," he said curtly, wanting Caroline and everyone else, including the Moorhouse sisters, to know that his problems with Jane were his business…and hers. No one else's.

"Cal, listen—"

"I don't mean to be rude, but I'm in a hurry." Not

waiting for her reply, Cal locked his postal box and left the building.

When he'd first returned from California, people had naturally assumed that Jane had stayed on with the children to help Mrs. Dickinson. Apparently news of the separation had leaked out after Annie called Jane at her mother's home. From that point on, word had spread faster than a flash flood. What began as simple fact became embellished with each retelling. Family and friends knew more about what was happening— or supposedly happening—in his life than he did, Cal thought sardonically.

Only yesterday Glen had asked him about the letter from Paul. Cal hadn't heard one word from his wife or children, but then he hadn't collected his mail, either. When Cal asked how Glen knew about this letter, his brother briskly informed him that he'd heard from Ellie. Apparently Ellie had heard it from Dovie, and Dovie just happened to be in the post office when Caroline was sorting mail. That was life in a small town.

As soon as he stepped out of the post office, Cal quickly shuffled through the envelopes and found the letter addressed to him in Jane's familiar writing. The return address showed Paul's name.

Cal tore into the envelope with an eagerness he couldn't hide.

Dear Daddy,

Thank you for my blankey. I sleep better with it.
Mary Ann likes it, too, and I sometimes share with
her. Grandma still misses Grandpa. We're spending Thanksgiving with Uncle Ken and Aunt Jean.

Love,

Paul

Cal read the letter a second time, certain he was
missing something. Surely there was a hidden message
there from Jane, a subtle hint to let him know what she
was thinking. Perhaps the mention of Thanksgiving
was her way of telling him that she was proceeding
with her life as a single woman. Her way of inform-
ing him that she was managing perfectly well without
a husband.

Thanksgiving? Cal had to stop and think about the
date. It'd been nearly three weeks since he'd last talked
to Jane. Three weeks since he'd hugged his children.
Three weeks that he'd been walking around in a haze
of wounded pride and frustrated anger.

Not wanting to linger in town, Cal returned to the
ranch. He looked at the calendar and was stunned to
see that he'd nearly missed the holiday. Not that eating
a big turkey dinner would've made any difference to

him. Without his wife and children, the day would be just like all the rest, empty and silent.

Thanksgiving Day Cal awoke with a sick feeling in the pit of his stomach. Glen had tried to talk him into joining his family. Ellie's mother and aunt were flying in from Chicago for the holiday weekend, he'd said, but Cal was more than welcome. Cal declined without regrets.

He thought he might avoid Thanksgiving activities altogether, but should have known better. Around noon his father arrived. As soon as he saw the truck heading toward the house, Cal stepped onto the back porch to wait for him.

"What are you doing here, Dad?" he demanded, making sure his father understood that he didn't appreciate the intrusion.

"It's Thanksgiving."

"I know what day it is," Cal snapped.

"I thought I'd let you buy me dinner," Phil said blithely.

"I thought they served a big fancy meal at the retirement residence."

"They do, but I'd rather eat with you."

Cal would never admit it, but despite his avowals, he wanted the company.

"Where am I taking you?" he asked, coming down the concrete steps to meet Phil.

"Brewster."

Cal tipped back his hat to get a better look at his father. "Why?"

"The Rocky Creek Inn," Phil said. "From what I hear, they cook a dinner fit to rival even Dovie's."

"It's one of the priciest restaurants in the area," Cal muttered, remembering how his father had announced Cal would be footing the bill.

Phil laughed. "Hey, I'm retired. I can't afford a place as nice as the Rocky Creek Inn. Besides, I have something to tell you."

"Tell me here," Cal said, wondering if his father had news about Jane and the children. If so, he wanted it right now.

Phil shook his head. "Later."

They decided to leave for Brewster after Cal changed clothes and shaved. His father made himself at home while he waited and Cal was grateful he didn't mention the condition of the house. When he returned wearing a clean, if wrinkled, shirt and brand-new Wranglers, Phil was reading Paul's letter, which lay on the kitchen table, along with three weeks' worth of unopened mail. He paused, expecting his father to lay into him about leaving his family behind in California, and was relieved when Phil didn't. No censure was necessary; Cal had called himself every kind of fool for what he'd done.

The drive into Brewster took almost two hours and was fairly relaxing. They discussed a range of topics, everything from politics to sports, but avoided anything to do with Jane and the kids. A couple of times Cal could have led naturally into the subject of his wife, but didn't. No need to ruin the day with a litany of his woes.

The Rocky Creek Inn had a reputation for excellent food and equally good service. They ended up waiting thirty minutes for a table, but considering it was a holiday and they had no reservation, they felt that wasn't bad.

Both men ordered the traditional Thanksgiving feast and a glass of wine. Cal waited until the waiter had poured his chardonnay before he spoke. "You had something you wanted to tell me?" He'd bet the ranch that whatever it was involved the situation with Jane. But he didn't mind. After three frustrating weeks, he hoped Phil had some news.

"Do you remember when I had my heart attack?"

Cal wasn't likely to forget. He'd nearly lost his father. "Of course."

"What you probably don't know is that your mother and I nearly split up afterward."

"You and Mom?" Cal couldn't hide his shock. As far as he knew, his parents' marriage had been rock-solid from the day of their wedding until they'd lowered his mother into the ground.

"I was still in the hospital recovering from the surgery and your mother, God bless her, waltzed into my room and casually said she'd put earnest money down on the old Howe place."

Cal reached for his wineglass in an effort to stifle a grin. He remembered the day vividly. The doctors had talked to the family following open-heart surgery and suggested Phil think about reducing his hours at the ranch. Shortly after that, his parents decided to open a bed-and-breakfast in town. It was then that Cal and his brother had taken over the operation of the Lonesome Coyote Ranch.

"Your mother didn't even *ask* me about buying that monstrosity," his father told him. "I was on my death bed—"

"You were in the hospital," Cal corrected.

"All right, all right, but you get the picture. Next thing I know, Mary comes in and tells me, *tells* me, mind you, that I've retired and the two of us are moving to town and starting a bed-and-breakfast."

Cal nearly burst out laughing, although he was well aware of what his mother had done and why. Getting

Phil to cut back his hours would have been impossible, and Mary had realized that retirement would be a difficult adjustment for a man who'd worked cattle all his life. Phil wasn't capable of spending his days lazing around, so she'd taken matters into her own hands.

"I didn't appreciate what your mother did, manipulating me like that," Phil continued. "She knew I never would've agreed to live in town, and she went ahead and made the decision, anyway."

"But, Dad, it was a brilliant idea." The enterprise had been a money-maker from the first. The house was in decent condition, but had enough quirks to keep his father occupied with a variety of repair projects. The bed-and-breakfast employed the best of both his parents' skills. Phil was a natural organizer and his mother was personable and warm, good at making people feel welcome.

His father's eyes clouded. "It *was* brilliant, but at the time I didn't see it that way. I don't mind telling you I was mad enough to consider ending our marriage."

Cal frowned. "You didn't mean it, Dad."

"The hell I didn't. I would've done it, too, if I hadn't been tied down to that hospital bed. It gave me time to think about what I'd do without Mary in my life, and after a few days I decided to give your mother a second chance."

Cal laughed outright.

"You think I'm joking, but I was serious and your mother knew it. When she left the hospital, she asked me to have my attorney contact hers. The way I felt right then, I swear I was determined to do it, Cal. I figured there are some things a man won't let a woman interfere with in life, and as far as I was concerned at that moment, Mary had crossed the line."

Ah, so this was what Cal was meant to hear. In her lack of trust, Jane had crossed the line with him, too. Only, *he* hadn't been the one who'd chosen to break up the family. That decision had rested entirely with Jane.

"I notice you haven't pried into my situation yet," Cal murmured.

"No, I haven't," Phil said. "That's your business and Jane's. If you want out of the marriage, then that's up to you."

"Out of the marriage!" Cal shot back. "Jane's the one who wants out. She decided not to return to Promise. The day of her father's funeral, she told me she was staying with her mother…indefinitely."

"You agreed to this?"

"The hell I did!"

"But you left."

Cal had replayed that fateful night a hundred times, asking himself these same questions. Should he have stayed and talked it out with her? Should he have taken a stand and insisted she listen to reason? Three weeks later, he still didn't have the answer.

"Don't you think Jane might have been distraught over her father's death?" Phil wanted to know.

"Yeah." Cal nodded. "But it's been nearly a month and she hasn't had a change of heart yet."

"No, she hasn't," Phil said, and sighed. "It's a shame, too, a real shame."

"I love her, Dad." Cal was willing to admit it. "I miss her and the kids." He thought of the day he'd found Paul's blankey. After all the distress that stupid blanket had caused him, Cal was so glad to see it he'd brought it to his face, breathing in the familiar scent of his son. Afterward, the knot in his stomach was so tight he hadn't eaten for the rest of the day.

"I remember when Jennifer left you," Phil said, growing melancholy, "just a couple of days before the wedding. You looked like someone had stabbed a knife straight through your gut. I knew you loved her, but you didn't go after her."

"No way." Jennifer had made her decision.

"Pride wouldn't let you," Phil added. "In that case, I think it was probably for the best. I'm not convinced of it this time." His father shook his head. "I loved your mother, don't misunderstand me—it damn near killed me when she died—but as strong as my love for her was, we didn't have the perfect marriage. We argued, but we managed to work out our problems. I'm sure you'll resolve things with Jane, too."

Cal hoped that was true, but he wasn't nearly as confident as his father.

"The key is communication," Phil said.

Cal held his father's look. "That's a little difficult when Jane's holed up halfway across the country. Besides, as I understand it, communication is a two-way street. Jane has to be willing to talk to me and she isn't."

"Have you made an effort to get in touch with her?"

He shook his head.

"That's what I thought."

"Go ahead and say it," Cal muttered. "You think I should go after her."

"Are you asking my opinion?" Phil asked.

"No, but you're going to give it to me, anyway."

"If Jane was my wife," Phil said, his eyes intent on Cal, "I'd go back for her and settle this once and for all. I wouldn't return to Promise without her. Are you willing to do that, son?"

Cal needed to think about it, and about all the things that had been said. "I don't know," he answered, being as honest as he could. "I just don't know."

* * *

Nicole Nelson arrived for work at Tumbleweed Books bright and early on the Friday morning after Thanksgiving. With the official start of the Christmas season upon them, the day was destined to be a busy one. She let herself in the back door, prepared to open the bookstore for Annie, who was leaving more and more of the responsibility to her, which proved—to Nicole's immense satisfaction—that Annie liked and trusted her.

Nicole had taken a calculated risk over Thanksgiving and lost. In the end she'd spent the holiday alone, even though she'd received two dinner invitations. Her plan had been to spend the day with Cal. She would've made sure he didn't feel threatened, would have couched her suggestion in compassionate terms—just two lonely people making it through the holiday. Unfortunately it hadn't turned out that way. She'd phoned the ranch house twice and there'd been no answer, which made her wonder where he'd gone and who he'd been with. Needless to say, she hadn't left a message.

At any rate, the wife was apparently out of the picture. That had been surprisingly easy. Jane Patterson didn't deserve her husband if she wasn't willing to fight for him. Most women did fight. Usually their attempts were just short of pathetic, but for reasons Nicole had yet to understand, men generally chose to stay with their wives.

Those who didn't…well, the truth was, Nicole quickly grew bored with them. It was different with Cal, had always been different. Never before had she shown her hand more blatantly than she had with Dr. Jane. Nicole felt almost sorry for her. Really, all she'd done was enlighten Jane about a few home truths. The woman didn't value what she had if she was willing to let Cal go with barely a protest.

The phone rang. It wasn't even nine, the store didn't officially open for another hour, and already they were receiving calls.

"Tumbleweed Books," Nicole answered.

"Annie Porter, please." The voice sounded vaguely familiar.

"I'm sorry, Annie won't be in until ten."

"But I just phoned the house and Lucas told me she was at work."

"Then she should be here any minute." Playing a hunch, Nicole asked, "Is this Jane Patterson?"

The hesitation at the other end confirmed her suspicion. "Is this Nicole Nelson?"

"It is," Nicole said, then added with a hint of regret, "I'm sorry to hear about you and Cal."

There was a soft disbelieving laugh. "I doubt that. I'd appreciate it if you'd tell Annie I phoned."

"Of course. I understand your father recently passed away. I am sorry, Jane."

Jane paused, but thanked her.

"Annie was really upset about it. She seems fond of your family."

Another pause. "Please have her call when it's convenient."

"I will." Nicole felt the need to keep Jane on the line. *Know your enemy,* she thought. "My friend Jennifer Healy was the one who broke off her engagement with Cal. Did you know that?"

The responding sigh told Nicole that Jane was growing impatient with her. "I remember hearing something along those lines."

"Cal didn't go after Jennifer, either."

"Either?" Jane repeated.

"Cal never said who wanted the separation—you or him. It's not something we talk about. But the fact that he hasn't sent for you says a great deal, don't you think?"

"What's happening between my husband and me is none of your business. Goodbye, Nicole." Her words were followed by a click and then a dial tone.

So Dr. Jane had hung up on her. That didn't come as

a shock. If anything, it stimulated Nicole. She'd moved to Promise, determined to have Cal Patterson. Through the years, he'd never strayed far from her mind. She'd lost her fair share of married men to their wives, but that wasn't going to happen *this* time.

So far she'd been smart, played her cards right, and her patience had been rewarded. In three weeks, she'd only contacted Cal once and that was about a book order. Shortly after he'd returned from California alone, the town had been filled with speculation. The news excited Nicole. She'd planted the seeds, let gossip water Jane's doubts, trusting that time would eventually bring her hopes to fruition. With Jane still in California, Nicole couldn't help being curious about the status of the relationship, so she'd phoned to let him know the book Jane had ordered was in. Only Jane hadn't ordered any book...

Playing dumb, Nicole had offered to drop it off at the ranch, since she was headed in that direction anyway—or so she'd claimed. Cal declined, then suggested Annie mail it to Jane at her mother's address in California. Despite her efforts to keep Cal talking, it hadn't worked. But he'd been in a hurry; he must've had things to do. And he probably felt a bit depressed about the deterioration of his marriage. After all, no man enjoyed failure. Well, she'd just have to comfort him, wouldn't she? She sensed that her opportunity was coming soon.

It was always more difficult when there were children involved. In all honesty, Nicole didn't feel good about destroying a family. However, seeing how easy it'd been to break up this marriage made her suspect that the relationship hadn't been very secure in the first place.

She'd bide her time. It wouldn't be long before Cal needed someone to turn to. And Nicole had every intention of being that someone.

After speaking to that horrible woman, Jane felt wretched. Nicole had implied—no, more than implied—that she and Cal were continuing to see each other. Sick to her stomach, Jane hurried to her bedroom.

"Jane." Her mother stepped into the room. "Are you all right? Was that Cal on the phone? What happened? I saw you talking and all of a sudden the color drained from your face and you practically ran in here."

"I'm fine, Mom," Jane assured her. "No, it wasn't Cal. It wasn't anyone important."

"I finished writing all the thank-you notes and decided I need a break. How about if I take you and the children to lunch?"

The thought of food repelled her. "I don't feel up to going out, Mom. Sorry."

"You won't mind if I take the kids? Santa's arriving at the mall this afternoon and I know Paul and Mary Ann will be thrilled."

An afternoon alone sounded wonderful to Jane. "Are you sure it won't be too much for you?"

"Time with these little ones is *exactly* what I need."

"Is there anything you want me to do while you're out?" Jane asked, although she longed for nothing so much as a two-hour nap.

"As a matter of fact, there is," Stephanie said. "I want you to rest. You don't look well. You're tired and out of sorts."

That was putting it mildly. Jane felt devastated and full of despair, and given the chance, she'd delight in tearing Nicole Nelson's hair out! What a lovely Christian thought, she chastised herself. For that matter, what a cliché.

"Mom." Paul stood in the doorway to her bedroom.

"Aren't you going with Grandma?" Jane asked.

Paul nodded, then came into the room and handed her his blankey. "This is for you." Jane smiled as he placed the tattered much-loved blanket on her bed.

"Thank you, sweetheart," she said and kissed his brow.

Jane heard the front door close as the children left

with her mother. Taking them to a mall the day after Thanksgiving was the act of an insane woman, in Jane's opinion. She wouldn't be caught anywhere near crowds like that. As soon as the thought formed in her mind, Jane realized she hadn't always felt that way. A few years ago she'd been just as eager as all those other shoppers. Even in medical school she'd found time to hunt down the best buys. It'd been a competition with her friends; the cheaper an item, the greater the bragging rights.

Not so these days. None of that seemed important anymore. The closest mall was a hundred miles from the ranch, and almost everything she owned was bought in town, ordered through a catalog or purchased over the Internet. The life she lived now was based in small-town America. And she loved it.

She missed Promise. She missed her husband even more.

Her friends, too. Jane could hardly imagine what they must think. The only person she'd talked to after the funeral had been Annie, and then just briefly. When Annie had asked about Cal, Jane had refused to discuss him, other than to say they'd separated. It would do no good to talk about her situation with Annie, especially since Nicole worked for her now.

With her son's blanket wrapped around her shoulders, Jane did sleep for an hour. When she woke, she knew instantly who she needed to talk to—Dovie Hennessey.

The older woman had been her first friend in Promise, and Jane valued her opinion. Maybe Dovie could help her muddle her way through the events of the past few months. She was sorry she hadn't talked to her before. She supposed it was because her father's death had shaken her so badly; she'd found it too difficult to reach out. Dealing with the children depleted what energy she had. Anything beyond the most mundane everyday functions seemed beyond her. As a physician, Jane should have recognized the signs of depression earlier, but then, it was much harder to be objective about one's own situation.

To her disappointment Dovie didn't answer. She could have left a message but decided not to. She considered calling her husband, but she didn't have the courage yet. What would she say? What would *he* say? If Nicole answered, it would destroy her, and just now Jane felt too fragile to deal with such a profound betrayal.

Her mother was an excellent housekeeper, but Jane went around picking up toys and straightening magazines, anything to keep herself occupied. The mail was on the counter and Jane saw that it included a number of sympathy cards. She read each one, which renewed her overwhelming sense of loss and left her in tears.

Inside one of the sympathy cards was a letter addressed to her mother. Jane didn't read it, although when she returned it to the envelope, she saw the signature. Laurie Jo. Her mother's best friend from high school. Laurie Jo Spencer was the kind of friend to her mother that Annie had always been to Jane. Lately, though, Annie had been so busy dealing with the changes in her own life that they hadn't talked nearly as often as they used to.

Laurie Jo had added a postscript asking Stephanie to join her in Mexico over the Christmas holidays. They were both recent widows, as well as old friends; they'd be perfect companions for each other.

Jane wondered if her mother would seriously consider the trip and hoped she would. It sounded ideal. Her father's health problems had started months ago, and he'd required constant attention and care. Stephanie was physically and emotionally worn out.

If her mother did take the trip, it'd be a good time for Jane to find her own apartment. That way, her moving out would cause less of a strain in their relationship. So far, Stephanie had insisted Jane stay with her.

In another four weeks it'd be Christmas. Jane would have to make some decisions before then. Painful decisions that would force her to confront realities she'd rather not face. This lack of energy and ambition, living one day to the next, was beginning to feel like the norm. Beginning to feel almost comfortable. But for her own sake and the sake of her children, it couldn't continue.

Jane glanced at the phone again. She dialed Dovie's number, but there was still no answer.

It occurred to her that Dovie's absence was really rather symbolic. There didn't seem to be anyone—or anything—left for her in Promise, Texas.

Eight

Cal had never been much of a drinking man. An occasional beer, wine with dinner, but he rarely broke into the hard stuff. Nor did he often drink alone. But after six weeks without his family, Cal was considering doing both. The walls felt like they were closing in on him. Needing to escape and not interested in company, Cal drove to town and headed straight for Billy D's, the local watering hole.

The Christmas lights were up, Cal noticed when he hit Main Street. Decorations were everywhere. Store windows featured Christmas displays, come of them quite elaborate. Huge red-and-white-striped candy canes and large wreaths dangled from each lamppost. Everything around town looked disgustingly cheerful, which only depressed him further. He'd never been all that fond of Christmas, but Jane was as bad as his

mother. A year ago Jane had decided to make ornaments for everyone in the family. She'd spent hours
pinning brightly colored beads to red satin balls, each
design different, each ornament unique. Even Cal had
to admit they were works of art. His wife's talent had
impressed him, but she'd shrugged off his praise, claim-
ing it was something she'd always planned to do.

Last Christmas, Paul hadn't quite understood what
Christmas was about, but he'd gotten into the spirit
of it soon enough. Seeing the festivities through his
son's eyes had made the holidays Cal's best ever. This
year would be even better now that both children—the
thought pulled him up short. Without Jane and his family, this Christmas was going to be the worst of his life.

Cal parked his truck outside the tavern and sat there
for several minutes before venturing inside. The noise
level momentarily lessened when he walked in as people noted his arrival, then quickly resumed. Wanting
to be alone, Cal chose a table at the back of the room,
and as soon as the waitress appeared, he ordered a beer.
Then, after thirty minutes or so, he had another. Even
this place was decorated for Christmas, he saw, with
inflated Santas and reindeer scattered about.

He must have been there an hour, perhaps longer,
when an attractive woman made her way toward him

and stood, hands on her shapely hips, directly in front of his table.

"Hello, Cal."

It was Nicole Nelson. Cal stiffened with dread, since it was this very woman who'd been responsible for most of his problems.

"Aren't you going to say it's nice to see me?"

"No."

She wore skin-tight jeans, a cropped beaded top and a white Stetson. At another time he might have thought her attractive, but not in his present frame of mind.

"Mind if I join you?"

He was about to explain that he'd rather be alone, but apparently she didn't need an invitation to pull out a chair and sit down. He seemed to remember she'd done much the same thing the night she'd found him at the Mexican Lindo. The woman did what *she* wanted, regardless of other people's preferences and desires. He'd never liked that kind of behavior and didn't understand why he tolerated it now.

"I'm sorry to hear about you and Jane."

His marriage was the last subject he intended to discuss with Nicole. He didn't respond.

"You must be lonely," she went on.

He shrugged and reached for his beer, taking a healthy swallow.

"I think it's a good idea for you to get out, mingle with friends, let the world know you're your own man."

She wasn't making any sense. Cal figured she'd leave as soon as she realized he wasn't going to be manipulated into a conversation.

"The holidays are a terrible time to be alone," she said, leaning forward with her elbows on the table. She propped her chin in her hands. "It's hard. I know."

Cal took another swallow of beer. She'd get the message eventually. At least he hoped she would.

"I always thought you and I had a lot in common," she continued.

Unable to suppress his reaction, he arched his eyebrows. She leaped on that as if he'd talked nonstop for the past ten minutes.

"It's true, Cal. Look at us. We're both killing a Saturday night in a tavern because neither of us has anyplace better to go. We're struggling to hold in our troubles for fear anyone else will know the real us."

The woman was so full of malarkey it was all Cal could do not to laugh in her face.

"I can help you through this," she said earnestly.

"Help me?" He shouldn't have spoken, but he couldn't even guess what Nicole had to offer that could possibly interest him.

"I made a terrible mistake before, when Jennifer

broke off the engagement. You needed me then, but I was too young to know that. I'm mature enough to have figured it out now."

"Really?" This entire conversation was laughable.

Her smile was coy. "You want me, Cal," she said boldly, her unwavering gaze holding him captive. "That's good, because I want you, too. I've always wanted you."

"I'm married, Nicole." That was a little matter she'd conveniently forgotten.

"Separated," she corrected.

This woman had played no small part in that separation, and Cal was seeing her with fresh eyes.

"I think you should leave," he said, not bothering to mince words. Until now, Cal had assumed Jane was being paranoid about Nicole Nelson. Yes, they'd bumped into each other at the Mexican Lindo. Yes, she'd baked him a casserole and delivered it to the house. Both occasions meant nothing to him. Until today, he'd believed that Jane had overreacted, that she'd been unreasonable. But at this moment, everything Jane had said added up in his mind.

"Leave?" She pouted prettily. "You don't mean that."

"Nicole, I'm married and I happen to love my wife and children very much. I'm not interested in an affair with you or anyone else."

"I…I hope you don't think that's what I was saying." She revealed the perfect amount of confusion.

"I know exactly what you were saying. What else is this 'I want you' business? You're right about one thing though—I know what I want and, frankly, it isn't you."

"Cal," she whispered, shaking her head. "I'm sure you misunderstood me."

He snickered softly.

"You're looking for company," she said, "otherwise you would've done your drinking at home. I understand that, because I know what it's like to be alone, to want to connect with someone. You want someone with a willing ear."

Cal had any number of family and friends with whom he could discuss his woes, and he doubted Nicole had any viable solutions to offer. He groaned. Sure as hell, Jane would get wind of this encounter and consider it grounds for divorce.

"All right," Nicole said, and pushed back her chair. "I know this is a difficult time. Separation's hard on a man, but when you want to talk about it, I'll be there for you, okay? Call me. I'll wait to hear from you."

As far as Cal was concerned, Nicole would have a very long wait. He paid his tab, and then, because he didn't want to drive, he walked over to the café in the bowling alley.

"You want some food to go with that coffee?" Denise asked pointedly.

"I guess," he muttered, realizing he hadn't eaten much of anything in days. "Bring me whatever you want. I don't care."

Ten minutes later she returned with a plate of corned-beef hash, three fried eggs, plus hash browns and a stack of sourdough toast. "That's breakfast," he said, looking down at the plate.

"I figured it was your first meal of the day. Your first decent one, anyhow."

"Well, yeah." It was.

Denise set the glass coffeepot on the table. "You okay?"

He nodded.

"You don't look it. You and I went all the way through school together, Cal, and I feel I can be honest with you. But don't worry—I'm not going to give you advice."

"Good." He'd had a confrontation with his brother earlier in the day about his marriage. Then he'd heard from Nicole. Now Denise. Everyone seemed to want to tell him what to do.

"I happen to think the world of Dr. Jane. So work it out before I lose faith in you."

"Yes, Denise." He picked up his fork.

Cal was half finished his meal when Wade McMillen slipped into the booth across from him. "Hi, Cal. How're you doing?"

Cal scowled. This was the very reason he'd avoided coming into town until tonight. People naturally assumed he was looking for company, so they had no compunction about offering him that—and plenty of unsolicited advice.

"Heard from Jane lately?" Wade asked.

Talk about getting straight to the point.

"No." Cal glared at the man who was both pastor and friend. At times it was hard to see the boundary between the two roles. "I don't remember inviting you to join me," he muttered and reached for the ketchup, smearing a glob on the remains of his corned-beef hash.

"You didn't."

"What is it with people?" Cal snapped. "Can't they leave me the hell alone?"

Wade chuckled. "That was an interesting choice of words. Leave you *the hell alone*. I imagine that's what it must feel like for you about now. Like you're in hell and all alone."

"What gives you that impression?" Cal dunked a slice of toast into the egg yolk, doing his best to appear unaffected.

"Why else would you come into town? You're going stir-crazy on that ranch without Jane and the kids."

"Listen, Wade," Cal said forcefully, "I wasn't the one who wanted a separation. Jane made that decision. I didn't want this or deserve it. In fact, I didn't do a damn thing."

His words were followed by silence. Then Wade said mildly, "I'm sure that's true. You didn't do a damn thing."

Cal met his gaze. "What do you mean by that?"

"That, my friend, is for you to figure out." Wade stood up and left the booth.

For the tenth time that day, Dovie Hennessey found herself staring at the phone, willing it to ring, willing Jane Patterson to call from California.

"You're going to do it, aren't you?" Frank said, his voice muted by the morning paper. "Never mind everything you said earlier—you're going to call Jane."

"I don't know what I'm going to do," Dovie murmured, although she could feel her resolve weakening more each day. When she learned that Cal and Jane had separated, Dovie's first impulse had been to call Jane. For weeks now, she'd resisted. After all, Jane was with her mother and certainly didn't need advice from Dovie. If and when she did, Jane would phone her.

Everything was complicated by Harry Dickinson's death. Jane was grieving, and Dovie didn't want to intrude on this private family time. First her father and then her marriage. Her friend was suffering, but she'd hoped that Jane would make the effort to get in touch with her. She hadn't, and Dovie was growing impatient.

Few people had seen Cal, and those who did claimed he walked around in a state of perpetual anger. That sounded exactly like Cal, who wouldn't take kindly to others involving themselves in his affairs.

Dovie remembered what he'd been like after his broken engagement. He'd hardly ever come into town, and when he did, he settled his business quickly and was gone. He'd been unsociable, unresponsive, impossible to talk to. Falling in love with Jane had changed him. Marrying Dr. Texas was the best thing that had ever happened to him, and Dovie recalled nostalgically how pleased Mary had been when her oldest son announced his engagement.

"Go ahead," Frank said after a moment. "Call her."

"Do you really think I should?" Even now Dovie was uncertain.

"We had two hang-ups recently. Those might've been from Jane."

"Frank, be reasonable," Dovie said, laughing lightly. "Not everyone likes leaving messages."

"You could always ask her," he said, giving Dovie a perfectly reasonable excuse to call.

"I could, couldn't I?" Then, needing no more incentive, she reached for the phone and the pad next to it and dialed the long-distance number Annie Porter had given her.

On the third ring Jane answered.

"Jane, it's Dovie—Dovie Hennessey," she added in case the dear girl was so distraught she'd forgotten her.

"Hello, Dovie," Jane said, sounding calm and confident.

"How are you?" Dovie cried, unnerved by the lack of emotion in her friend. "And the children?"

"We're all doing fine."

"Your mother?"

Jane sighed, showing the first sign of emotion. "She's adjusting, but it's difficult."

"I know, dear. I remember how excruciating everything was those first few months after Marvin died. Give your mother my best, won't you?"

"Of course." Jane hesitated, then asked, "How's everyone in Promise?"

Dovie smiled; it wasn't as hopeless as she'd feared. "By everyone, do you mean Cal?"

The hesitation was longer this time. "Yes, I suppose I do."

"Oh, Jane, he misses you so much. Every time I see that boy, it's all I can do not to hug him…."

"So he's been in town quite a bit recently." Jane's voice hardened ever so slightly. The implication was there without her having to say it.

"If that's your way of asking whether he's seeing Nicole Nelson, I can't really answer. However, my guess is he's not."

"You don't know that, though, do you? I...I spoke with Nicole myself and, according to her, they've been keeping each other company."

"Hogwash! What do you expect her to say? You and I both know she's after Cal."

"You think so, too?" Jane's voice was more emotional now.

"I didn't see it at first, but Frank did. He took one look at Nicole and said that woman was going to be trouble."

"Frank said that? Oh, Dovie, Cal thinks..." Jane inhaled a shaky breath. Then she went quiet again. "It doesn't matter anymore."

"What do you mean? Of course it matters!"

"I made an appointment with a divorce attorney this morning."

Stunned, Dovie gasped. "Oh, Jane, no!" This news was the last thing she'd wanted to hear.

"Cal made his choice."

"I don't believe that. You seem to be implying that

he's chosen Nicole over you and the children, and Jane, that simply isn't so."

"Dovie—"

"You said Nicole claimed she was seeing Cal. Just how trustworthy do you think this woman is?"

"Annie trusts her."

"Oh, my dear, Annie hasn't got a clue what's happening. Do you seriously believe she'd stand by and let Nicole ruin your life if she knew what was going on? Right now all she's thinking about is this pregnancy and the changes it'll bring to *her* life. I love Annie, you know that. She's a darling girl, but she tends to see the best in everyone. Weren't you the one who told me about her first husband? You said everyone knew what kind of man he was—except Annie. She just couldn't see it."

"I…I haven't discussed this with her."

"I can understand why. That's probably a good idea, the situation being what it is," Dovie said. "Now, let's get back to this business about the lawyer. Making an appointment—was that something you really *wanted* to do?"

"Actually, my uncle Ken suggested I get some advice. He's right, you know. I should find out where I stand legally before I proceed."

"Proceed with what?"

"Getting my own apartment, joining my uncle's medical practice and…" She didn't complete the thought.

"Filing for divorce," Dovie concluded for her.

"Yes." Jane's voice was almost inaudible.

"Is a divorce what you want?"

"I don't know anymore, Dovie. I just don't know. Cal and I have had plenty of disagreements over the years, but nothing like this."

"All marriages have ups and downs."

"I've been gone nearly six weeks and I haven't even heard from Cal. It's almost as…as if he's blotted me out of his life."

Dovie suspected that was precisely what he'd been trying to do, but all the evidence suggested he hadn't been very successful. "What about you?" she asked. "Have you tried to reach him?"

Jane didn't want to answer; Dovie could tell from the length of time it took her to speak. "No."

"I see." Indeed she did. Two stubborn, hurting people, both intent on proving how strong and independent they were. "What about the children? Do they miss their father?"

"Paul does the most. He asks about Cal nearly every day. He…he's taken to sucking his thumb again."

"And Mary Ann?"

"She's doing well. I don't think she realizes her father's out of the picture."

"You don't seriously believe that, do you?"

Jane breathed in deeply and Dovie could tell she was holding back tears. "I'm not sure anymore, Dovie." There was a pause. "She's growing like a weed, and she looks so much like Cal."

"She deserves to know her father."

"And I deserve a husband."

"Exactly," Dovie said emphatically. "Then what are you doing seeing an attorney?"

"Cal will never do it. He'll be content to leave things as they are. He seems to think if he ignores me long enough, I'll come to my senses, as he puts it, and return home. But if I did that, I'm afraid everything would go back the way it was before. My feelings wouldn't matter. He'd see himself as the long-suffering husband and me as a jealous shrew. No, Dovie, I'm not going to be the one to give in. Not this time."

"So this is a battle of wills?"

"It's much more than that."

Dovie heard the tears in her voice, and her heart ached for Jane, Cal and those precious children. "This is all because of Nicole Nelson," she said.

"Partially. But there's more."

"There's always more," Dovie agreed.

"I guess Nicole crystallized certain…problems or made them evident, anyway." Jane paused. "She as good as told me she wants him."

That Dovie could believe. "So, being the nice accommodating woman you are, you're just stepping aside and opening the door for her?"

This, too, seemed to unsettle Jane. After taking a moment to consider her answer, she said, "Yes, I guess I am. You and everyone else seem to think I should fight for Cal, that I have too much grit to simply step aside. At one time I did, but just now…I don't. If she wants him and he wants her, then far be it from me to stand between them."

"Oh, Jane, you don't mean that!"

"I do. I swear to you, Dovie, I mean every word." She stopped and Dovie heard her blowing her nose then, a murmured "I'm fine, sweetheart, go watch Mary Ann for me, all right?"

"That was Paul?" Dovie asked. The thought of this little boy, separated from his father for reasons he didn't understand, brought tears to her eyes.

"Yes. He gave me a tissue." She took a deep breath. "Dovie, I have to go now."

"Sounds like you've made up your mind. You're keeping that appointment with the divorce attorney, then?"

"Yes. I'll be getting an apartment right after Christmas, and I'll move in the first of the year."

"You aren't willing to fight for Cal," she said flatly.

"We've been over this, Dovie. No, as far as I'm concerned, he's free to have Nicole if he wants, because he's made it quite plain he isn't interested in me."

"Now, you listen, Jane Patterson. You're in too much pain to deal with this right now. You've just lost your father. That's trauma enough without making a decision about your marriage. And isn't it time you thought about your children?"

"My children?"

"Ask yourself if they need their father and if he needs them. You won't have to dig very deep to know the answers to those questions. Let them be your guide."

To Dovie's surprise, Jane started to laugh. Not the bright humorous laughter she remembered but the soft knowing laughter of a woman who's conceding a point. "You always could do that to me, Dovie."

"Do what?"

Jane sniffled. "Make me cry until I laugh!"

Cal knew something was wrong the minute Grady Weston pulled into the yard. The two men had been neighbors and best friends their whole lives. As kids, they'd discovered a ghost town called Bitter End, which had since become a major focus for the community. Along with Nell Bishop and the man she'd married, writer Travis Grant, they'd uncovered the secrets of the long-forgotten town. It was the original settlement— founded by Pattersons and Westons, among others— and later re-established as Promise.

Grady jumped out of his pickup, and Cal saw that he had a bottle of whiskey in his hand.

"What's that for?" Cal asked, pointing at the bottle.

"I figured you were going to need it," Grady said. "Remember when I was thirteen and I broke my arm?"

Cal nodded. They'd been out horseback riding, and Grady had taken a bad fall. Both boys had realized the bone was broken. Not knowing what to do and fearful of what would happen if he left his friend, Cal had ridden like a madman to get help.

"When you brought my dad back with you, he had a bottle of whiskey. Remember?"

Cal nodded again. Grady's dad had given him a couple of slugs to numb the pain. It was at this point that Cal made the connection. "You've got something to tell me I'm not going to want to hear."

Grady moved onto the porch, and although it was chilly and the wind was up, the two of them sat there.

"I'm not getting involved in this business between

you and Jane," Grady began. "That's your affair. I have my own opinion, we all do, but what happens between the two of you…well, you know what I mean."

"Yeah."

"Savannah was in town the other day and she ran into Dovie."

Cal was well aware that Dovie and Jane were good friends, had been for years. "Jane's talked to Dovie?"

"Apparently so."

"And whatever Jane told Dovie, she told Savannah and Savannah told Caroline and Caroline told you. So, what is it?"

Grady hesitated, as though he'd give anything not to be the one telling him this. "Jane's filing for divorce."

"The hell she is." Cal bolted upright, straight off the wicker chair. "That does it." He removed his hat and slapped it against his thigh. "Enough is enough. I've tried to be patient, wait this out, but I'm finished with that."

"Finished?"

"We start getting lawyers involved, and we'll end up hating each other, sure as anything."

Grady chuckled. "What are you going to do?"

"What else can I do? I'm going after her." He barreled into the house, ready to pack his bags.

"You're bringing her home?" his friend asked, following him inside. The screen door slammed shut behind Grady.

"You bet I'm bringing her home. Divorce? That's just crazy!" So far, Cal had played it cool, let Jane have the distance she seemed to need. Obviously that wasn't working. He hadn't thought out his response to the situation, had merely reacted on an emotional level. In the beginning he was too angry to think clearly; then his anger had turned to bitterness, but that hadn't lasted long. Lately, all he'd been was miserable, and he'd had about as much misery as a man could take.

Grady gave him a grin and a thumbs-up. "Good. I wasn't keen on handing over my best bottle of bourbon, so if you have no objection, I'll take this back with me."

"You do that," Cal said.

"Actually this is perfect."

"How do you mean?"

Grady laughed. "A Christmas reunion. Just the kind of thing that makes people feel all warm and fuzzy." The laughter died as Grady looked around the kitchen.

"What?" Cal asked, his mood greatly improved now that he'd made his decision. He loved his wife, loved his children, and nothing was going to keep them apart any longer.

"Well…" Grady scratched his head. "You've got a bit of a mess here."

Cal saw the place with fresh eyes and realized he'd become careless again with Jane away. Their previous reunion had been tainted by a messy house. "I'd better do some cleaning before she gets home. She was none too happy about it the last time."

"You're on your own with this," Grady said. He headed out the door, taking his whiskey with him.

"Grady," Cal said, following him outside. His friend turned around. Cal was unsure how to say this other than straight out. "Thank you."

Grady nodded, touched the brim of his hat and climbed into his truck.

Almost light-headed with relief, Cal went back to the kitchen and tackled the cleaning with enthusiasm. He started a load of dishes, put away leftover food, took out the garbage, mopped the floor. He was scrubbing away at the counter when it occurred to him that after three weeks of caring for her parents, Jane must have been completely worn out. Upon her return to Promise, she'd faced a gigantic mess. *His* mess.

Cal hadn't understood why she'd been so upset over a few dishes and some dirty laundry. He recalled the comments she'd made and finally grasped what she'd really been saying. She'd wanted to be welcomed home for herself and not what she could do to make his life more comfortable. He'd left her with the wrong impression, hadn't communicated his love and respect.

He had to do more than just straighten up the place, Cal decided now. Glancing around, he could see plenty of areas that needed attention. Then it hit him—what Grady had said about a Christmas reunion. God willing, his family would be with him for the holidays, and when Jane and the children walked in that door, he wanted them to know they'd been in his thoughts every minute of every day.

Christmas. Jane was crazy about Christmas. She spent weeks decorating the house, and while he didn't have time for that, he could put up the tree. Jane and the kids would love that.

Hauling the necessary boxes down from the attic was no small task. He assembled the tree and set it in the very spot Jane had the year before. The lights were his least-favorite task, but he kept thinking of Jane as he wove the strands of tiny colored bulbs through the bright green limbs.

Several shoe boxes were carefully packed with the special beaded ornaments she'd made. He recalled the time and effort she'd put into each one and marveled anew at her skill and the caring they expressed. In that moment, his love for her nearly overwhelmed him.

When he'd finished with the tree, he hung a wreath

on the front door. All this activity had made him hungry, so he threw together a ham sandwich and ate it quickly. As he was putting everything back in the fridge—no point in undoing the work of the past few hours—he remembered his conversation with Wade McMillen a week earlier. Cal had stated vehemently that he hadn't "done a damn thing," and Wade had said that was the problem. How right his friend had been.

This separation was of his own making. All his wife had needed was the reassurance of his love and his commitment to her and their marriage. Until now, he'd been quick to blame Jane—and of course the manipulative Nicole—but he'd played an unsavory role in this farce, too.

Because of the holidays, he had to pay an exorbitant price for a plane ticket to California the next day, December twenty-second. The only seat available was in business class; and considering that he was plunking down as much for this trip as he would for a decent horse, he deserved to sit up front.

The next phone call wasn't as easy to make. He dialed his mother-in-law's number and waited through four interminable rings.

Voice mail came on. He listened to the message, taken aback when Harry Dickinson's voice greeted him. Poor Harry. Poor Stephanie.

He took a deep breath. "Jane, it's Cal. I love you and I love my children. I don't want to lose you. I'll be there tomorrow. I just bought a ticket and when I arrive, we can talk this out. I'm willing to do whatever it takes to save our marriage and I mean that, Jane, with all my heart."

Nine

"Dovie! Have you heard anything?" Ellie asked, making her way along the crowded street to get closer to Dovie and Frank Hennessey. She had Johnny by the hand and Robin in her stroller. Both children were bundled up to ward off the December cold.

The carolers stood on the opposite corner. Glen was with the tenors, and Amy McMillen, the pastor's wife, served as choral director. Carol-singing on the Saturday night before Christmas had become a tradition for Promise Christian Church since the year Wade married Amy. The event was free of charge, but several large cardboard boxes were positioned in front of the choir to collect food and other donations for charity.

"I did talk to Jane," Dovie murmured for Ellie's ears only.

"Again?" Ellie asked, unable to hide her excitement.

Dovie nodded. "She's feeling very torn. I gather her mother's relying on her emotionally."

"But..."

"Don't worry, Ellie," Dovie whispered. "She's half-way home already. I can just feel it!"

"How do you mean?" Ellie was anxious to learn what she could. This episode between Cal and Jane had taken a toll on her own marriage. Glen was upset, so was she, and they'd recently had a heated argument over it, each of them taking sides.

It'd all started when Ellie and Glen decorated their Christmas tree, and Ellie had found the beautiful beaded ornament Jane had made for her the previous year. She'd felt a rush of deep sadness and regret and had said something critical of Cal. Glen had instantly defended his brother.

She was baffled by how quickly their argument had escalated. Within minutes, what had begun as a mere difference of opinion had become a shouting match. Not until later did Ellie realize that this was because they were so emotionally connected to Cal and Jane. She wasn't sure she could ever put that special orna-ment on the tree again and not feel a sense of loss, es-pecially if the situation continued as it was.

"Did she keep the appointment with the attorney?" Ellie asked. The fact that Cal and Jane had allowed their disagreement to escalate this far horrified her; at the same time it frightened her. Ellie had always viewed Cal and Jane's marriage as stable—like her own. If two people who loved each other could reach this tragic point so quickly, she had to wonder if the same sad future was in store for her and Glen.

The intensity of their own quarrel had shocked her, and only after their tempers had cooled were Ellie and Glen able to talk sensibly. Her husband insisted they had nothing to worry about, but Ellie still wondered.

Dovie shrugged. "I don't know what happened with the attorney. Doesn't Cal discuss these things with Glen?"

Ellie shook her head. "Cal won't, and every time Glen brings up the subject, they argue. When I told Glen about Jane seeing an attorney, he was furious."

"With Jane?"

"No, with Cal, but if Glen said anything to him, he didn't tell me."

"Oh, dear." Dovie wrapped her scarf around her neck.

The singing began and Ellie lifted Robin out of the stroller and held her up so the child could see her father. Johnny clapped with delight at the lively rendition of "Hark Go the Bells," and Robin imitated her brother.

Ellie's eyes met her husband's. Even though he stood

across the street, she could feel his love and it warmed her. This ordeal of Cal's had been difficult for him. They both felt terrible about it. She wished now that she'd done something earlier, *said* something.

A warning about Nicole Nelson, maybe. A reassurance that this problem would pass. Anything.

"I have a good feeling," Dovie said, squeezing Ellie's arm. "In my heart of hearts, I don't think Cal or Jane will ever let this reach the divorce courts."

"I hope you're right," Ellie murmured and shifted Robin from one side to the other.

The Christmas carols continued, joyful and festive, accompanied by a small group of musicians. The donation boxes were already filled to overflowing.

"You're bringing the children over for cookies and hot chocolate, aren't you?" Dovie asked.

Ellie sent her a look that suggested she wouldn't dream of missing it. So many babies had been born in Promise recently, and several years ago, Dovie and Frank started holding their own Christmas party for all their friends' children. Dovie wore a Mrs. Claus outfit and Frank Hennessey made an appearance as Santa. Even Buttons, their poodle, got into the act, sporting a pair of stuffed reindeer antlers. For a couple who'd never had children of their own, Dovie and Frank did a marvelous job of entertaining the little ones.

"Johnny and Robin wouldn't miss it for the world," Ellie assured her. "I wish…"

Ellie didn't need to finish that thought; Dovie knew what she was thinking. It was a shame that Paul and Mary Ann wouldn't be in Promise for the Hennesseys' get-together.

"I'm just as hopeful as you are that this will be re- solved soon," Ellie said, forcing optimism in her words. She wanted so badly to believe it.

"Me, too," Nell Grant said, standing on the other side of Dovie. "The entire community is pulling for them." She blushed. "I hope you don't mind me jumping into the middle of your conversation."

"Everyone's hoping for the best," Dovie said with finality. Then, looking over at the small band of mu- sicians, she turned back to Nell. "Don't tell me that's Jeremy playing the trumpet? It can't be!"

Nell nodded proudly. "He's quite talented, isn't he?"

"Yes, and my goodness, he's so tall."

"Emma, too," Nell said, pointing at the flute player.

"That's Emma?" Ellie asked, unable to hide her shock. Heavens, it hadn't been more than a couple of months since she'd seen Nell's oldest daughter, and the girl looked as though she'd grown several inches.

With this realization came another. It'd been nearly six weeks since Cal had seen his children. At their ages, both were growing rapidly, changing all the time. She could only guess how much he'd missed—and felt sad that he'd let it happen.

Despite her disagreement with Glen, Ellie still blamed Cal. Eventually he'd come to his senses. She hoped that when he did, it wouldn't be too late.

Her mother's mournful expression tugged at Jane's heart as she finished packing her suitcase.

"You're sure this is what you want?" Stephanie Dickinson asked. Tears glistening in her eyes, she stood in the doorway of Jane's old bedroom.

"Yes, Mom. I love my husband. Things would never have gone this far if—"

"It's my fault, isn't it, honey?"

"Oh, Mom, don't even think that." Jane moved away from the bed, where the suitcases lay open, and hugged her mother. "No one's to blame. Or if anyone is, I guess I am. I let everything get out of control. I should've fought for my husband from the first. Cal was angry that I doubted him."

"But he—" Her mother stopped abruptly and bit her lip.

"You heard his message. He loves me and the children, and Mom…until just a little while ago I didn't realize how *much* I love him. It's taken all this time for us both to see what we were doing. I love you and Derek and Uncle Ken, but Los Angeles isn't my home anymore. I love Promise. My friends are there, my home and my husband."

Jane could tell that it was difficult for her mother to accept her decision. Stephanie gnawed on her lower lip and made an obvious effort not to weep.

"You talked to Cal? He knows you're coming?"

"I left him a message."

"But he hasn't returned your call?"

"No." There was such wonderful irony in the situation. Her mother had taken the children on an outing while Jane was scheduled to meet with the attorney. But as she'd sat in the waiting room, she'd tried to picture her life without Cal, without her family and friends in Promise, and the picture was bleak. She could barely keep from dissolving in tears right then and there.

Everything Dovie had said came back to her, and she'd known beyond a doubt that seeing this attorney was wrong. Paul and Mary Ann needed their father, and she needed her husband. For the first time since her father's illness, Jane had felt a surge of hope, the desire to win back her husband. If Nicole thought Jane would simply walk away, she was wrong. At that moment, she'd resolved to fight for her marriage.

Without a word of explanation, Jane left the attorney's office and rushed home. The message light alerted her to a call, and when she listened to it, Cal's deep voice greeted her. His beautiful loving voice, telling her the very things she'd longed to hear.

In her eagerness to return his call, her hand had shaken as she punched out the number. To her consternation she'd had to leave a message. She'd tried his cell phone, too, but Cal was notorious for never remembering to turn it on. Later phone calls went unanswered, as well. Her biggest fear was that he'd already boarded a plane, but she still hoped to stop him, and fly home with the children and meet him in San Antonio. With that in mind, she'd booked her flight.

"I'll try to call him again."

"You could all spend Christmas here," her mother suggested hopefully.

"Mom, you're going with Laurie Jo to Mexico and that's the end of it."

"Yes, I know, but—"

"No buts, you're going. It's exactly what you need."

"But your father hasn't even been gone two months."

Jane shook her head sternly. "Staying here moping is the last thing Dad would want you to do."

Her mother nodded. "You're right…but I'm worried about you and the children."

"Mom, you don't have to be. We'll be fine."

"But you can't go flying off without knowing if Cal will be at the airport when you arrive!"

"I'll give Glen and Ellie a call. They'll see he gets the message. And if they can't reach him, don't worry—*someone* will be at the airport to pick us up." Jane sincerely hoped it would be Cal. And this time she'd make sure their reunion was everything the previous one wasn't.

Her mother frowned and glanced at her watch. "You don't have much time. I really wish you weren't in such a rush."

"Mother, I've been here nearly two months. Anyone would think you'd be glad to get rid of me." This wasn't the most sensitive of comments, Jane realized when her mother's eyes filled with tears and she turned away, not wanting Jane to see.

"I shouldn't have depended on you and the children so much," Stephanie confessed. "I'm sorry, Jane."

"Mom, we've already been through this." She closed the largest of the suitcases, then hugged her mother again. "I'll call Ellie right now and that should settle everything. She'll let Cal know which flight I'm on, or die trying."

She wished her husband would phone. Jane desperately wanted to speak to him, and every effort in the past three hours had met with failure. Funny, after all

these weeks of no communication, she couldn't wait
to speak with him.

"Mommy, Mommy!" Paul dashed into the bedroom
and stuffed his blankey in the open suitcase. Then,
looking very proud of himself, he smiled up at his
mother. "We going home?"

"Home," she echoed and knelt to hug her son. She
felt such joyful anticipation, it was all she could do to
hold it inside.

Luckily, reaching Ellie wasn't difficult. Her sister-
in-law was at the feed store and picked up on the second ring. "Frasier Feed," Ellie said in her no-nonsense
businesswoman's tone of voice.

"Ellie, it's Jane."

"Jane!" Her sister-in-law nearly exploded with excitement.

"I'm coming home."

"It's about time!"

"Listen," Jane said, "I haven't been able to get hold
of Cal. He left a message that he's flying to California,
but he didn't say when. Just that he's coming today."

"Cal phoned you?"

"I wasn't here. This is so crazy and wonderful. Ellie,
I was sitting in the attorney's office and all of a sud-
den I knew I could't go through with it. I belong with
Cal in Promise."

"Whatever you need, I'll find a way to do it," Ellie said. "You have no idea how much we've all missed you. None of us had any idea what to think when we didn't hear from you."

"I know. I'm so sorry. It's just that…" Jane wasn't sure how to explain why she hadn't called anyone in Promise for all those weeks. Well, she'd tried to reach Dovie, but—

"Don't apologize. I remember what it was like after my father died. One night I sat and watched some old westerns he used to love and I just cried and cried. Even now I can't watch a John Wayne movie and not think of my dad."

"You'll make sure Cal doesn't leave Promise?" That was Jane's biggest concern. She hated the thought of getting home and learning he was on his way to California. If that did happen, he'd find an empty house, because her mother would be in Mexico.

"You can count on it."

"And here, write down my flight information and give it to Cal—if you catch him in time."

"I'll find him for you, don't you worry."

Jane knew her sister-in-law would come through.

Cal spent the morning completing what chores he could, getting ready to leave. Glen was attending a cattlemen's conference in Dallas and would be home that evening, but by then Cal would be gone.

Now that his decision was made, he wondered what had taken him so long to own up to the truth. His love for Jane and their children mattered more than any-thing—more than pride and more than righteousness. His friends and family had tried to show him that, but Cal hadn't truly grasped it until he learned how close he was to losing everything that gave his life meaning.

His father had urged him to listen to reason with that conversation during Thanksgiving dinner, and Phil's advice hadn't come cheap. Not when Cal was paying the bill at the Rocky Creek Inn.

Glen had put in his two cents' worth, and his com-ments had created a strain in their relationship. Cal hadn't been able to listen to his younger brother, couldn't accept his judgment or advice—although he wished he was more like Glen, easygoing and quick to forgive.

Even Wade McMillen had felt obliged to confront Cal. Every single thing his friends and family said had eventually hit home, but the full impact hadn't been made until the night Cal had gone to Billy D's.

Only when Nicole Nelson had approached his table had he seen the situation clearly. He'd been such a fool, and he'd nearly fallen in with her schemes. His wife was right: Nicole *did* want him. Damned if he knew why. It still bothered Cal that Jane hadn't trusted him. He hadn't even been tempted by Nicole, he could say that in all honesty, but he'd allowed her to flatter him.

Cal had made his share of mistakes and was more than willing to admit it. He regretted the things he'd said and done at a time when Jane had been weakest and most vulnerable. Thinking over the past few months, Cal viewed them as wasted. He wanted to kick himself for waiting so long to go after his family.

As he headed toward the house, he saw Grady's truck come barreling down the driveway. His neighbor eased to a stop near Cal, rolled down his window and shouted, "Call Ellie!"

"Ellie? What about?"

"No idea. Caroline called from town with the message."

"All right," he said, hurrying into the house.

Grady left, shouting "Merry Christmas" as his truck rumbled back down the drive.

When Cal reached his front door, he saw a large piece of paper taped there. "CALL ELLIE IMMEDIATELY," it read. "Good Luck, Nell and Travis."

What the hell? Cal walked into his house and grabbed the phone. He noticed the blinking message light, but not wanting to be distracted, he ignored it.

"Is that you, Cal?" Ellie asked, answering the phone herself.

"Who else were you expecting?"

"No one."

She sounded mighty cheerful.

"You doing anything just now?" his sister-in-law asked.

"Yeah, as a matter of act, I am. I've got a plane to catch. It seems I have some unfinished business in California."

He'd thought Ellie would shriek with delight or otherwise convey her approval, since she'd made her opinion of his actions quite clear.

But all she said was "You're going after Jane?"

He'd be on the road this very minute if he wasn't being detained. He said as much, although he tried to be polite about it. "What's with the urgency? Why is it so important that I call you?"

"Don't go!"

"What?" For a moment Cal was sure he'd misunderstood.

"You heard me. Don't go," Ellie repeated, "because Jane and the kids are on their way home."

"If this is a joke, Ellie, I swear to you—"

She laughed and didn't let him finish. "When was the last time you listened to your messages?"

The flashing light condemned him for a fool. He should have realized Jane would try to reach him. In his eagerness he'd overlooked the obvious.

"What flight? When does she land?" He'd be there to meet her and the children with flowers and chocolates and whatever else Dovie could recommend. Ah yes, Dovie. Someone else who'd been on his case. He smiled, remembering her less-than-subtle approach.

Ellie rattled off the flight number and the approximate time Jane and the children would land, and Cal scribbled down the information. "How did she manage to get a flight so quickly?" With holiday travel, most flights were booked solid.

"I don't know. You'll need to ask Jane."

Cal didn't care what she'd had to pay; he wanted her home. And now that the time was so close, he could barely contain himself.

As soon as he finished his conversation with Ellie, Cal listened to his messages. When he heard Jane's voice, his heart swelled with love. He could hear her relief, her joy and her love—the same emotions he was experiencing.

With his steps ten times lighter than they'd been a mere twenty-four hours ago, Cal jumped into the car and drove to town. Before he left, though, he carefully surveyed the house, making sure everything was perfect for Jane and the children. The Christmas tree looked lovely, and he'd even bought and wrapped a few gifts to put underneath. Not a single dirty dish could be seen. The laundry was done, and the sheets on the bed were fresh. This was about as good as it got.

Cal dropped in at Dovie's, and then—because he couldn't resist—he walked over to Tumbleweed Books. Sure enough, Nicole was behind the counter. Her face brightened when he entered the store.

"Cal, hello," she said with an eagerness she didn't bother to disguise.

"Merry Christmas."

"You, too." People were busy wandering the aisles, but Nicole headed directly toward him. "It's wonderful to see you."

He forced a smile. "About our conversation the other night…"

Nicole placed her hand on his arm. "I was more blunt than I intended, but that's only because I know what it's like to be lonely, especially at Christmastime."

"I'm here to thank you," Cal said, enjoying this.

Nicole flashed her baby blues at him with such adoration it was hard to maintain a straight face.

"You're right, I have been terribly lonely."

"Not anymore, Cal, I'm here for you."

"Actually," he said, removing her fingers from his

forearm, "it was after our conversation that I realized how much I miss my wife."

"Your...wife?" Nicole's face fell.

"I phoned her and we've reconciled. You helped open my eyes to what's important."

Nicole's mouth sagged. "I...I wish you and Jane the very best," she said, obviously struggling to hide her disappointment. "So you decided to go back to her." She shrugged. "Too bad. It could have been great with us, Cal."

Her audacity came as a shock. She'd actually believed he'd give up his wife and family for her. If he hadn't already figured out exactly the kind of woman she was and what she'd set out to do, he would have known in that instant. He should have listened to Jane—and just about everyone else.

"Stay out of my life, Nicole. Don't *just happen* to run into me again. Don't seek me out. Ever."

"I'm sorry you feel this way," she mumbled, not meeting his eyes.

During the course of his life, Cal had taken a lot of flack for being too direct and confrontational. Today he felt downright pleased at having imparted a few unadorned facts to a woman who badly needed to hear them. He walked out of the bookstore, and with a determination that couldn't be shaken, marched toward his parked car. He was going to collect his wife and children.

Jane's flight landed in San Antonio after midnight. Both children were asleep, and she didn't know if anyone would be at the airport to meet her. During the long hours on the plane, she'd fantasized about the reunion with her husband, but she'd begun to feel afraid that she'd been too optimistic.

All the passengers had disembarked by the time she gathered everything from the overhead bins and awakened Paul. The three-year-old rubbed his eyes, and Jane suspected he was still too dazed to understand that they were nearly home. Dragging his small backpack behind him, he started down the aisle. Mary Ann was asleep against her shoulder.

Their baggage was already on the carousel, and with a porter's assistance, she got it all piled on a cart. Then she moved slowly into the main area of the airport. Her fear—that Cal might not be there—was realized when she didn't see him anywhere. Her disappointment was so intense she stopped, clutching her son's hand as she tried to figure out what to do next.

"Jane…Jane!" Cal's voice caught her and she whirled around.

He stood at the information counter, wearing the biggest smile she'd ever seen. "I didn't know what to think when you weren't here. I thought you—"

"This is your family?" the woman at the counter interrupted.

"Yes," he said happily.

Paul seemed to come fully awake then and let out a yell. Dropping his backpack, the boy hurled himself into Cal's waiting arms.

Cal wrapped his son in his embrace. Jane watched as his eyes drifted shut and he savored this hug. Then Paul began to chatter until his words became indistinguishable.

"Just a minute, Paul," Cal said as he walked toward Jane.

With their children between them—Paul on his hip, Mary Ann asleep on her shoulder—Cal threw one arm around Jane and kissed her. It was the kind of deep open kiss the movies would once have banned. A kiss that illustrated everything his phone message had already explained. A real kiss, intense and passionate and knee-shaking.

The tears, which had been so near the surface moments earlier, began to flow down her cheeks. But they were no longer tears of disappointment; they were tears of joy. She found she wasn't the least bit troubled about such an emotional display in the middle of a busy airport with strangers looking on.

"It's all right, honey," Cal whispered. He kissed her again, and she thought she saw tears in his eyes, too.

"I love you so much," she wept.

"Oh, honey, I love you, too. I'm sorry."

"Me, too— I made so many mistakes."

"I've learned my lesson," he said solemnly.

"So have I. You're my home, where I live and breathe. Nothing's right without you."

"Oh, Jane," he whispered and leaned his forehead against hers. "Let's go home."

They talked well into the night, almost nonstop, discussing one subject after another. Cal held her and begged her forgiveness while she sobbed in his arms. They talked about their mistakes and what they'd learned, and vowed never again to allow anyone— man, woman, child or beast—to come between them.

Afterward, exhausted though she was from the flight and the strain of the past months, Jane was too keyed up to sleep. Too happy and excited. Even after they'd answered all the questions, resolved their doubts and their differences, Jane had something else on her mind. When her husband reached for her, she went into his arms eagerly. Their kisses grew urgent, their need for each other explosive.

"Cal, Cal," she whispered, reluctantly breaking off the kiss.

"Yes?" He kissed her shoulder and her ear.

"I think you should know I stopped taking my birth control pills."

Cal froze. "You what?"

She sighed and added, "I really couldn't see the point."

It was then that her husband chuckled. "In other words, there's a chance I might get you pregnant again?"

She kissed his stubborn wonderful jaw. "There's always a chance."

"How would you feel about a third child?"

"I think three's a good number, don't you?"

"Oh, yes—and if it's a boy we'll name him after your father."

"Harry Patterson?" she asked, already picturing a little boy so like his father and older brother. "Dad would be pleased."

Two nights later Cal, Jane and the children drove into town to attend Christmas Eve services. Their appearance generated considerable interest from the community, Jane noted. Every head seemed to turn when they strolled into the church, and plenty of smiles were sent in their direction. People slipped out of their seats to hug Jane and slap Cal on the back or shake his hand.

When Wade stepped up to the pulpit, he glanced straight at Cal, grinned knowingly and acknowledged him with a brief nod. Jane saw Cal return the gesture and nearly laughed out loud when Wade gave Cal a discreet thumbs-up.

"You talked to Wade?" she asked, whispering in his ear.

Her husband squeezed her hand and nodded.

"What did he say?"

"I'll tell you later."

"Tell me now," Jane insisted.

Cal sighed. "Let's just say the good pastor's words hit their mark."

"Oh?" She raised her eyebrows and couldn't keep from smiling. Being here with her husband on Christmas Eve, sharing the music, the joy, love and celebration with her community, nearly overwhelmed her.

Not long after Jane and Cal had settled into the pew, Glen, Ellie and their two youngsters arrived, followed by her father-in-law. Phil's eyes met Jane's and he winked. Jane pressed her head to her husband's shoulder.

Cal slid his arm around her and reached for a hymnal, and they each held one side of the book. Organ music swirled around them, and together they raised their voices in song. "O, Come All Ye Faithful." "Silent Night." "Angels We Have Heard on High." Songs celebrating a birth more than two thousand years ago. Songs celebrating a rebirth, a reunion, a renewal of their own love.

The service ended with a blast of exultation from the trumpet players, and finally the "Hallelujah" chorus from the choir. More than once, Jane felt Cal's gaze on her. She smiled up at him, and as they gathered their children and started out of the church, she was sure she could feel her father's presence, as well.

Phil was waiting for them outside. Paul ran to his grandfather and Phil lifted the boy in his arms, hugging him.

"We have a lot to celebrate," he said quietly.

"Yes, Dad, we do," Cal agreed. He placed one arm around his father and the other around Jane, and they all headed for home.

* * * * *

Can This Be Christmas?

For my dear friend Betty and her Judge
Many years of happiness, my friend
To the new
Mr and Mrs Jim Roper

One

"I'll Be Home for Christmas"

A robust version of "Little Drummer Boy" played in the background as Len Dawber glanced at his watch—for at least the tenth time in five minutes. He looked around the depot impatiently, hardly noticing the Christmas decorations on the windows and walls—the cardboard Santa's sleigh, the drooping garland and blinking lights.

Len was waiting with a herd of other holiday travelers to board the train that would take him to Boston. The snowstorm that had started last evening meant his early-morning flight out of Bangor, Maine, had been canceled and the airport closed. Although the airlines couldn't be blamed for the weather, they'd done everything possible to arrange transportation out of Maine. Len suspected more than a few strings had been pulled to get seats on the already full midmorning train. Maybe some of the original passengers canceled, he thought with faint hope.

Because, unfortunately, that crowded train was his only chance of making it to Boston in time to connect with his flight home for Christmas.

Len got to his feet, relinquishing his place on the hard station bench to a tired-looking man. He walked quickly to the door and stepped outside. He lifted his gaze toward the sky. Huge flakes of snow swirled in the wind, obscuring his view. His shoulder muscles tensed with frustration until he could no longer remain still. This was exactly what he'd feared would happen when he'd awakened that morning. Even then the clouds had been dark and ominous, threatening his plans and his dreams of a reunion with Amy.

Despite the snow that stung his eyes and dampened his hair, Len began to pace back and forth along the platform, peering down the tracks every few seconds. No train yet. Damn it! Stuck in New England on Christmas Eve.

This was supposed to be the season of joy, but there was little evidence of that in the faces around him. Most people were burdened with luggage and armfuls of Christmas packages. Some of the gift wrap was torn, the bows limp and tattered. The children, sensing their parents' anxiety, were cranky and restless. The younger ones whined and clung to their mothers.

Worry weighed on Len's heart. He *had* to catch the Boston flight, otherwise he wouldn't make it home to Rawhide, Texas, today. He'd miss his date with Amy and the family's Christmas Eve celebration. Part of his precious leave would be squandered because of the snowstorm.

There was another reason he yearned for home. Len didn't intend this to be an ordinary Christmas. No, this Christmas would be one of the best in his entire life. It had everything to do with Amy—and the engagement ring burning a hole in his uniform pocket.

Len had enlisted in the navy following high-school graduation and taken his submarine training in New London, Connecticut. Afterward, he'd been assigned to the sub base in Bangor, Maine. He thoroughly enjoyed life on the East Coast, so different from anything he'd known in Texas, and wondered if Amy would like it, too....

Len was proud to serve his country and seriously considered making the navy his career, but that decision depended on a number of things. Amy's answer, for one.

A real drawback of military life was this separation from his family. On his most recent trip home last September, he'd come to realize how much he loved Amy Brent. In the weeks since, he'd decided to ask her to marry him. They planned to be together that very night, Christmas Eve—the most wonderful night of the year. Once they were alone, away from family and friends, Len intended to propose.

He loved Amy; he had no doubts about that. He wasn't a man who gave his heart easily, and he'd made sure, in his own mind at least, that marriage was what he truly wanted. In the weeks since their last meeting, he'd come to see that loving her was for real and for always.

They hadn't talked about marriage, not the way some couples did, but he was confident she loved him, too. He paused for a moment and held in a sigh as the doubts came at him, thick as the falling snow. Lately Len had noticed that Amy seemed less like her normal self. They hadn't talked much, not with him saving to buy the diamond. And it was difficult for Amy to call him at the base. So they'd exchanged letters—light newsy letters with little mention of feelings. He had to admit he found their letters enjoyable to read—and even to write—and the cost of stamps was a lot more manageable than some of his phone bills had been. The truth was, he couldn't afford to spend money on long-distance calls anymore, not the way he had in previous months. His airfare home hadn't been cheap, either.

It wasn't as if he'd put off traveling until the last minute, which Amy seemed to suspect. He'd been on duty until the wee hours of this morning; he'd explained all that in a letter he'd mailed earlier in the week, when he'd sent her his flight information. Although Amy hadn't come right out and said it, he knew she'd been disappointed he couldn't arrive earlier, but that was navy life.

He hadn't received a letter from her in ten days, which was unusual. Then again, perhaps not. After all, they'd be seeing each other soon. Amy and his parents were scheduled to pick him up in Dallas, and together they'd drive home to Rawhide. He closed his eyes and pictured their reunion, hoping the mental image would help calm his jangled nerves. It did soothe him, but not for long.

He had to get home for Christmas. He just had to.

This was Cathy Norris's first Christmas without Ron, and she refused to spend it in Maine. She'd buried her husband of forty-one years that October; her grief hadn't even begun to abate. The thought of waking up Christmas morning without him had prompted her to accept her daughter's invitation. She'd be joining Madeline and her young family in Boston for the holidays.

Cathy had postponed the decision until last week for a number of reasons. To begin with, she wasn't a good traveler and tended to stay close to home. Ron, on the other hand, had adored adventure and loved trekking through the woods and camping and fishing with his friends. Cathy was more of a homebody. She'd never flown or taken the train by herself before—but then, she was learning, now, to do a great many unfamiliar things on her own. In the past Ron had always been with her, seeing to their tickets, their luggage and any unforeseen problems. He had been such a dear husband, so thoughtful and generous.

The battle with cancer had been waged for a year. Ron had put up a gallant fight, but in the end he'd been ready to die, far more ready than she was to let him go. Trivial as it seemed now, she realized that subconsciously she'd wanted him to live until after the holidays.

Naturally she'd never said anything. How could she, when such a request was purely selfish? It wasn't as if Ron could choose when he would die. Nevertheless, she'd clung to him emotionally far longer than she should have—until she'd painfully acknowledged that her fears were denying her husband a peaceful exit from life. Then with an agony that had all but crippled her, she'd kissed him one final time. Holding his limp hand between her own, she'd sat by his bedside, loving him with her entire being, and waited until he'd breathed his last.

Ron's death clouded what would otherwise have been her favorite month of the year. She found it devastating to be around others celebrating the season while she struggled to shake her all-consuming grief. She'd accepted Madeline's invitation as part of a concerted effort to survive the season of peace and goodwill.

Charting a new course for herself at this age was more of a challenge than she wanted. Life, however, had seen fit to make her a widow one month, then thrust her into the holiday season the next.

She was doing her best, trying to cope with her grief, finding the courage to smile now and again for her children's sake. They realized how difficult the holidays were for her of course, but her daughters were grieving, too.

This snowstorm had been an unwelcome hitch in her careful plans. Madeline had urged her to come sooner, but Cathy had foolishly resisted, not wanting to overstay her welcome. She'd agreed to visit until the twenty-seventh. Ron had always said that company, like fish, began to smell after three days.

"Mom," Madeline had said when she'd phoned early that morning, "I heard on the news there's a huge snowstorm headed your way."

"I'm afraid it arrived last night." The wind had moaned audibly outside her window as she spoke.

"What are you going to do?" Madeline, her youngest, tended to worry; unfortunately she'd inherited that trait from her mother.

"Do?" Cathy repeated as if a fierce winter blizzard was of little concern. "I'm taking the train to Boston to join you, Brian and the children for Christmas. What else is there to do?"

"But how will you get to the station?"

Cathy had already worked that out. "I've phoned for a taxi."

"But, Mom——"

"I'm sure everything will be fine," Cathy said firmly, hoping she sounded confident even though she was an emotional wreck. She felt as though her life was caving in around her. Stuck in Bangor over Christmas, grieving for Ron——that would have been more than Cathy could handle. If spending the holiday with family meant taking her chances in the middle of a snowstorm, then so be it.

The first hurdle had been successfully breached. Listening to Andy Williams crooning a Christmas ballad,

Cathy stood in line at the Bangor train depot, along with half the town, it seemed. The taxi fare had been exorbitant, but at least she was here, safe and sound. She'd packed light, leaving plenty of room in her suitcase for gifts for her two youngest granddaughters. Shopping had been a chore this year, so she'd decided simply to give Madeline and Brian a check and leave it at that, but she couldn't give money to her grandchildren. They were much too young for that. The best gifts she could think to bring them were books, plus a toy each.

Madeline had consented to let Lindsay and Angela, aged three and five, open their presents that evening following church services. Then the children could climb onto Cathy's lap and she'd read them to sleep. The thought of holding her grandchildren close helped ease the ache in her heart.

Everything would be all right now that she was at the depot, she reassured herself. Soon she'd be with her family. The train might be late, but it would get there eventually.

All her worries had been for nothing.

Matthew McHugh hated Christmas. And he didn't have a problem expressing that opinion. As for the season of goodwill—what a laugh. Especially now, when he was stuck in an overcrowded train depot, waiting for the next train to Boston where he'd catch the flight into LAX. The timing of this snowstorm had been impeccable. Every seat in the station was taken, and people who weren't sitting nervously paced the confined area, waiting for the train, which was already fifteen minutes late. Some, like that guy in the navy uniform, were even prowling the platform—as though *that* would make the train come any faster.

Christmas Eve, and the airports, train depots and bus stations were jammed. Everyone was in a rush to get somewhere, him included. As a sales rep for a Los Angeles-based software company, Matt was a seasoned traveler. And he figured anyone who spent a lot of time in airports would agree: Christmas was the worst. Crying babies, little old ladies, cranky kids—he'd endured it all. Most of it with ill grace.

His boss, Ruth Shroeder, who'd been promoted over him, had handed him this assignment early in the week. She'd purposely sent him to the other side of the country just so he'd know *she* was in charge. Rub his face in it, so to speak. This could easily have been a wasted trip; no one bought computer software three days before Christmas. Fortunately he'd outfoxed her and made the sale. By rights, he should be celebrating, but he experienced little satisfaction and no sense of triumph.

Ruth had been expecting him to make a fuss, demand that the assignment go to one of the junior sales reps. Matt had merely smiled and reached for the plane tickets. He'd sold the software, but was left feeling that although he'd won the battle, he was destined to lose the war.

And a whole lot more.

Pam, his wife of fifteen years, hadn't been the least bit understanding about this trip. If ever he'd needed her support it was now, but all she'd done was add to his burden. "Christmas, Matt? You're leaving three days before Christmas?"

What irritated him most was her complete and total lack of appreciation for his feelings. It wasn't like he'd *asked* for this trip or wanted to be away from the family. The fact that Pam had chosen the evening of his departure to start an argument revealed how little she recognized the stress he'd been under since the promotions were announced.

"I already said it couldn't be helped," he'd explained calmly as he packed his bag. His words were devoid of emotion, although plenty of it simmered just below the surface. He carefully placed an extra shirt in his bag.

Pam had gone strangely quiet.

"I'll be home Christmas Eve in time for dinner," he'd promised, not meeting her eyes. "My flight gets into LAX at four, so I'll be back here by six." He spoke briskly, reassuringly.

Silence.

"Come on, Pam, you have to know I don't like this any better than you do," he said, and forcefully jerked the zipper on his garment bag closed.

"You're going to miss Jimmy in the school play."

He was sorry about that, but there were worse things in life than not seeing his six-year-old son as an elf. "I've already talked to him about it, and Jimmy understands." Even if his wife didn't.

"What was he supposed to say?" Pam demanded.

Matt's shrug was philosophical.

"You were away when Rachel had the lead in the Sunday-school program, too."

Matt frowned, trying to remember missing that. "Rachel was in a Sunday-school program?"

"Three years ago… I see you've already forgotten. It broke her heart, but I notice you've conveniently let it slip your mind."

Matt had heard enough. He folded his garment bag over his arm and reached for his coat and briefcase.

"You don't have anything else to say?" Pam cried as she stormed after him.

"So you can shovel more guilt at me? Do you want

me to confess I'm a rotten father? Okay, fine." His voice gained volume. "Matthew McHugh is a rotten father."

Pam blinked back tears. Matt longed to hold her, but they'd gone too far for that.

"You aren't a bad father," she said after a moment, and his heart softened. A fight now was the last thing either of them needed. He was about to tell her so when she continued. "It's as a husband that you've completely failed."

Matt swore under his breath. Any tenderness he'd felt earlier shattered.

"You're leaving me to deal with Christmas, the shopping, dinners, everything. I can't take it anymore."

"Take it?" he shouted. "Do you know how many women would love to be able to stay home with their families? You have it easy compared to working mothers who're out there competing in a man's world. If you think shopping and cooking dinner is too much for you, then—"

Pam's expression grew mutinous. "My not working was a decision we made together! I can't believe you're throwing that in my face now. If you're saying you want me to get a job, fine, consider it done."

Matt's fist tightened around his briefcase handle. That wasn't what he wanted, and Pam knew it.

"All I'm saying is I could use a little support."

"It wouldn't hurt you to support me, either," she snapped.

They glared at each other, neither willing to give in.

"Have a good time," she said flippantly. "Just go. I'll do what I always do and make excuses for you with the children and your parents. I'll be at the school for Jimmy, so don't worry—not that you ever have."

If Matt heard about this stupid Christmas pageant one more time, he'd blow a fuse. Rather than continue the argument, he headed out the door. "I'll call you in the morning."

"Don't bother," she exploded, and slammed the door in his wake.

Matt had taken his wife at her word and hadn't phoned once in the past three days. It was the first time in fifteen years on the road that he hadn't called his family. Pam had the number of his hotel, and she hadn't made the effort to call him, either. They'd argued before, all couples did, but they'd never allowed a disagreement to go on this long.

Now as he stood in the crowded depot, waiting for the train to arrive, Matt was both tired and bored. For a man who'd purposely avoided any contact with his wife, he was in an all-fired hurry to get home.

This should be the happiest Christmas of Kelly Berry's life. After a ten-year struggle she and Nick were first-time parents. She liked to joke that her labor had lasted five years. That was how long they'd been on the adoption waiting list. Five years, two months and seventeen days, to be exact. Then the call had finally come, and twenty hours later they'd brought their daughter home from the hospital.

In less than a day, their entire existence had been turned upside down. After the long frustrating years of waiting, they were parents at last.

This would be their first trip home to Macon, Georgia, since they'd signed the adoption papers. Brittany Ann Berry's grandparents were eager to meet her.

The infant fussed in her arms and let loose with a piercing cry that cut into Neil Diamond's rendition of "Jingle Bells." A businessman scowled at them; Nick, muttering under his breath, grabbed the diaper bag. Doing the best she could, Kelly gently placed the baby over her shoulder and rubbed her tiny back.

"She's all right," Kelly said, smiling to reassure her husband while he rummaged through the diaper bag in search of the pacifier.

As Nick sat upright, he dragged one hand down his face, already showing signs of stress. They hadn't so much as left the train depot and already their nerves were shot. Despite their eagerness to be parents, the adjustment was a difficult one. Nick had proved to be a nervous father. Kelly wasn't all that adept at parenthood herself. She smiled again at Nick, accepting the pacifier. Everything would be easier once Brittany slept through the night, she was sure of that.

Her two older sisters were much better at this mothering business than she was. Never had Kelly missed her family more; never had the need to talk out her fears and doubts been more pressing.

This flight home was an extravagance Nick and Kelly could ill afford. Then the storm had blown in, with all its complications, and they'd been rerouted to Boston by train.

A whistle sang from the distance, and the sound of it was as beautiful as church bells.

The train was coming, just like the man at the ticket counter had promised. She listened to the announcement listing the destinations between here and Boston as people stood and reached for their bags. Nick automatically started gathering the baby paraphernalia.

They were headed home, each and every one of them. A little snow wasn't going to stand in their way.

Two

"I Wonder as I Wander"

The train filled up quickly, and Len was fortunate to find a seat next to a grandmotherly woman who pulled out her knitting the moment she'd made herself comfortable. Mesmerized, he watched her fingers expertly weave the yarn, mentally counting stitches in an effort to keep his mind off the time and how long it was taking his fellow passengers to get settled.

The nervousness in the pit of his stomach began to ease as the conductor, an elderly white-haired gentleman, shuffled slowly down the aisle, checking tickets.

"Will we reach Boston before noon?" That question came from the woman with the baby seated across from him.

Len was grateful she'd asked; he was looking for answers himself.

"Hard to say with the snow and all."

"But it has to," she groaned, again voicing his own concerns. "We'll never catch our flight otherwise."

"I heard the airports are closed between Bangor and Boston," he said amiably. He scratched the side of his white head as if that would aid his concentration. "The train's running, though, and you can rest assured we'll do our best to see you make it to Boston in time."

His words reassured more than the young couple with the baby. Len's anxious heart rested a little easier, too. Glancing at the older woman in the seat next to him, he decided some conversation might help distract him.

"Are you catching a flight in Boston?"

"Oh, no," she said, tugging on the red yarn. "My daughter and her family live in Boston. I'm joining them for Christmas. Where are you headed?"

"Rawhide, Texas," Len said, letting his pride in his state show through his words.

"Texas," she repeated, not missing a stitch. "Ron and I visited Texas once. Ron wanted to see the Alamo. He's my husband...was my husband. He died this October."

"I'm sorry."

"So am I," she murmured with such utter sadness that Len had to look away. She recovered quickly and continued. "It's mind-boggling that people can fly across this country in only a few hours, isn't it?"

It was a fact that impressed Len, too, but he was more grateful than astonished. He felt even more appreciative when the whistle pierced the chatter going on about him. Almost immediately the train started to move, then quickly gained speed. Everyone aboard seemed to give a collective sigh of relief.

Len and the widow chatted amicably for several minutes and eventually exchanged names. Cathy asked him a couple of questions, about Texas and the navy, and he asked her a few. After a while, their conversation died down and they returned to their own thoughts.

The train traveled at a slow but steady pace for an hour or so. The unrelenting snow whirled around them, but the passengers were warm and cozy. For all the worry this storm had caused earlier, it didn't seem nearly as intimidating from inside the train. Relaxed, Len stretched out his legs, confident that with a little luck, he'd connect with the flight out of Logan International.

The train stopped now and then at depots on the way. Each stop resulted in a quick exchange of passengers. Len noticed that the storm appeared to have changed people's holiday plans; far more exited the train than entered. The brief stops lasted no more than ten minutes, and soon there were a number of vacant seats in the passenger car. Before long Len heard the conductor say they'd be crossing into New Hampshire.

Len figured you could fit all of these tiny New England states inside Texas. He'd seen cattle ranches that were larger than Rhode Island! The thought produced a pang of homesickness. The song sure got it right—there's no place like home for the holidays. His life belonged to the navy now, but he was a Texas boy through and through.

"Do you have someone at home waiting for you?" Cathy asked him.

"My family," Len told her, and added, prematurely, "and my fiancée." Saying the words produced a happiness in him that refused to be squelched.

"How nice for you."

"Very nice," he said. Then thinking it might help ease his mind, he opened the side zipper of his carry-on bag and pulled out Amy's most recent letter, dated two weeks earlier.

Dear Len,

I waited until ten for you to phone, then realized it was eleven your time and you probably wouldn't be calling. I was feeling low about it, then received your letter this afternoon. I'm glad you decided to write. You say you're not good at writing letters, but I disagree. This one was very sweet. It's nice to have something to hold in my hand, that I can read again and again, unlike a telephone conversation. While it's always good to hear the sound of your voice, when we hang up, there's nothing left.

Everything's going along fine here at home and at work. For all my complaining about not finding a more glamorous job, I've discovered I actually enjoy being part of the nursing-home staff. The travel agency that didn't hire me is the one to lose out.

Did I tell you we had quite a stir last week? Mr. Perkins exposed himself in the middle of a pinochle game. All the ladies were outraged, but I noticed that the sign-up sheet for pinochle this Thursday is full. Mrs. MacPherson lost her teeth, but they were eventually found. (You don't want to know where.) I still have my lunch in Mr. Danbar's room; he seems to enjoy my company, although he hasn't spoken a word in three years. I chatter away and tell him all about you and me and how excited I am that you're coming home for Christmas.

I was pleased that your mother asked me if I wanted to tag along when she and your dad pick you up at the airport on Christmas Eve. I'll be there, you know I will—which brings me to something else. Something I've been wanting to ask you for a long time.

Do you remember my joke about sailors having a woman in every port? You laughed and reminded me that, as a submariner, you didn't see that many ports above water. Bangor's a long way from Rawhide, though, isn't it? I guess I'm asking you about other women.

Well, I'd better close for now. I'll see you in two weeks and we can talk more then.

Love,
Amy

Len folded the letter and slipped it back inside the envelope. Amy shouldn't need to ask him about other women. He didn't know what had made her so insecure, but he'd noticed the doubt in her voice ever since he returned in September.

The diamond ring should relieve her worries. He smiled just thinking about it. He could hardly wait to see the look on her face.

Cathy set her knitting aside and stared sightlessly out the train window. The snow obliterated everything, not that the scenery interested her. Try as she might, she couldn't stop thinking about Ron.

Other years, she'd been working in her kitchen Christmas Eve day, baking cookies and pies, getting ready for the children and grandchildren to arrive. As a surprise—although it had long since ceased to be one—she'd always baked Ron a lemon meringue pie, his favorite. And he'd always pretend he was stunned that she'd go to all that trouble just for him.

Christmas had been the holiday her husband loved most. He was like a kid, decorating the outside of the house with strand upon strand of colorful lights. Last year he'd outdone all his previous efforts, as if he'd known even then that he wouldn't be here this Christmas.

She remembered how, every year, Ron had wanted to put up the tree right after Thanksgiving. She was lucky if she could hold him off until it was officially December.

It took them an entire day to decorate the tree. Not that they ever chose such a large one. Trimming their Christmas tree was a ritual that involved telling each other stories about past Christmases, recalling where each decoration came from—whether it was made by one of the girls or bought on vacation somewhere or given to them by a friend. It wasn't just ornaments, baubles of glass and wood and yarn, that hung from the evergreen branches but memories. They still had several from when they were first married, back in 1957. And about ten years ago, Cathy had cross-stitched small frame ornaments with pictures of everyone in the family. It'd taken her months and Ron was as proud of those tiny frames as if he'd done the work himself.

Memories… Cathy couldn't face them this Christmas. All she could do was hope they brought her comfort in the uncertain future.

Since he'd retired from the local telephone company four years ago, Ron had used his spare time puttering around his wood shop, building toys for the grandchildren. Troy and Peter had been thrilled with the race cars he'd fashioned from blocks of wood. Ron had taken such pride in those small cars. Angela and Lindsay had adored the dollhouse he'd carefully designed and built for them. The end table he'd started for Cathy remained in his wood shop unfinished. He'd longed to complete it, but the chemotherapy had drained away his strength, and in the months that followed, it was enough for him just to make it through the day.

Ron wouldn't be pleased with her, Cathy mused. She'd made only a token effort to decorate this year. No tree, no lights on the house. She'd set out a few things—a crèche on the fireplace mantel and the two cotton snowmen Madeline had made as a craft project years ago when she was in Girl Scouts.

Actually Cathy couldn't see the point of doing more. Not when it hurt so much. And not when she'd be leaving, anyway. She did manage to bake Madeline's favorite shortbread cookies, but that had been the only real baking she'd done.

Resting her head against the seat, Cathy closed her eyes. She tried to let the sound of the train lull her to sleep, but memories refused to leave her alone, flashing through her mind in quick succession. The sights and sounds of the holidays in happier times. Large family dinners, the house filled with the scents of mincemeat pies and sage dressing. Music, too; there was always plenty of music.

Madeline played the piano and Gloria, their oldest, had been gifted with a wonderful voice. Father and daughter had sung Christmas carols together, their voices blending beautifully. At least one of their three daughters had made it home for the holidays every year. But Gloria couldn't afford the airfare so soon after the funeral, and Jeannie was living in New York now and it was hard for her to take time off from her job, especially when she'd already asked for two weeks in order to be with her father at the end. Madeline would have come, Cathy guessed, if she'd asked, but she'd never do that.

Dear God, she prayed, *just get me through the next three days.*

Matthew McHugh's patience was shot. The cranky baby from the station was in the same car and hadn't stopped fussing yet. Matthew's head throbbed with the beginnings of a killer headache. His argument with Pam played over and over in his mind until it was so distorted he didn't know what to think anymore.

If Pam was upset about his being gone this close to Christmas, he could only imagine what she'd say when he arrived home hours later than scheduled.

He could picture it now. His parents, Pam and the kids, all waiting for him to pull into the driveway so they could eat dinner. When he did walk in the house, they'd glare at him as though he'd stayed away just to inconvenience them. He'd seen it happen before. As though he were somehow personally responsible for weather conditions and canceled flights.

As for Pam's complaining about having to do all the shopping and cooking herself, he didn't understand it. If she preferred, they could order one of those take-out Christmas dinners from the local diner. She didn't need to do all this work if she didn't want to. The choice was hers. He couldn't care less if the jellied salad was homemade or came out of a container. Pam was putting pressure on herself.

The same thing applied to inviting his parents for Christmas Eve dinner. He wasn't the one who'd asked them. That had been Pam's doing. His mom and dad lived less than an hour away; they could stop by the house any time they wanted. To make a big deal out of having a meal together on Christmas Eve was ridiculous to him, especially if Pam was going to bitch about it.

The baby cried again. Matt clenched his fists and tried to hold on to his patience. The infant wasn't the only irritation, either. A little girl, five or so, was standing on the seat in front of his, staring at him.

"What's your name?" she asked.

"Scrooge."

"My name's Kate."

"Shouldn't you be sitting down, Kate?" he asked pointedly, hoping the kid's mother heard him and took action. She didn't.

"It's going to be Christmas tomorrow," she said, ignoring his question.

"So I hear." He attempted to look busy, too busy to be bothered.

The kid didn't take the hint.

"Santa Claus is coming to Grandma's house."

"Wonderful." His voice was thick with sarcasm. "Don't you know it's impolite to stare?"

"No." The kid flashed him an easy smile. "I can read."

"Good for you."

"Do you want me to read you *How the Grinch Stole Christmas*? It's my favorite book."

"No."

An elderly black couple sat across the aisle from him. The woman scowled disapprovingly, her censure at his attitude toward the kid obvious. "Why don't you read to her?" Matt suggested, motioning to the woman. "I've got work to do."

"You're working?" shrieked Kate-the-pest.

"Yes," came his curt reply, "or trying to." He couldn't get any blunter than that.

"Can I read you my story?" Kate asked the biddy across the aisle from him. Matt flashed the old woman a grin. Served her right. Let *her* deal with the kid. All Matt wanted was a few moments' peace and quiet while he mulled over what was going to happen once he got home.

Some kind of commotion went on in front of him. The little girl whimpered, and he felt a sense of righteousness. Kate's mother had apparently put her foot down when the kid tried to climb out of her seat. Good, now maybe she'd leave him and everyone else alone. If he'd been smart he would have pretended he was asleep like the man sitting next to him.

"Mom said I have to stay in my seat," Kate said, tears glistening as she peered over the cushion at him. All he could see was her watery blue eyes and the top of her head with a fancy red bow.

Matt ignored her.

"Santa's going to bring me a—"

"Listen, kid, I don't care what Santa's bringing you. I've got work to do and I don't have time to chat with you. Now kindly turn around and stop bothering me."

Kate frowned at him, then plunked herself back in her seat and started crying.

Several people condemned him with their eyes, not that it concerned Matt. If they wanted to entertain the kid, fine, but he wanted no part of it. He had more important things on his mind than what Santa was bringing a spoiled little brat with no manners.

The train had been stopped for about five minutes. "Where are we now?" Kelly asked, gently rocking Brittany in her arms. The baby had fussed the entire time they'd been on the train. Nothing Kelly did calmed her. She wasn't hungry; her diaper was clean. Kelly wondered if she might be teething. A mother was supposed to know these things, but Kelly could only speculate.

It helped that the train was becoming less crowded. With the storm, people seemed to be short-tempered and impatient. The guy who looked like a salesman was the worst; in fact, he was downright rude. She felt sorry for Kate and her mother. Kelly appreciated what it must be like traveling alone with a youngster. She'd never be able to do this without Nick. Frankly, she didn't know how anyone could travel with a baby and no one to help. An infant required so much *stuff*. It took hours just to organize and pack it all.

"According to the sign, we're in Abbott, New Hampshire," Nick informed her.

Kelly glanced out the window, through the still-falling snow. "Oh, Nick, look! This is one of those old-fashioned stations." The redbrick depot had a raised platform with several benches tucked protectively against the side, shielded from the snow by the roof's overhang. A ticket window faced the tracks and another window with many small panes looked into the waiting room.

"Hmm," Nick said, not showing any real interest.

"It's so quaint."

He didn't comment.

"I didn't know they had any of these depots left anymore. Do you think we could get off and look around a bit?"

She captured his attention with that. "You're joking, right?"

"We wouldn't have to take everything with us."

"The baby shouldn't be out in the cold."

Her enthusiasm faded. "Of course…she shouldn't."

The conductor walked down the center aisle and nodded pleasantly in Kelly's direction.

"That's a lovely old depot," she said.

"One of the last original stations in Rutherford County," he said with a glint of pride. "Built around 1880. Real pretty inside, too, with a potbellied stove and hardwood benches. They don't make 'em like this anymore."

"They sure don't," Kelly said, smiling.

"Shouldn't we be pulling out soon?" the man in the navy uniform asked, glancing at his watch.

"Anytime now," the conductor promised. "Nothing to worry about on this fine day. Snow or no snow, we're going to get you folks to Boston."

Three

"Have Yourself a Merry Little Christmas"

"It's been twenty minutes," Len said, straining to see what had caused the delay. Cupping his face with his hands, he pressed against the window and squinted at the station. The snow had grown heavier and nearly obliterated the building from view. The train had been sitting outside the depot in Abbott twice as long as it had at any previous stop. Apparently the powers-that-be didn't fully grasp the time constraints he and several other passengers were under to reach Logan International. Too much was at stake if he missed his flight.

"I'm sure everything will be all right," Cathy assured him, but he noticed that she was knitting at a frantic pace. She jerked hard on the yarn a couple of times, then had to stop and rework stitches, apparently because of a mistake.

Len saw that he wasn't the only one who seemed concerned. The cranky businessman got out of his seat and walked to the end of the compartment. He leaned over to peer out the window at the rear of the train car, as if that would tell him something he didn't already know.

"Someone's coming," he announced in a voice that said he wasn't going to be easily pacified. He wanted answers, and so did Len. Under normal circumstances Len was a patient man, but this was Christmas Eve and he had an engagement ring in his pocket.

The wind howled and snow blew into the compartment as the elderly conductor opened the door. He stepped quickly inside, then made his way to the front. "Folks, if I could have your attention a moment…"

Even before the man spoke, Len's gut told him it wasn't good news.

"We've got a problem on the line ahead."

"What kind of problem?" the sales rep demanded.

"Track's out."

A chorus of mumbles and raised voices followed.

The conductor raised his hands and the passengers fell silent. "We're doing the best we can."

"How long will it take to get it fixed?" The shout came from a long-haired guy at the front of the car. With his leather headband and fringed jacket, he resembled an overgrown hippie. He sat with a woman whose appearance complemented his—straight center-parted hair that reached the middle of her back and a long flower-sprigged dress under her heavy coat.

The conductor's face revealed doubt. "Couple of hours, possibly longer. Can't really say for sure."

"Hours!" Len exploded.

"We have a plane to catch," the young father cried, his anger spilling into outrage.

"The airlines arranged for us to be on the train for *this?*" the businessman shouted, not bothering to disguise his disgust. "We were better off waiting out the storm in Bangor."

"I'm sorry, but—"

"Does this podunk town have a car-rental agency?" someone asked. Len couldn't see who.

"Not right here. There's one in town, but with the storm, I'd strongly recommend none of you…"

Len didn't stick around to hear the rest. As best he could figure, he was less than sixty miles from Boston. If he could rent a car, there was a chance he might still make it to the airport on time. Moving faster than he would've thought possible, Len reached for his bag and raced off the train.

The moment he jumped onto the depot platform, a sudden blast of cold jolted him. He hunched his shoulders and kept his face down as he struggled against the icy wind to open the door. Not surprisingly, the inside of the depot was as quaint as the outside, with long rows of hardwood benches and a potbellied stove.

The stationmaster looked up as people started to flood inside. Apparently he handled the sale of tickets and whatever was available to buy—a few snack items, magazines, postcards and such. Three phones were positioned against the far wall. One bore an Out of Order sign.

A long, straggling line had already formed in front of the two working phones. Len counted ten people ahead of him and figured he had a fair chance of getting a vehicle until he remembered a friend telling him you needed to be twenty-five to rent one. His hopes sagged yet again. He was a year too young. Discouraged, he dropped out of line.

His nerves twisting, he sat on a hard wooden bench away from the others. It was hopeless. Useless to try. Even if the train had arrived anywhere close to its scheduled time, there was no guarantee he'd actually have a seat on the plane. Because of the storm, the airline had tried to get him on another flight leaving four hours later. But he was flying standby, which meant the only way he would get on board was if someone didn't show.

The reservation clerk had been understanding and claimed it wasn't as unlikely as it sounded. According to her, there were generally one or two seats available and he was at the top of the list. It had all sounded promising—and now this.

Cathy Norris sat down on the bench next to him. "I guess I should call my daughter," she said.

Len didn't know if she was speaking to him or not. "I suppose I should phone home, too."

The line for the phones had dwindled to five people. Len rejoined the group and impatiently waited his turn. It seemed to take forever before he was finally able to use the phone. He thought about contacting his parents, but he'd already spoken to them once that day.

Placing the charges on a calling card, he dialed Amy's number and prayed she was at home.

"Hello."

His relief at the sound of her soft drawl was enough to make him want to weep. "Hello, Amy Sue."

"Len?" Her voice rose with happy excitement. "Where are you?" Not giving him time to answer, she continued, "Your mother phoned earlier and said your flight had been canceled. Are you in Boston?"

"Abbott, New Hampshire."

"New Hampshire? Len, for mercy's sake, what are you doing there?"

"I wish I knew. The airline put us on a train."

"Your mother told me about the storm and how they

closed the airport and everything," she said. He was distracted by the people lining up behind him, but her voice sounded...sad, almost as if she knew in advance what he was about to tell her.

"There's something wrong with the tracks. It's going to take a couple of hours to repair, so there's no telling what time I'll get to Boston."

"Oh, Len." Her voice was more breath than sound. "You're not going to make it home for Christmas, are you?"

He opened his mouth to insist otherwise, but the truth was, he no longer knew. "I want to, but..."

He could feel Amy's disappointment vibrate through the telephone wire. It was agony to be so far away and not able to hold her. "I'll do whatever I can to get to the airport on time, but there's no guarantee. You know I'd do anything to be with you right now, don't you?"

She didn't answer.

"Amy?" Talking with a lineup of people waiting to use the phone was a little inhibiting.

"I'll get in touch with your parents and let them know," she whispered, and her voice broke.

"I'll call you as soon as I hear anything," he said. Then, despite a dozen people eavesdropping on his conversation, he added, "I love you, Amy."

Unfortunately the line was already dead.

* * *

He should phone home, Matt decided, and even waited his turn in the long line that formed outside the telephone booth. He was three people away when he suddenly changed his mind. He had no idea why; then again, maybe he did.

It went without saying that Pam would be furious. He could hear her lambaste him now, and frankly, he wasn't in the mood for it.

He crossed to one of the vacant benches and sat down. These old seats might look picturesque, but they were a far sight from being comfortable. He shifted his position a number of times, crossed and uncrossed his legs.

As bad luck would have it, the couple with the baby sat directly opposite him. Matt didn't understand it. He seemed to attract the very people who irritated him most. Thankfully the infant was peacefully asleep in her mother's arms.

Matt studied the baby, remembering his own children at that age and how happy he and Pam had been in the early years of their marriage. That time seemed distant now. His dissatisfaction with his job didn't help. He felt as if he was struggling against everything that should make life good—his family, his marriage, his work. As if he stood waist-deep in the middle of a fast-flowing stream, fighting the current.

His wife had no comprehension of the stress he experienced day in and day out. According to her, he went out of his way to make her life miserable. Lately all she did was complain. If he went on the road, she complained; if he was home, she found fault with that, too.

The thought had come to him more than once these past few days that maybe they'd be better off living apart. He hadn't voiced it, but it was there in the back of his mind. Unhappy as she was, Pam must be entertaining these same thoughts. He couldn't remember the last time they'd honestly enjoyed each other's company.

Restless now, he stood and walked about. The depot had filled up, and there wasn't room enough for everyone to sit. The stationmaster was on the phone, and Matt watched the old man's facial expressions, hoping to get a hint of what was happening.

The man removed his black hat, frowned, then nodded. Matt couldn't read anything into that. He waited until the old guy had replaced the receiver. No announcement. Apparently there wasn't anything new to report. Matt checked his watch and groaned.

Thinking he might be more comfortable back on the train, he hurried outside, rushing through the bone-chilling wind and snow to the security of the train itself. The conductor and other staff had disappeared, Matt didn't know where. Probably all snug in the comfort of some friend's home. Not so for the passengers. The wind and snow nearly blinded him. He wasn't on board more than twenty minutes when the young father hurried inside and reached for a diaper bag tucked under the seat.

"Your first kid?" Matt asked, bored and miserable. A few minutes of conversation might help pass the time. The answer was fairly obvious. He was no expert when it came to infants, but it was clear to him that this couple was far too high-strung about parenthood. To his way of thinking, once these two relaxed, their baby would, too.

The man nodded, then sat down abruptly. "I had no idea it would be like this."

"Nothing's the same after you have kids," Matt said. The train, now that it'd shut down, wasn't heated, and the piercing cold had quickly permeated the interior.

"Do you have kids?"

"Two," Matt said, and despite his mood, he grinned. "Matt McHugh." He held out his hand.

"Nick Berry."

"This isn't exactly how I expected to spend Christmas Eve."

"Me, neither," Nick said. He lifted his shoulders and rubbed his bare hands. "If it was up to me, we'd never have left Bangor, but Kelly's parents haven't seen the baby yet."

Matt grunted in understanding.

"I'd better get back inside," Nick said. "Kelly's waiting."

"I might as well go in with you." It was obvious that he wouldn't be able to stay on the train much longer. He'd come for peace and quiet and found it not worth the price of having to sit alone in the cold. The temperature wasn't the only source of discomfort; he didn't like the turn his thoughts had taken. He didn't want a divorce, but he could see that was the direction he and Pam were headed.

Matt and Nick sprinted back into the depot just as the stationmaster walked to the center of the room. Nick rejoined his wife and handed her the diaper bag.

"Folks," the old man said, raising his arms to attract their attention. "My name's Clayton Kemper and I'm here to give you as much information as I can about the situation."

"How much longer is this going to take?" the long-haired guy demanded.

"Yeah," someone else shouted. "When do we get out of here?"

"Now, folks, that's something I can't predict. The

problem involves more than the storm. The tracks are out."

His words were followed by low dissatisfied murmurs.

"I realize you're anxious to be on your way, seeing it's Christmas Eve and all. But no one can tell us just how long it'll be before the repairs are finished. Our first estimate was two hours, but the repair crew ran into difficulties."

The murmurs rose in volume. "We need answers," Matt said loudly, his fists clenched. "Some of us are booked on flights."

Clayton Kemper held up his hands. "I'm sorry, folks, I really am, but like I said before, there's just no way of predicting this sort of thing. It could be another hour… or it could be till morning."

"Morning!" The grumbling erupted into a flurry of angry shouts.

"What about hotel rooms?" an older man asked, placing a protective arm around the woman beside him.

Matt watched Nick glance at his wife as he stepped forward. "That's a good question. Should we think about getting a hotel room?" It went without saying that a young family would be far more comfortable in one. "And what's available here?"

"There's a hotel in town and a couple of motels that

should have a few rooms left. I can call and they'll send their shuttle vans for anyone who wants to be picked up. Same goes for the car rental agency. But—" Mr. Kemper rubbed the side of his jaw "—I can't tell you what would be best. When the repairs are finished, the train's pulling out. We won't have time to call all over town and round people up. If you're here, you go. If not, you'll need to wait for the next train."

Matt weighed his options and decided to wait it out. He was probably being too optimistic, but he'd rather take his chances at the depot. His choice wasn't the popular one. The majority of those on the train decided to get hotel rooms. Within ten minutes, the depot had emptied, leaving twenty or so hardy souls willing to brave the rest of the afternoon.

"What about you two?" Matt asked Nick, glancing at the younger man's wife and baby. He'd expected Nick to be among the first to seek more comfortable accommodations.

"Kelly thinks we should stay."

"It could be a long hard afternoon," Matt felt obliged to remind him. Later, when Nick and his wife changed their minds, there likely wouldn't be any rooms left. But that was none of his affair.

Matt's gaze went to the telephones. He probably should phone Pam, but the prospect brought him no pleasure. He'd wait until he had a few more pertinent details. No use upsetting her this soon. She had four hours yet before she needed to know he wasn't on his scheduled flight. In this instance ignorance was bliss.

"Mother...oh dear, this isn't working out the way I'd hoped." Madeline's distress rang over the wire.

Cathy's thoughts echoed her daughter. She pressed the telephone to her ear. "I don't want you to worry."

"I have every right to worry," Madeline snapped. "I should have come up there and gotten you myself."

"Nonsense." As far as Cathy was concerned, that would only have made matters worse. The last thing she wanted was to take her daughter away from her family on Christmas Eve.

"But Daddy would—" Madeline abruptly cut off the rest of what she was about to say.

"I'm perfectly fine."

"You're in the middle of a snowstorm on Christmas Eve. You're stuck without family, alone in some train depot in a dinky town in New Hampshire. You are not fine, Mother."

Alone. The word leaped out of her daughter's mouth and hit Cathy hard. Hard enough that she took an involuntary step backward. Alone. That was how she'd felt since Ron's death. It seemed as though she wandered from day to day without purpose, linked to no one, lost, confused. And consumed by a grief so painful it virtually incapacitated her. All she had was the promise that time would eventually ease this ache in her heart.

"The entire situation is horrible," Madeline continued.

"What would you have me do? Scream and shout? Yell at the stationmaster who's done nothing but be as helpful and kind as possible? Is that what you want?"

Her question was followed by Madeline's soft unhappy sigh.

"I feel so incredibly guilty," her daughter confessed after a moment.

"Why in heaven's name should you feel anything of the sort?" It was ludicrous that Madeline was blaming herself for these unfortunate circumstances.

"But, Mother, you're with strangers, instead of family, and I'd hoped—"

"Now stop," Cathy said in her sternest voice. "None of this is your fault. In any case, I'm here in Abbott and perfectly content. I brought my knitting with me and there are plenty of others for company."

"But it's Christmas Eve," Madeline protested.

Cathy closed her eyes and inhaled sharply. "Do you honestly believe any Christmas will ever be the same for me without your father?"

"Oh, Mom." Her daughter's voice fell. "Don't mention Daddy, please. It's so hard without him."

"But life goes on," Cathy said, doing her best to sound brave and optimistic.

"I'd wanted to make everything better for you."

"You have," Cathy told her gently. "I couldn't have stayed at the house alone. I'd rather be in this depot with strangers than spending Christmas with memories I'm not ready to face. And sometime tonight or tomorrow, I'll be with all of you. Now let's stop before we both embarrass ourselves."

"You'll phone as soon as the tracks are repaired?"

"The minute I hear, you'll be the first to know."

"Brian and I and the girls will come down to the depot for you."

"Fine, sweetheart. Now don't you worry, okay?"

Madeline hesitated, then whispered, "I love you, Mom."

"I love you, too. Now promise me you won't fret."

"I'll try."

"Good." After a few words of farewell, Cathy replaced the receiver and returned to her seat. The depot was warm, thanks to the small stove. Those who'd stayed had taken up residence on the hardwood benches. As Cathy reached for her knitting, she battled back a fresh wave of depression.

Madeline was right. It was a dreadful situation, being stuck in a train depot this day of all the days in the year. She glanced around at the others. They appeared just as miserable as she.

Could this really be Christmas?

Four

"Hi." A little girl with pigtails and a charming tooth-less smile sauntered up to Cathy.

"Hello," Cathy said in a friendly voice. Not includ-ing the baby, two children remained in the depot. A girl and a boy. The girl bounced about the room like a red rubber ball, but the boy remained glued to his par-ents' sides.

"What are you doing?" the child asked, slipping onto the wooden bench next to her.

"Knitting. This is a sweater for my granddaughter. She's about your age."

"I'm five."

"So is Lindsay."

"I can read. The kindergarten teacher told Mommy I'm advanced for my age."

"That's wonderful. I'll bet your mother and father are very proud of you." Cathy smiled at the youngster while her fingers continued to work the colorful yarn.

The little girl's head drooped slightly. "My mommy and daddy are divorced now."

Cathy felt the child's confusion and pain. "That's too bad."

She nodded, looking wise beyond her years. "We're going to spend Christmas with my grandma Gibson in Boston."

"Kate." A frazzled young woman approached the little girl. "I hope you weren't bothering this lady."

"Not at all," Cathy assured her.

"My grandma said Santa was coming tonight and bringing me lots of presents." Kate's sweet face lit up with excitement. "Santa'll still come, won't he, even if the train is late?"

"Of course he will," the child's mother told her in a tone that suggested this wasn't the first time she'd reassured her daughter.

"He'll find us even in the storm?"

"He has Rudolph's nose to guide his sleigh, remember?"

Kate nodded.

Cathy let her knitting rest in her lap.

"Can I read to you?" the youngster asked, her eyes huge. "Please?"

"Why, I can't think of anything I'd enjoy more." Cathy could, but it was clear the restless child needed something to take her mind off the situation, and she was happy to listen. Having grandchildren, she could well appreciate the difficulty of keeping a five-year-old entertained in conditions such as these.

Kate raced for her backpack and returned a moment later with her precious book.

"Thank you," Kate's mother whispered. "I'm Elise Jones."

"Hello, Elise. Cathy Norris."

Kate scooted onto the bench between Cathy and her mother and eagerly opened the book. She placed her finger on the first word and started reading aloud with a fluency that suggested this was a much-read and much-loved story.

Cathy smiled down on the little girl. Soon all this frustration and delay would be over. Mr. Kemper would come out from behind his desk and announce that the tracks had been repaired and they'd be on their way. In a few hours she'd be with Madeline and her family, all of this behind her. Somehow, listening to Kate read soothed her, made her feel that today's problems were tolerable. Inconvenient but definitely tolerable.

Kate's voice slowly faded and her eyes closed. She slumped over, her head against Cathy's side. Seconds later the book slipped from her lap and onto the floor.

"Oh, thank heaven, she's going to take a nap, after all," Elise whispered, getting carefully to her feet. She lifted Kate's small legs onto the bench and tucked a spare sweater beneath her head.

"Children can be quite a handful," Cathy murmured, remembering the first time she and Ron had watched their two granddaughters for an entire day while Madeline and Brian attended an investment workshop. The kids had been picked up by four that afternoon, but she and Ron went to bed before eight o'clock, exhausted.

"Being a single mother is no piece of cake," Elise told her. "When Greg and I divorced, I didn't have a clue what would happen. Then he lost his job and had to manage on his unemployment check. He just started working again—but he's so far behind on everything. Now he's having trouble making the child-support payments on time, which only complicates things." Embarrassed she looked away as if she regretted what she'd said. "We wouldn't have Christmas if it wasn't for my mother. I certainly can't afford gifts this year."

The pain that flashed in the younger woman's eyes couldn't be hidden. Cathy realized that, in many ways, Elise's divorce had been as devastating as a death. Feeling a kinship with her, she reached over and squeezed her hand.

Elise recovered quickly, then said with forced enthusiasm, "I've always wanted to know how to knit."

"Would you like me to teach you?" Cathy asked, seizing upon the idea. She'd successfully taught her own three daughters and carried an extra set of needles in her knitting bag. Now was ideal, seeing as they had nothing but time on their hands and Kate was sleeping.

"Now?" Elise asked, flustered. "I mean, I'd love to, but are you sure it isn't too much trouble?"

"Of course not. I've found knitting calms my nerves, especially these past few months since my husband died."

"I'm sorry about your husband," Elise said, real sympathy in her voice.

"Yes, I am, too. I miss him dreadfully." With a sense of purpose Cathy reached for her spare needles. "Would you like to start now?"

Elise nodded. "Why not?"

Cathy pulled out a ball of yarn. "Then let me show you how to cast on stitches. It isn't the least bit difficult."

Len had trouble not watching the clock. They'd been in Abbott a total of four hours, with no further word regarding their situation. The stationmaster, Clayton Kemper, had turned out to be a kindhearted soul. He'd made a fresh pot of coffee and offered it to anyone who wanted a cup, free of charge.

Len had declined. Stressed as he was, the last thing he needed was caffeine. Plenty of others took advantage of Kemper's generosity, though. They were a motley group, Len noted. The widow, dressed in her gray wool coat with her knitting and her sad but friendly smile. The divorced mother and her little girl. The grumpy sales rep. The young couple with the baby, the hippie and his wife, the elderly black couple plus an assortment of others.

Kemper walked by with the coffeepot on a tray. "You sure I can't interest you in a cup, young man?"

"I'm sure."

"I found a deck of cards. How about that?"

Len nodded eagerly. "That'd be great." Cards would be a welcome way to pass the time. He sometimes played solitaire and enjoyed two or three different versions of the game. At the mention of cards, the sales rep, who sat close by, looked up from his laptop. Maybe Len could talk two or three of the others into a game of pinochle or poker.

"You play pinochle?" he asked Matt.

"And canasta, hearts, bridge—whatever you want."

"I wouldn't mind playing," Nick volunteered.

"Come to think of it, I've got an old card table in the back room," Kemper said when he returned with the cards. "And a couple of chairs, too, if you need 'em. I should have thought of this earlier. You folks must be bored out of your minds."

A fourth man joined them, and with a little rearranging they soon had the table set up. That was followed by the sound of cards being shuffled and the occasional scrape of a chair as they settled down to a friendly game of pinochle.

Kelly Berry's arms ached from holding the baby. The carrier seat was still on the train, but she hadn't asked Nick to bring it in. He'd already gone outside once and seemed reluctant to venture into the storm again. Besides, he was busy playing cards.

Kelly wondered, not for the first time, if they'd *ever* adjust to parenthood. The whole experience was so… different from what she'd expected. Desperately longing for a child of their own, they'd dreamed and hungered to the point that Kelly felt their marriage would be incomplete without a family. Now, after three months with a fussy, colicky infant, she was ready to admit her spirits were the lowest they'd been in years.

She'd always believed a baby would bring her and

Nick closer together. The baby would be a living symbol of their love and commitment to each other, the culmination of their marriage. Instead, Brittany seemed to have driven a wedge between them. Not long ago their world had revolved entirely around each other; these days, it revolved around Brittany. Caring for the baby demanded all their energy, all their time.

Her arms tightened around her daughter, and a surge of love filled her heart. She and Nick felt overwhelmed because this was so new, Kelly told herself. In a few months everything would be easier-for both of them. While confident of Nick's love, Kelly knew he found it difficult to deal with the changes that had come into their marriage since the adoption.

"Would you like me to hold the baby for a while?" The older woman sat down next to her. "I'm Cathy Norris. You must be exhausted."

"Kelly Berry." She hesitated. "You wouldn't mind?"

"Not at all," Cathy said, taking the sleeping infant from her arms. She gazed down at Brittany and smiled. "She's certainly beautiful, and her little red outfit is delightful."

"Thank you," Kelly said, truly grateful. She'd enjoyed dressing Brittany for the holiday season. She could've spent a fortune if Nick had let her, but her ever-practical husband had been the voice of reason. Not that *he* wasn't guilty of spoiling their daughter.

"She certainly resembles your husband."

Kelly glowed with happiness. "I think so, too."

With an ease that Kelly envied, Cathy Norris held Brittany against her shoulder, gently rubbing her back. Brittany shifted her head to one side and her tiny mouth made small sucking sounds. Once more Kelly's heart stirred with love.

She felt someone's gaze and glanced up to find Nick watching her. When he realized he had her attention, he smiled. His eyes softened as he looked at their daughter.

They *would* be all right, Kelly thought. This was their dream; it was just that after waiting and planning all these years, they hadn't been quite as ready for the reality as they'd assumed.

Clayton Kemper walked out of the station and returned almost immediately, a shovel in his hand. "Good news!" he shouted.

Every head in the room shot up, every face alight with expectation, Kelly's included. Some people were already on their feet, reaching for bags of colorfully wrapped gifts.

"The storm's died down. It's stopped snowing."

"Does that mean we can get out of here any sooner?" Matt McHugh demanded.

"Well, it's bound to help the repair crew."

The happy anticipation sank to the pit of Kelly's stomach. *Oh, please,* she prayed, *don't let us end up spending our first Christmas with Brittany stuck in a train depot. Don't let this be our Christmas.*

Five

"O Christmas Tree"

The news that the snow had stopped falling should have cheered Len Dawber, but it didn't. Instead, his mood took an immediate dive. He'd figured that with the storm passing, the train would leave soon. It didn't appear to be the case.

His interest in the card game died and he got up to give his seat to someone else, but no one seemed keen to play anymore. Before long, Nick Berry had the deck of cards and sat alone, flipping through them in a listless game of solitaire.

His frustration mounting, Len approached the counter. Clayton Kemper glanced up. "Can I get you anything?"

"How about some information?" Matt McHugh asked, moving to Len's side. "We've been here six hours. There must be *something* you can tell us by now." He clenched his fist and rested it on the counter. "You've got to realize how impossible this situation is for us."

Kemper shrugged helplessly. "I don't know what to tell you."

"Isn't there someone you could phone?" The plaintive voice of a woman came from behind them. Len looked over his shoulder and recognized the mother of the little boy, who still clung to her side.

"Find out what you can," Matt insisted. "You owe us that much."

"Surely there's someone you can call," the elderly black man said.

Tension filled the room as more people stood up and started walking about. The baby Cathy Norris held awoke suddenly and shattered the air with a piercing cry. Cathy tried to quiet the infant, but it did no good. The young mother couldn't do any better. The baby's cries clawed at already taut nerves.

"Kindly keep that baby quiet, would you?" Len wasn't sure who'd said that; painful as the baby's shrieking was, he felt a fleeting sympathy for the mother.

"Do something," Nick snapped at his wife.

"I'm trying," Kelly said, glaring back at him with a hurt look.

"I've got to get out of here," Nick said, and stalked outside, letting the door slam in his wake.

"We need information," Len pressed Kemper again.

"At least give us an idea how much longer it could be," Matt added. "In case you've forgotten, it's Christmas Eve."

Kemper was clearly at a loss and for an instant Len felt sympathy for him, too, but he felt even worse for himself. He'd been looking forward to this night for weeks. He wanted it to be the most beautiful and romantic evening of his life. Instead, he'd probably be spending it in this train station somewhere in New Hampshire.

Kemper raised his hands to quiet the murmurs of discontent. "I'll make a few phone calls and see what I can find out."

"You should have done that long before now," Matt said irritably.

Len was in full agreement. This damned waiting had gone on long enough. The minute he had a definite answer, he'd call Amy again. Even if he *didn't* have an answer, he was phoning Amy. He needed to hear the sound of her voice, needed to know this nightmare would soon be over and they'd be together—if not for Christmas, then soon.

Len returned to his seat and Matt followed him.

"This isn't exactly my idea of Christmas Eve," the older man muttered, more to himself than his companion.

"I don't think any of us could have anticipated this."

It didn't take Kemper long to connect with someone, Len noticed. The stationmaster was on the phone five minutes. He nodded once in a while, then scowled and wrote something down on a piece of paper. When he'd finished, he walked toward the potbellied stove.

Every eye in the room followed him. "Well," he said, with a deep expressive sigh, "there really isn't any news I can give you."

"No news is good news?" Cathy suggested hopefully.

"No news is no news," Matt McHugh returned tartly.

"You were talking to someone," Len said. "They must've had something to say...."

"Only what I found out earlier, that the break in the line is more serious than was originally determined."

"Isn't there anything you can suggest? How long should we expect to wait? Give us your best estimate. Surely you've seen breakdowns like this before." Len's voice thinned with frustration. He noticed a number of people nodding as he spoke.

"Well," Kemper said thoughtfully, "you're right, I have seen plenty of breakdowns over the years. Each one's different. But we've got a full crew working on this one, despite the fact that it's Christmas Eve."

"That's encouraging, anyway," Elise Jones said. "It isn't like any of us planned to spend the holidays here, you know."

"I know, I know." Kemper looked out over the group and seemed to recognize that he wouldn't be off the hook until he gave these people some kind of answer. "My best guess is sometime after midnight."

"Midnight!" Matt shouted.

He wasn't the only one who reacted with anger. But Len barely reacted at all; he felt as though the wind had been knocked clear out of him. Slowly he sank onto the bench and closed his eyes. He no longer knew if the airline could even get him a seat. Because of the snow-storm he'd missed his original flight. Because of the train's delay, he hadn't made the standby flight, either. Nor could he book another. Not until he could give the airline a time.

This felt like the worst day of his life.

Nick knew he was a fool, snapping at his wife in front of a room full of strangers and then stalking out of the train depot like a two-year-old having a tantrum. He'd caught the shocked look in Kelly's eyes. It was unchar-acteristic behavior for him, but he'd just been feeling so…on edge. Then he'd lost control because someone had shouted at Kelly to keep Brittany quiet.

What upset him was that he'd been thinking the same thing himself. He wanted her to do something, anything, to stop Brittany's crying. The baby had been contentedly asleep for a few hours, and he supposed he'd been lulled into a false sense of peace. Then she'd awakened, and it seemed that every ounce of composure he'd managed to scrape together had vanished.

He'd say one thing for his daughter. She had an incredible sense of timing. Why she'd pick that precise moment to start wailing, he'd never know. She was a fragile little thing, but obviously had the lungs of a tuba player.

It had felt as though everyone in the room was glaring at him and Kelly with malice, although in retrospect, he thought his own frustrations had probably made him misread their reactions. Everything in life had come hard for Nick; why should fatherhood be any different? He'd been raised in a series of foster homes and the only reason he'd been able to go on with his schooling was because of a scholarship. He'd graduated while holding down two part-time jobs and now worked as a scientist for a pharmaceutical company. He'd met Kelly when they were both in college. He still considered it a miracle that this beautiful woman loved him. For years now, her love had been the constant in his life, his emotional anchor, his sanctuary.

The intense cold had soaked through his coat. He kicked at the snow, depressed and angry with himself. Kelly deserved a better husband, and Brittany sure as hell needed a more loving father.

He was about to go back inside the station when the door opened and Clayton Kemper walked out.

"You're leaving?" Nick asked, shocked that the stationmaster would desert them at a time like this.

Clayton Kemper looked more than a little guilty. "My shift was over an hour ago and the missus is wanting me home."

Talk about deserting the ship. "Someone else is coming, right?"

"Oh, sure. Don't you worry. Someone'll be by to check up on you folks, but it might not be for a while." Having said that, he headed down the steps, then glanced back over his shoulder and called, "Merry Christmas."

Nick stared at the man in disbelief. This had to be the worst Christmas of his entire life! Trapped with a cranky newborn and a wife who refused to see reason. If it'd been up to him, the three of them would at least have been in a motel room, comfortable and warm. But Kelly hadn't wanted to leave the station, certain the repairs wouldn't take long. Now it was too late. The guy with the long hair and his wife had already made inquiries. Apparently every hotel for miles around was full.

This optimistic bent of Kelly's had always been a problem. He'd been ready to give up on the fertility clinic long before she agreed. The expense had been horrific, and he didn't mean just the financial aspects. Emotionally Kelly was a wreck two weeks out of every month. Only when he was able to talk her into accepting their situation and applying to an adoption agency had she gotten off the emotional roller coaster.

Nick had almost given up hope himself—and then they received the phone call about Brittany. That five-minute conversation had changed their lives forever.

He found himself grinning at the memory. Kelly was the one who'd been cool and calm while he'd sat there trembling. He'd never experienced any excitement even close to what he'd felt when he learned they finally had a baby.

The first instant he saw Brittany, he'd been swept by a love so powerful it was beyond comprehension. Yet here he was, three months later, acting like a dolt and snapping at his wife in public.

That wasn't his only offense, either. For most of the afternoon, he'd ignored Kelly and the baby, wanting to escape them both. He wasn't proud of himself; he'd ignored their needs, leaving Kelly to care for their daughter on her own while he brooded and behaved like a spoiled child.

With that in mind, he boarded the train, walked down

the narrow aisle and got the baby seat down from the storage compartment. Kelly's arms must be tired from holding Brittany. He wished he'd thought of this sooner.

Hauling in a deep breath, he walked back into the station and stomped the snow from his boots. When he looked up, he discovered Kelly staring at him, her lips tight, but her eyes forgiving.

"I'm sorry," he whispered as he sat beside her. He gazed down at Brittany, who gazed back at him, her blue eyes wide and curious. His daughter seemed to recognize him, and she, at least, didn't know enough to realize what a cantankerous fool he'd been the past few hours. He offered her his finger, which she gripped eagerly with her little hand.

"I'm sorry, too," Kelly whispered back, sounding close to tears.

Nick set the baby seat on the floor and placed his arm around his wife's shoulders. She leaned her head against him. "I don't know what came over me," he murmured. "I wish we were anyplace but here."

"Me, too," Kelly said.

"Amy?"

Len felt a surge of relief and unmistakable joy at the sound of her "hello."

"Are you in Boston?" she asked excitedly. "When can you catch a flight home?"

"I'm still in Abbott," Len said, his happiness evaporating quickly with the reality of this long day. He was trapped, a hostage to circumstances beyond his control.

"You're still in Abbott?" Amy sounded ready to weep. "Oh, Len, will you ever get home for Christmas?"

"I don't know," he told her, trying to keep his own hopes alive—and failing. It seemed everything was against him.

"Yes," he said suddenly, emphatically. For a moment he didn't know where this optimism had come from. Then he did. It was his overwhelming need to be with Amy. "I *will* get home for Christmas." He wasn't about to let the storm, the damaged tracks or anything else ruin his leave. "I'll be home for Christmas, Amy. You can count on it."

He could almost feel her spirits rise. "Your girl in Rawhide will be waiting for you, sailor man."

"You're more than my girl in Rawhide," Len said. "You're my one and only girl. Period!"

She said nothing after his declaration. "Do you mean that, Len?" she finally asked.

"With all my heart." He was tempted to tell her about the diamond, but that would ruin his surprise, and he didn't want to propose over the phone. It just didn't seem near good enough. He wanted her to see the love in his eyes and watch her face when she saw the ring.

"Oh, Len," she whispered.

"Listen, would you call my mom and dad and tell them I still don't know when I'll be home?"

"Sure. Listen, since you can't be here, I'll go back to the nursing home tonight and play the piano for everyone. They wanted to sing Christmas carols but couldn't find any staff willing to take time away from their families."

Len loved her all the more for her generous heart.

"I can't see sitting around home and moping," she explained.

"Sing a Christmas carol for me."

"I will," she said, and her voice softened.

There was a beep in his ear and Len knew he had only a couple of minutes left on his calling card.

"Oh, Len," Amy said. "Time's running out."

"Remember, I'll see you as soon as I can," he said, ready to hang up.

"Len, Len…"

"Yes? What is it?"

"Len," she said, her voice catching, "I…love you. I was going to wait until tonight to tell you, but I want you to know right now. You might be in New Hampshire and me here in Rawhide, but that doesn't matter, because you have my heart with you wherever you are."

The line went dead. Len wasn't sure if she'd hung up or if the time had simply expired.

"I love you, too, Amy," he said into the silent phone, knowing she couldn't hear the words. Somehow he was certain she could feel his heart responding to hers. Soon she'd know how very much he loved his Amy Sue.

Len replaced the receiver and turned around to face the room. Everyone seemed in a dour mood.

The door burst open just then and a smiling, light-hearted Clayton Kemper walked in. He glanced around and beamed proudly at the group of weary travelers.

"I was on my way home when I ran across this," he said cheerfully. He stuck his hand out the door and dragged in the sorriest-looking Christmas tree Len had ever seen.

One side of the evergreen was bare, the top had split and two branches spiked in opposite directions, resembling bug antennae.

"The man in the Christmas-tree lot gave it to me for a buck."

"You got overcharged," Matt McHugh muttered. His words were followed by a few short laughs and a general feeling of agreement.

"That may well be," Kemper said, not letting their lack of enthusiasm dampen his spirit. "But it seemed to me that since you folks are stuck here on Christmas Eve, you might as well make the best of it."

"That tree looks like it's in the same shap? we're in," Elise Jones said dryly.

"The tree is yours to do with as you wish," Kemper told them. "Merry Christmas to you all."

No one thought to thank him, Len noticed.

The sad little tree stood in the center of the room, bare and forlorn, wounded and ugly. He'd have to go along with Elise. The Christmas tree did resemble them—and their attitude.

Five-year-old Kate Jones walked over to it and stood with her arms akimbo, staring at the limp branches. Then, apparently having come to some sort of decision, she turned to confront the disgruntled group.

"I think it's a beautiful tree," she announced. "It just needs a little help." She removed the red bow from the top of her head and pinned it to the nearest branch.

Despite himself, Len grinned. On closer examination, the kid was right. The tree wasn't nearly as ugly as he'd first thought.

Six

"Sing We Now of Christmas"

Most everyone ignored the Christmas tree, Cathy Norris mused sadly. Except for Kate... Then Kelly walked over and silently added a rattle. She took her time finding just the right spot for it, choosing to hang it directly in the middle, opposite Kate's hair bow.

Turning to the others, she smiled and said, "Come on, you guys, it's Christmas Eve."

"She's right," Nick said, and joined his wife. He bounced the baby gently in his arms, and Brittany grinned and reached for his bright green muffler. Nick removed it, handed the baby to Kelly and placed the muffler on the tree, stretching it out as if it were the finest decorative strand. He wove it between the lower branches of the fir, the wool fringe dangling like green wool tinsel.

Len surveyed the tree, then stepped up and added his white cap, settling it near the top, where it sat jauntily.

The elderly black man moved forward next and added his tie clasp. He clipped it to the branch in an upright position like a clothespin, stepped back and nodded once, apparently pleased with the effect. "Hey, this tree doesn't look so bad."

Soon others became creative about decorating the Christmas tree. Cathy cut strips of red yarn and with Kate's help draped the strands over as many branches as they could reach.

Even the grumpy salesman pitched in. Cathy saw him with the small pair of scissors on his Swiss Army knife, folding and cutting memos into paper snowflakes, then hanging them on the tree with dental floss. Actually they looked quite attractive against the backdrop of red yarn.

It wasn't long before every branch sprouted some sort of odd decoration. True, it wasn't a traditional Christmas tree, but it seemed to possess amazing powers. The scowls and complaints of moments earlier were now replaced by smiles and animated chatter.

"I think my daughter's right," Elise said, walking over to more closely examine their handiwork. "This is actually a beautiful tree."

The little boy, around three or four, who'd stayed close by his parents the entire day, clapped in delight.

Cathy noticed several smiles.

"I'm hungry," Kate whispered to her mother.

Worrying about their situation as she had for most of the day, Cathy hadn't given any thought to food until the youngster mentioned it. She apparently wasn't the only one.

"What about dinner?" Cathy asked, glancing about the room. It looked as though they'd been left to fend for themselves. Mr. Kemper had said someone would come by to check on them, but so far no one had.

"Nothing's going to be open tonight," Matt McHugh grumbled. "Not on Christmas Eve."

"Especially not with the storm and all earlier," Len put in.

Cathy could feel the mood of the room, so recently elevated, plunge. Already those who'd moved closer to the Christmas tree were sliding away to slump on benches by the walls.

"Now, that does bring up an interesting prospect," Cathy said, speaking to the entire group for the first time. "I'm Cathy Norris, by the way. I'm going to visit my daughter and her family in Boston, and I just happened to bring along four dozen of her favorite shortbread cookies. Somehow, I don't think she'd mind my sharing them with all of you."

She brought out the tin and pried open the lid.

"My wife and I have several oranges," the elderly

black man said. "We can share those. Since we're going to be eating together, it's only appropriate that we introduce ourselves. My name's Sam Givens and my wife's Louise."

"Thank you, Sam and Louise," Cathy said. "Anyone else?"

"I'm Matt McHugh. I was given a fruitcake on my last sales call," Matt surprised her by saying. "I would've thrown the damn thing out, but one of my kids likes the stuff. I can cut that up if anyone's interested."

"Well, I'm quite fond of fruitcake," Kelly Berry said.

Although the depot office was locked, the counter was free and Cathy placed the tin of cookies there. Matt took out the fruitcake and sliced it with his Swiss Army knife. Sam Givens brought over the oranges, then peeled and sectioned them.

Elise Jones collected paper towels from the rest room to use as napkins. Soon more and more food appeared. It seemed almost everyone had something to share. A plate of beautifully decorated chocolates. A white cardboard box filled with pink divinity and homemade fudge. Then a tin of peanuts and a bag of pretzels. Len added a package of cinnamon-flavored gum.

A crooked line formed and they all helped themselves, taking bits and pieces of each dish. It wasn't much, but it helped do more than dull the edge of their hunger. It proved, to Cathy at least, that there was hope for them. That banding together they could get through this and even have a good time.

"My mother's serving prime rib right about now," Elise lamented as she took an orange segment and a handful of peanuts.

"And to think she's missing out on Matt McHugh's fruitcake," Cathy said, and was delighted by the responding laugh that echoed down the line. Even Matt chuckled. An hour ago Cathy would have thought that impossible.

"I never thought I'd say this about fruitcake," the young sailor said, saluting Matt with a slice, "but this ain't half-bad."

"What about my peanuts?" the guy with long hair asked. "I spent hours slaving over a hot stove to make those."

Everyone smiled and the silly jokes continued.

"Quiet," Nick said suddenly, jumping to his feet. "I hear something."

"A train?" Matt teased.

"'Do you hear what I hear?'" Someone sang.

"I'm serious."

It didn't take Cathy long to pick up the faint sound of voices singing. "Someone's coming," she announced.

"Carolers?" Kelly asked. "On a night like this? For us?"

"No night more perfect," Cathy murmured. Years

ago she and Ron had been members of the church choir. Each holiday season the choir had toured nursing homes and hospitals, giving short performances. They'd been active in their church for a number of years. Unfortunately their attendance had slipped after Ron retired, then stopped completely when he became seriously ill. And afterward…well, afterward Cathy simply didn't have the heart for it.

For the first time since the funeral, she felt the need to return. This insight was like an unexpected gift, and it had come to her at the sound of the carolers' voices.

The door opened and a group of fifteen or so entered the train depot.

"Hello, everyone." A man with a bushy gray mustache and untamed gray hair stepped forward. "I'm Dean Owen. Clayton Kemper's a friend of mine and he mentioned you folks were stranded. This is the teen choir from the Regular Baptist Church. Since we weren't able to get out last night because of the snow, we thought we'd make a few rounds this evening. How's everyone doing?"

"Great."

"As good as can be expected."

"Hangin' in there."

"I love your Christmas tree," one of the girls said.

She was about sixteen, with long blond hair in a pony-tail and twinkling eyes.

"We decorated it ourselves," Kate said, pointing to her hair bow. "That's mine."

"Would anyone mind if I took a picture?" the girl asked, pulling a disposable camera from her coat pocket.

"This is something that's got to be seen to be believed," Matt whispered to Cathy. "Actually I wouldn't mind having a copy of it myself."

"Me, too."

"Shall we make it a family photo?" Elise asked.

A chorus of yes's and no's followed, but within a minute the ragtag group had gathered around the tree. Cathy ran a comb through her hair and added a dash of lipstick. Others, too, reviewed their appearance as they assembled for the photograph, jostling each other good-naturedly.

What amazed Cathy were the antics that went on before the picture was taken. They behaved like a group of teenagers themselves. Len held up the V for peace sign behind Nick's head. Even Matt managed a crooked smile. For that matter, so did Cathy. Someone joked and she laughed. That made her realize how long it'd been since she'd allowed herself to be happy. *Too long. Ron wouldn't want that.*

The girl took four snapshots. Before long the development of the film had been paid for and she had a list of names and addresses to send copies of the photo. Cathy's name was there along with everyone else's. She wanted something tangible to remember this eventful day—the oddest Christmas Eve she'd spent in her entire life.

"We thought we'd deliver a bit of cheer," Dean said, once the photo arrangements were finished.

Their coming had done exactly that. The travelers gathered around without anyone's direction, positioning the benches in a way that allowed them all to see the singers.

The choir assembled in three rows of five each and began with "Silent Night," sung in three-part harmony. Cathy had heard the old carol all her life, but never had it sounded more beautiful than it did this evening. Without accompaniment, without embellishment, simple, plain—and incredibly lovely. With the beautiful words came a sense of camaraderie and joy, a sense that this night was truly special.

This *was* a holy night.

"Silent Night" was followed by "The Little Drummer Boy," then "Joy to the World," one carol flowing smoothly into another, ending with "We Wish You a Merry Christmas."

While Cathy and the others applauded loudly, Kate

in a burst of childish enthusiasm spontaneously rushed forward and hugged Dean's knees. "That was so pretty," she squealed, her delight contagious.

Len jumped to his feet, continuing the applause. Soon the others stood, too, including Cathy.

The small choir seemed overwhelmed by their appreciation.

"This is the first time we ever got a standing ovation," the girl with the camera said, smiling at her friends. "I didn't realize we were that good."

"Sing more," Kate pleaded. "Do you know 'Rudolph the Red-Nosed Reindeer'?"

"Can you sing it with us?" Dean bent down and asked Kate.

The child nodded enthusiastically, and Dean had her stand in front of the choir. "Sing away."

"Join in, everyone," he suggested next, turning to face his small audience.

Cathy and the others didn't need any encouragement. Their voices blended with those of the choir as if they'd sung together for weeks. "Rudolph" led to other Christmas songs—"Silver Bells,"

"Deck the Halls," and the time passed quickly.

When they finished, the choir members brought out paper cups and thermoses of hot chocolate. No sooner had the hot drink been poured than the station door opened again.

"So Clayton was right." A petite older woman, with a cap of white hair and eyelids painted the brightest shade of blue Cathy had ever seen, entered the room. Two other women filed in after her.

"I'm Greta Barnes," the leader said, "and we're from the Veterans of Foreign Wars Women's Auxiliary."

"We've brought you folks dinner," another woman told them.

"Now you're talking!" Len Dawber shouted. "Sorry, folks, but a slice of fruitcake and a few pretzels didn't quite fill me up."

"Made for a great appetizer, though," Nick said.

"The food's out in the car. Would someone help carry it in?" Greta asked. She didn't have to ask for volunteers a second time. Nick, Matt and Len were up before any of the other men had a chance. A couple of minutes later they were back inside, their arms loaded with boxes.

"It's not much," one of the other women said apologetically as she set a huge pot of soup on the counter. "We didn't get much notice."

"We're grateful for whatever you brought us," Sam assured the women. Louise nodded in agreement.

"Luckily the family had plenty of clam chowder left over," the older of Greta's friends said. "The soup's a Christmas Eve tradition in our house, and I can't help it, I always cook up more than enough."

"Eleanor's soup is the best in the state," Greta declared.

"There's sandwiches, too," the third woman said, unpacking one of the smaller boxes.

"And seeing that no one knows when the repairs on those tracks are going to be finished," the spry older woman added, "we decided to bring along some blankets and pillows."

"All the comforts of home," Matt muttered, but the caustic edge that had laced his comments earlier in the day had vanished.

"I must say you folks are certainly good sports about all this."

Considering that this change in attitude had only recently come about, none of them leaped to their feet to accept credit.

"Like I said earlier," Matt told her, speaking for the group, "we're making the best of it."

"We're very grateful for the pillows and blankets," Cathy put in.

"The food, too," several others said.

The church choir stayed and helped pass around the sandwiches, which were delicious. Cathy ate half a tuna-salad sandwich, then half a turkey one. She was amazed at how big her appetite was. Food, like almost everything since Ron's death, had become a necessity and not an enjoyment.

When the teen choir left, it was with a cheery wave and the promise that everyone who'd asked for a picture would be sure to receive one. With a responsible kindhearted man like Dean Owen as their leader, Cathy was confident it would come about.

The soup and sandwiches disappeared quickly. Three other men helped pack up the leftovers and carted the boxes out to the car.

"You sure we can't get you anything else?" Greta asked before she headed outside.

"You've done more than enough."

"Thank Mr. Kemper for us," Len said, ready to escort the older women to their vehicle.

With many shouts of "Merry Christmas," everyone waved the Auxiliary ladies goodbye.

Len returned, leaning against the door when it closed. Cathy watched as he paused and glanced about the room. "You know," he said, not speaking to anyone in particular, "I almost feel sorry for all those people who decided to stay in hotels. They've missed out on the best Christmas Eve I can ever remember."

Seven

"Santa Claus Is Coming to Town"

The station seemed unnaturally quiet after the choir and the members of the VFW Women's Auxiliary had left. The lively chatter and shared laughter that had filled the room died down to a low hum.

Matt knew he should phone home, that he'd delayed it as long as he dared. With the time difference between the east and west coasts, it wasn't quite four in the afternoon in Los Angeles. The dread that settled over him depleted the sense of well-being he'd experienced over the past few hours.

He didn't look forward to a telephone confrontation with Pam, but as far as he could see there was no avoiding one. He could almost hear her voice, starting low and quickly gaining volume until it reached a shrill, near-hysterical pitch.

He wished things could be different, but he knew she'd start in on him, and then, despite his best efforts, he'd retaliate. Soon their exchange would escalate into a full-blown fight.

His feet felt weighted as he crossed the station to the row of pay phones. He slipped his credit card through the appropriate slot, punched in his home number and waited for the line to connect.

The phone rang twice, three times, then four before the answering machine came on. Bored, he tapped his foot while he listened to the message he'd recorded earlier in the year. When he heard the signal, he was ready. "Pam, it's Matt. I'm sorry about this, but I got caught in the snowstorm that struck Maine yesterday. The flights out of Bangor were canceled, so the airline put me on a train for Boston. Now the train tracks are out and I don't have a clue when I'll be home. As soon as I reach Boston, probably sometime Christmas morning, I'll phone and let you know when to expect me. I'm sorry about this, but it's out of my control. Kiss the kids for me and I'll see you as soon as I can."

The relief that came over him at not getting caught in a verbal battle with his wife was like an unexpected gift. This wasn't how it should be, but he felt powerless to change the dynamics of their marriage. Somewhere along the road the partnership they'd once shared had fallen apart. He wasn't the only one who felt miserable; he knew that. The look in Pam's eyes as he'd walked through the house, suitcase in hand, had told him he wasn't the only one thinking about a separation.

His mood was oppressive by the time he returned to his seat.

"What about Santa?" Matt heard Kate ask her mother.

"Honey, he's still coming to Grandma's house." Kate's mother was busy making up a bed for her daughter. She placed a pillow at one end of the bench and arranged the blanket so the little girl could sleep between its folds.

"But, Mom, I'm *not* at Grandma Gibson's house— I'm *here.* Santa might not know."

Elise apparently needed a minute to think about that. "Grandma will have to tell him."

"But what if Santa decides to try to find me here, instead of leaving my presents with Grandma?"

"Kate, please, can't you just trust that you're going to get your gifts?"

Arms crossed, the child shook her head stubbornly. "No, I can't," she said, her voice as serious as the expression on her face. "You told me Daddy was going to come see me before we left and he didn't."

"Honey, I don't have any control over what your father says and does. I'm sorry he disappointed you."

Her look said it wasn't the first time mother and child had been let down.

Kate started to whimper.

"Sweetheart, please," Elise whispered. She seemed close to breaking down herself. She picked up her daughter and held her close. As she gently rocked the little girl, her eyes shone with unshed tears. "Santa won't forget you."

"Daddy did."

"No, honey, I'm sure he didn't, not really."

"Then why didn't he come like he said?"

"Because..." Elise began, then hesitated and forcefully expelled her breath. "It's complicated."

"Everything's complicated since you and Daddy divorced."

Matt felt like an eavesdropper, yet he couldn't tune out the conversation between mother and child. Part of him yearned to let Kate use his credit card to phone her father, but if he suggested that, Elise would know he'd been listening in.

Hearing Kate cry about being forgotten by her dad left Matt to wonder if this would be his own children's future should he and Pam decide to split up. He didn't want a divorce, never had. But it was obvious they couldn't continue the way they'd been going—belittling each other, arguing, eroding the foundation of their love and commitment.

"Why didn't Daddy come see me like he said he would?" Kate persisted.

Elise took her time answering. "Your daddy was embarrassed."

"Embarrassed?"

"He felt bad."

"About what?"

"Being late helping to pay the bills. He didn't come see you because...well, because I don't think he could afford to buy you anything for Christmas, and he didn't want you to be disappointed in him because he didn't have a gift."

Kate mulled that over for a while, nibbling her bottom lip. "I love him and I didn't have a gift for him, either."

"Your daddy loves you, Kate, that much I know."

"Can I talk to him myself?"

Elise took a deep breath. "You can phone him when we reach Grandma's house, and you can tell him about spending the night in the train depot. He'll want to hear about all your adventures on Christmas Eve."

Matt considered what would happen to his relationship with his children if he and Pam went their separate ways. The love he felt for Rachel and Jimmy ran deep, and the idea of Pam having to make excuses for him…

His thoughts tumbled to an abrupt halt. That was exactly what Pam had been forced to do the afternoon he'd left for Maine. Jimmy had been counting on him to attend the school Christmas program and, instead, he'd raced off to the airport. Matt's stomach knotted, and he sat back, wiping a hand down his face.

A whispered discussion broke out between the widow and the elderly couple who'd supplied the oranges. Matt had no idea what was going on and, caught up in his own musing, didn't much care.

Not long afterward, he discovered that a few of the senior crowd had decided to take this matter of Christmas for the two children into their own hands.

Cathy walked by Kate, paused suddenly and held one hand to her ear. "Did you hear something?" she asked the youngster.

"Not me," Kate answered.

"I think it's bells."

Elise cupped her ear. "Reindeer feet?"

"Bells," Cathy returned pointedly.

"Yes," Louise piped up. "It's definitely the sound of bells. What could it be?"

They weren't going to get any Academy Award nominations, but they did manage to convince the children.

"I hear bells!" the other child called. "I do, I do."
It was the first time the little boy had spoken all day.

Kate sat up straight on her mother's lap. "I hear them, too."

Matt had to admit the two old ladies really had him going; he could almost hear them himself. Then he realized he really *could* hear the jingle of bells.

A knock sounded loudly on the station door. "I'll get it." Sam eagerly stepped to the door. He opened it a couple of inches, nodded a few times and looked over his shoulder. "Do we have a little girl named Kate here and a boy…Charlie?"

"Charles," his mother corrected.

"Kate and Charles," Sam informed the mysterious visitor no one was allowed to see. "As a matter of fact, Kate and Charles *are* here," Sam said loudly. "You do… of course. I'll see to it personally. Now don't you worry, you have plenty of other deliveries to make tonight. You'd best be on your way."

Matt glanced around and noticed that Nick Berry was missing…and he seemed to remember that their baby had a rattle with bells inside.

The room went quiet as Sam closed the door, and the jingling receded. He had a pillowcase in one hand, with a couple of wrapped gifts inside. "That was Santa Claus," he announced. "He heard that Kate and Charles were stuck here on Christmas Eve. Santa wanted them to know he hadn't forgotten them."

"Did he bring my presents?" Kate sprang off her mother's lap and ran toward Sam, still standing near the door.

Charles joined her, gazing up at the man with hopeful eyes.

"Santa wanted me to tell you he left plenty of gifts at your Grandma Gibson's house, Kate, but he didn't want you to worry that he'd missed you, so he dropped this off." He thrust his arm into the pillowcase and produced a wrapped box.

Matt recognized it right away as one he'd seen poking out of Cathy Norris's carry-on bag when she'd removed the tin of cookies.

"I believe this one is for you, Charles," Sam said. The second gift went to the four-year-old. The boy raced back to his parents and dropped to his knees. He tore into the wrapping paper, scattering pieces in all directions. The minute Charles saw the rubber dinosaur, he cried out in delight and hugged it to his chest.

Kate, on the other hand, opened her present with delicate precision, carefully removing the ribbon first and placing it on the tree. Next came the wrapping paper. Matt couldn't figure out how she did it, but she managed to pull off the Christmas wrap without tearing it even once. When she saw the Barbie doll, she looked up at her mother and smiled wonderingly.

"Daddy must have given it to Santa. This is what I told him I wanted."

"I'm sure he did." Elise was gracious enough to concur.

Matt didn't know what had gone wrong in this woman's marriage, but it wasn't difficult to see the pain that divorce had brought into her life. Could bring into his own, if he allowed it to happen.

Cathy and the elderly couple exchanged smiles that their small ploy had worked. Actually Matt was touched by their generosity; they'd obviously given up Christmas presents meant for their own grandchildren.

He wasn't sure what prompted the idea, but he reached for his briefcase. "As a matter of fact, Santa left a few goodies with me, too. Is anyone interested in a sample of the latest software from MicroChip International?"

It didn't take long to discover that a number of people were.

"Are you sure, man?" the ex-hippie asked. "This is worth a good two hundred bucks in the store."

"Five hundred, actually," Matt said. "Consider it compliments of the company."

"We've got extra pictures of the baby, if anyone would like," Nick offered.

"Sure," Len said. "Amy—my fiancée—is crazy about babies." He took one and so did Cathy, Elise and several others.

As had happened earlier with the food, a variety of gifts, some wrapped and others not, started to appear. The joking and laughter continued during the impromptu gift exchange. By the end, everyone had both given and received at least one gift.

Sam, who'd stayed in the background most of the day, stepped forward with a worn Bible in his hand. "This being the night of our Savior's birth," he said, "I thought we might like to listen to the account of the first Christmas."

Most people nodded in silent agreement. Sam pulled out a chair and set it close to their Christmas tree, then perched a pair of glasses on his nose.

The room hushed as he began to read. His rich resonant voice echoed through the depot. Everyone listened with an attentiveness Matt found amazing.

When he'd finished, Sam reverently closed the Bible and removed his glasses, tucking them into his shirt pocket. "It seems to me that we all have something in common with Mary and Joseph. They, too, were weary travelers and there wasn't any room for them at the inn." He paused and held up one hand. "I checked earlier and every room in this town has been booked for the night."

There were grins and murmurs at his remark. Sam got to his feet and sang the first words of "Silent Night." Everyone joined in, their voices rising in joyful sound. Matt thought he'd never heard anything so achingly beautiful, so…sincere.

As the last line died away, Sam walked over to the wall and turned out the light. The room went dim, but the outside lights cast a warm glow into the station's interior.

"It's nine o'clock," the ex-hippie announced. "I haven't been to bed this early in twenty years, but I'm more than ready to hit the hay."

His wife giggled. The two of them cuddled awkwardly on the hard bench, kissing and whispering.

Matt felt a pang of regret at seeing the closeness they shared, a closeness so sadly lacking in his own marriage. He glanced at his watch, certain that Pam would be home now, probably seething about the brief message he'd left. Nevertheless he wanted to talk to her. No, he corrected himself, he *needed* to talk to her.

Light from the window guided him to the far wall of the station, to the phones. Because it was still early, people continued to talk. He slipped his credit card through the slot and waited for the line to connect.

Pam answered on the first ring. "Hello." Her clipped tone told him she was angry, as he'd expected.

"It's Matt," he said.

"Matt?" She paused. "Matt?" she said again. "Where—"

"Merry Christmas, sweetheart," he whispered.

"How can you 'Merry Christmas' me with the kids screaming in my ear? Your parents are due any minute, and the house is a mess. The cat tipped over the Christmas tree and you're…you're…" She burst into tears.

"Pam," he said softly. "Honey, don't cry."

"I can't help it! I suppose you're in some posh hotel, ogling the cocktail waitress, while I'm here—"

"I'm not in any hotel."

"Then where are you?"

"A hundred-year-old train depot with…" Now it was his turn to pause. "With friends who were strangers not that long ago."

"A train depot?" She sniffled and sounded unsure.

"It's a long story and I'll tell you about it when I get home."

"You didn't phone all week."

"I know and I'm sorry, sweetheart, really sorry. It was childish and silly of me to let our argument stand in the way of talking to you and the kids."

"You haven't called me sweetheart in a long time."

"Too long," Matt said. "I've done a lot of thinking these past few days, and once I'm home I want to talk to you about making some changes."

"I've been a terrible wife," she sobbed into the phone.

"Pam, you haven't. Now stop. I love you and you love me, and we're going to make it, understand?"

"Yes," she mumbled, her reply quavery with emotion.

"Listen, I want you to think about two things."

"Okay."

"First, I want to quit my job." Not until he said the words did Matt recognize how right it was to leave MicroChip. He should have known it when he was passed over for a promotion he'd earned. Being undervalued and underappreciated had cut into his self-confidence, and inevitably, his dissatisfaction with his job had affected his family life. He couldn't, wouldn't, allow that to continue.

"Quit your job?" Pam gasped.

"It isn't as bad as it sounds. I'm going to send out a couple of feelers right after New Year's. I've got a good reputation in the industry. I can get something else. The main thing is that I spend more time at home with you and the kids. It's unfair to have you chained down with all the responsibility for them and the house while I travel. I'm going to be looking for a sales position that won't take me away for more than a day at a time."

"That sounds wonderful."

"The other thing we need is a vacation, just the two

of us. I've got vacation time coming, and it's been far too long since you and I got away without the kids."

"I'd love that, Matt, more than anything."

"How about a Caribbean cruise?" he suggested.

"Yes… Oh, Matt, I love you so much and I've felt so awful about the way our marriage has been going."

"Me, too. We'll talk about that some more. Maybe it wouldn't be such a bad idea to see a counselor, either."

"Yes," she whispered.

Over the phone Matt heard a chorus of background shouts.

"Your parents just arrived," Pam told him.

"Let them wait. I want to say Merry Christmas to my wife."

Eight

"Silent Night"

Cathy made up a small bed for herself using the blankets and pillows the VFW Women's Auxiliary had distributed. By all rights, she should be exhausted. She'd been up since dawn and the day had been filled with uncertainty and tension.

Instead, she lay with her eyes wide-open, mulling over the events of the past twenty-four hours. Apparently she wasn't the only one having difficulty sleeping. Matt, the sales rep, had carefully made his way across the darkened room and used the phone. It could be her imagination, but his steps seemed lighter on the return trip, as though his mood had improved. Cathy felt pleased for him. She'd lost patience with him earlier, and later…well, later, he'd proved to be an ally and a friend.

She'd witnessed more than one transformation today. The young sailor had been nervous and excited about this trip home; he'd chattered like a five-year-old when they'd first started out.

Then troubles developed, and he'd withdrawn into himself. But over the next few hours, Cathy had watched as Len recovered from his disappointment and frustration. Before the night was over he'd been an encouragement to others.

Nick and Kelly, the young couple with the newborn, were struggling to be good parents and still hold on to the closeness they'd once had in their marriage. Those two reminded Cathy of Ron and her about thirty years ago, after the birth of their first daughter. Eventually, like most couples, Nick and Kelly would learn to work together and ease gracefully into parenthood.

Sam and Louise had kept to themselves all day, offering no advice and little comment until Cathy shared her shortbread cookies. It was then that they'd kindly come forward and contributed their oranges. Later Sam had read the Christmas story from the Bible in a way that had stirred her beyond any Christmas Eve church service she'd ever attended.

She thought again of Matt McHugh. In the beginning he'd been quite disagreeable. Easily irritated, his few remarks cynical. One would assume that as a seasoned traveler he'd be better able to deal with frustrations of this sort. Unfortunately that wasn't the case until… Cathy couldn't put her finger on the precise moment she'd noticed the change in him. About the time they'd decorated the tree, she decided, when he'd opened his briefcase and started folding and clipping memos into paper snowflakes. She'd sensed a genuine enthusiasm in him from that point on.

Cathy had been just as affected by the unusual events of this Christmas Eve as her fellow passengers. That morning, when she'd phoned for a taxi in the middle of the snowstorm, she hadn't been looking forward to the trip. She'd dreaded it less, however, than spending the holiday alone in the house where she'd lived all those years with Ron.

She'd known Christmas would be difficult. After living first with the approach of death and then the aftermath of it, she'd anticipated nothing but pain and loneliness during the Christmas season. And she'd been right. But today, for the first time since standing over her husband's grave, she'd experienced what it meant to be alive. Sharing, encouraging, laughing. Damn, but it felt good.

"Are you awake?" Matt whispered from the bench directly across from her.

"Yes. You, too." She smiled at the obviousness of the comment.

"I just spoke to my wife." He sounded excited. "It was the first time we've connected all day."

"I imagine she was relieved to hear from you."

She saw his nod, and then he said the oddest thing.

"You loved your husband very much, didn't you?" he asked, sitting up and leaning toward her, bracing his elbows on his knees.

"Yes." Her voice wavered slightly, surprised as she was by his question and the instant flash of pain it produced.

"I want my wife and me to have the same kind of relationship you did with your husband."

The comment touched her heart. "Thank you," she whispered, warmed by the praise of this stranger who'd become her friend. "How'd you know… I didn't mention Ron, I don't think."

"Ah, but you did," he said quietly, nestling against his pillow. "You told Kate about the dollhouse your husband built for his granddaughters. It was easy to read between the lines and…well, I could see this Christmas was difficult for you."

"It's better now," she whispered.

He sighed and curled up against the pillow before closing his eyes. "It's better for me, too."

"Merry Christmas, Matt."

"Merry Christmas, Cathy."

Len purposely waited until the depot was silent. The even rhythm of breathing told him that almost everyone was asleep. His watch said eleven-thirty, which made it ten-thirty in Rawhide. Amy had mentioned playing the piano at the rest home, and he'd waited until he was fairly confident she'd be home.

The phone card he'd paid for on base had long since expired, so he had to use his credit card. The transaction seemed loud enough to wake the entire room, but as far as Len could see, no one stirred.

When the line connected, the phone rang three times, three of the longest rings Len could ever remember hearing. He was about to give up hope when Amy answered.

"Hello." Her voice sounded breathless and excited at once.

"Merry Christmas, Amy," he said, speaking in a whisper for fear of disturbing the others.

"Len, Len, is that you?"

"It's me."

"Where are you?"

"The train depot," he said, wishing he had other news to give her.

"Still? Oh, Len, are you ever going to make it home?"

"And miss seeing my girl? Are you nuts? I'll walk from here to Rawhide if I have to."

"Oh, Len! I can't believe this is happening."

He'd felt much the same way himself most of the day, but somehow everything had changed after Mr. Kemper brought in the Christmas tree. And after the choir had come and the ladies had brought them a meal. And Sam had read the Christmas story...

In the beginning tempers had flared and folks were impatient and short with each other. Then the kind-hearted stationmaster had brought that bare sad-looking tree and placed it in the center of the room.

Someone had commented that the stupid tree wasn't worth the buck Kemper had paid for it.

Len had agreed. It'd taken a five-year-old child to teach them. The minute Kate had placed her hair bow on one sagging limb, the Christmas tree had been magically transformed into something beautiful. Not because of what they'd used to decorate its branches, but because of the effect it'd had on all of them, the way it had brought them together.

Everything had changed from then on. Suddenly they weren't strangers anymore. Suddenly it was a Christmas like those he'd enjoyed when he was a boy. He'd spent Christmas Eve with strangers who'd become so much more. Strangers who'd become family. Granted, it wasn't the same as if he'd spent Christmas Eve with Amy, but then he expected to be with her for the rest of his life.

"I'll be home before you know it," he promised.

"I'll be here," she whispered.

The line was quiet a moment while Len gathered his courage. He'd rather propose when he could look into her eyes and see her reaction as he said the words, but that wasn't possible. He didn't think he could wait any longer.

"Did you mean what you said earlier?" he asked. "Do you really love me, Amy Sue?"

"Yes," she admitted as though confessing to a fault. "I...I probably shouldn't have said it."

"Why not?" he asked, raising his voice before he could stop himself.

"Because...well, because we've never talked about our feelings and—"

"I love you, too, Amy."

She didn't say anything for so long Len feared they'd been disconnected.

"Amy?"

"I'm here."

He could tell from the tremble in her voice that she was close to tears. "Amy, listen, I never intended it to happen like this, but then life doesn't always go the way we plan it. I decided to come home for another reason besides spending Christmas with my family."

"What?"

"I was hoping…" Despite rehearsing his proposal, he was tongue-tied and nervous.

"You were hoping…" she encouraged.

"To talk to you about something important."

"Yes?"

"About the two of us." He continued to improvise, forgetting the carefully worded proposal he'd practiced a hundred times. "I was thinking you and I…that is, if you were interested…that maybe we should get married."

There was a silence that seemed to go on and on.

"Married," she finally repeated, sounding stunned.

Len's hand tightened around the telephone receiver. His nerves were stretched to the limit. "Say something," he pleaded, all the while wondering if it was possible to get a refund on the diamond if she refused him. His heart sank to his knees; he hadn't considered Amy's refusal. In his arrogance he'd assumed she'd scream with delight, maybe even cry a little. The last thing he'd anticipated was no response.

"Amy?" he asked, humble now, wondering how he could have made such a mistake in judgment. He'd noted the reserve in her recently, the fact that he hadn't gotten a letter in almost two weeks. Other things didn't add up, either, but he'd pushed his concerns aside each time he spoke with her—although of course their phone calls had been less frequent lately. But whenever he managed to call she'd always sounded so glad to hear from him.

"Is there someone else?" he demanded, his pride rescuing him. "Is that it?"

"Oh, Len, how can you think such a thing?"

"Then what's it to be?" A proposal was a straightforward enough question. "Yes or no?"

"Who told you?"

"Told me?" he echoed. "Told me what?"

"About the baby."

Nine

"Baby?" Len's knees went weak and to remain upright he braced his shoulder against the wall.

"Who told you?" Amy repeated.

"No one…" Len's thoughts twisted around in his mind until he was convinced he'd misunderstood her. "To make sure I understand what's happening here, I need to ask you something. Are you telling me you're pregnant?"

"Yes."

"Don't you think you should've mentioned this before now?" he demanded, not caring who heard him. "You must be at least three months along."

"Three and a half… I love you, Len, but you've never said how you felt about me. I didn't want you to feel obligated to marry me. My dad married my mother because she was pregnant and the marriage was a disaster. I refuse to repeat my mother's mistakes, although I certainly seem to have started out on the same path."

"Amy, listen, I swear I didn't know about the baby. No one told me a damn thing." He took a deep breath. "As for you being like your mom…this is different. I love you. I want us to get married. I wanted it even before I knew about the baby." It hurt to think Amy had held back, not telling him she was pregnant. "Who else knows?"

"Jenny."

"You'd tell your best friend before you'd tell me?" he said, hardly able to believe his ears.

"Why'd you ask me to marry you?" she returned, equally insistent. "Is it just because of the baby?"

"No… I already told you that. Isn't loving you and wanting to spend the rest of my life with you reason enough?"

"Yes," she whispered, whimpering now. "It's more than enough."

"Listen, Amy. I want to be with you. And I want my baby. We're getting married, understand? Soon, too, next week if it can be arranged, and when I go back to Maine, I'm going to ask for married housing. Next month I'll come down and get you."

"Len…"

That was the reason she'd asked if she was just "his

girl in Rawhide." He hated the thought of her worrying and fretting all these weeks, wondering how he'd react once he learned the truth.

"You said you love me. Are you taking that back now?" he asked.

"No…"

"I love you. I knew it after my last visit home. I should have said something then. I regret now that I didn't." Then, remembering how he didn't enjoy having his life dictated to him, he asked again, "Will you marry me, Amy?"

Her hesitation was only momentary this time. "Yes, Len, oh, yes."

He could hear her sob softly in the background.

"I knew tonight would be special," she murmured.

"How's that?" Len's mind continued to spin with Amy's news, but it wasn't unwelcome. He was ready to be a husband and had always loved children. His own parents had been wonderful and he was determined to be a good husband and father himself.

"Mr. Danbar came out of his room tonight when I sat down at the piano," Amy told him.

Len could only vaguely recall the man's name. "Mr. Danbar?"

"He's the one who hasn't spoken a word since his wife died three years ago. The man I eat my lunch with every day. I'm the one who does all the talking, but that's all right."

"He came out of his room?" This was big news, Len realized. He remembered now that Amy had written to him about the older gentleman.

"His wife used to play the piano and when he heard the music, he climbed out of bed and came into the recreation room. He sat down on the bench beside me and smiled. Oh, Len, it was the most amazing thing."

His wife-to-be was pretty darn amazing herself, he thought proudly. She could coax a lonely old man from his room and brighten his life with her music and kindness. Len meant what he'd said, about their marrying as soon as possible. Their marriage would be a strong one, based on love and mutual respect.

He felt like the luckiest man alive.

"Are you awake?" Nick whispered to Kelly in the dead of night. He thought he'd heard her stir and realized they were both accustomed to Brittany waking and needing to be fed around this time.

Nick had been wide-awake for the better part of an hour. Sleeping upright with his head propped against the wall had been awkward, but he'd managed to get some rest. It helped to have his arm around Kelly and hold her close to his side. They hadn't held each other nearly enough lately, but that was something he hoped to remedy.

In response to his question, Kelly yawned. "What time is it?"

"About two."

"Already?" His wife smothered a second yawn. "How's Brittany?"

"Better than either of us."

Nick grinned into the darkness and gently squeezed her shoulder.

"I never thought we'd spend our first Christmas as parents stuck in some train depot," Kelly said, her words barely audible.

"Me, neither."

"It hasn't been so bad."

Nick pressed his face into her hair and inhaled, delighting in her warm female scent. He loved Kelly and Brittany more than he'd thought it was possible to love anyone. More than it seemed reasonable for any human heart to love. Little in his life had come easy, and this parenting business might well be his greatest challenge yet. But his struggles had taught him to appreciate what he did have. Tonight, Christmas Eve, had taught him to *recognize* what he had.

He'd considered the trip home to Georgia unnecessary, but Kelly had wanted to introduce Brittany to her grandparents. Besides, traveling in winter was a mistake, he'd told her over and over. In the end he'd agreed only because Kelly had wanted it so badly. He hadn't been gracious about it, and when troubles arose, it was all he could do not to leap up and tell her how right he'd been.

Nick felt differently now. Being with these people on Christmas Eve hadn't been a mistake at all. Nor was taking Brittany to meet her extended family. They needed each other. He'd stood alone most of his life, but he wasn't alone anymore. He had a wife and daughter. Family. And friends.

More friends than he'd realized.

At six o'clock Christmas morning, Clayton Kemper received word that the tracks had been repaired. He hurriedly dressed and rushed down to the train depot, not sure what he'd find. It came as a pleasant surprise to discover everyone waking up in a good mood, grateful to hear his news. While the travelers stretched and yawned, Clayton put on a pot of coffee, then dragged out the phone book and called the hotels in town to alert the passengers there that the tracks had been repaired.

"I don't imagine this will be a Christmas you'll soon forget," Clayton said as he led the small band from the depot to the train. The engine hummed, ready to race down the tracks toward Boston.

Mrs. Norris was the first to board. She smiled as she placed her hand in his. "Thank you again for all your kindness, Mr. Kemper. And Merry Christmas."

"I was glad I could help," he said as she climbed onto the train.

The couple with the baby followed, along with the young navy man who lugged his own bag as well as the infant seat. It never ceased to amaze Clayton that one baby could need this much equipment. Time was, a bottle or two and a few diapers would suffice. These days it took the mother and two full-grown men to cart everything in. Clayton was pleased to see that the couple had struck up a friendship with the sailor. They certainly seemed to have a great deal to talk about.

The sales rep boarded next, after helping an elderly black couple with their luggage. This was the man who'd spent a large portion of the day before scowling and muttering under his breath. Kemper didn't know what had happened to him, but this morning the man grinned from ear to ear and was about as helpful as they come.

"We appreciate everything you did for us, Kemper," he said as he made his way into the train.

Five-year-old Kate bounced onto the first step and told Clayton, "Santa came last night and dropped off a present for me and Charles."

"Did he now?" Clayton asked, catching Elise Jones's eyes.

"Indeed he did," Elise said with a wide smile.

Apparently the adults had arranged something for the

children. Clayton was glad to hear it. He wished he'd been able to do more himself, but he had his own family and plenty of obligations. It was a sad case when the railroad had to put people up in a depot for the night, especially when that night happened to be Christmas Eve.

He waited until everyone was on board before he stepped away from the train. Glancing inside the compartment, he watched fascinated as the group of once-cantankerous travelers cheerfully teased one another. Anyone looking at them would assume they were lifelong friends, even family.

Was it possible, Clayton wondered, that this small band of strangers had discovered the true meaning of Christmas? Learned it in a train depot late on Christmas Eve in the middle of a snowstorm?

The question seemed to answer itself.

* * * * *

Can't get enough of Christmas?

Turn the page for an exclusive extract from
Debbie Macomber's

ON A SNOWY NIGHT

One across. A four-letter word for fragrant flower. Rose, naturally. Noelle McDowell penciled in the answer and moved to the next clue. A prickly feeling crawled up her spine and she raised her head. She disliked the short commuter flights. This one, out of Portland, carried twenty-four passengers. It saved having to rent a vehicle or asking her parents to make the long drive into the big city to pick her up.

The feeling persisted and she glanced over her shoulder. She instantly jerked back and slid down in her seat as far as the constraints of the seat belt allowed. It couldn't be. *No, please,* she muttered, closing her eyes. *Not Thom.* Not after all these years. Not now. But it was, it had to be. No one else would look at her with such complete, unadulterated antagonism. He had some nerve after what he'd done to her.

Long before she was ready, the pilot announced that the plane was preparing to land in Rose. On these flights, no carry-on bags were permitted, and Noelle hadn't taken anything more than her purse on board. Her magazines would normally go in her briefcase, but that didn't fit in the compact space beneath her seat, so the flight attendant had stowed it. She had a *Weight Watchers* magazine and a crossword puzzle book marked *EASY* in large letters across the top. She wasn't going to let Thom see her with either and stuffed them in the outside pocket of her purse, folding one magazine over the other.

Her pulse thundered like crazy. The man who'd broken her heart sat only two rows behind her, looking as sophisticated as if he'd stepped off the pages of *GQ*. He'd always been tall, dark and handsome—like a twenty-first century Cary Grant. Classic features that were just rugged enough to be interesting and very, very masculine. Dark eyes, glossy dark hair. An impeccable sense of style. Surely he was married. But finding out would mean asking her sister or one of her friends who still lived in Rose. Coward that she was, Noelle didn't want to know. Okay, she did, but not if it meant having to ask.

The plane touched down and Noelle braced herself against the jolt of the wheels bouncing on tarmac. As soon as they'd coasted to a stop, the Unfasten Seat Belt sign went off, and the people around her instantly leaped to their feet. Noelle took her time. Her hair was a fright. Up at three that morning to catch the 6:00 a.m. out of Dallas/Ft. Worth, she'd run a brush through the dark tangles, forgoing the usual routine of fussing with mousse. As a result, large ringlets fell like bedsprings about her face. Normally, her hair was shaped and controlled and coerced into gentle waves. But today she had the misfortune of looking like Shirley Temple in one of her 1930s movies—and in front of Thom Sutton, no less.

When it was her turn to leave her seat, she stood, looking staunchly ahead. If luck was with her, she could slip away unnoticed and pretend she hadn't seen him. Luck, however, was on vacation and the instant she stepped into the aisle, the handle of her purse caught on the seat arm. Both magazines popped out of the outside pocket and flew into the air, only to be caught by none other than Thom Sutton. The crossword puzzle magazine tumbled to the floor and he was left holding the *Weight Watchers* December issue. As his gaze slid over her, she immediately sucked in her stomach.

"I read it for the fiction," she announced, then added, "Don't I know you?" She tried to sound indifferent—and to look thin. "It's Tim, isn't it?" she asked, frowning as though she couldn't quite place him.

"Thom," he corrected. "Good to see you again, Nadine."

"Noelle," she said bitterly.

He glared at her until someone from the back of the line called, "Would you two mind having your reunion when you get off the plane?"

"Sorry," Thom said over his shoulder.

"I barely know this man." Noelle wanted her fellow passengers to hear the truth. "I once thought I did, but I was wrong," she explained, walking backward toward the exit.

"Whatever," the guy behind them said loudly.

"You're a fine one to talk," Thom said. His eyes were as dark and cold as those of the snowman they'd built in Lions' Park their senior year of high school—like glittering chips of coal.

"You have your nerve," she muttered, whirling around just in time to avoid crashing into the open cockpit. She smiled sweetly at the pilot. "Thank you for a most pleasant flight."

He returned the smile. "I hope you'll fly with us again."

"I will."

"Good to see you, Thom," the pilot said next.

Placing her hand on the railing of the steep stairs that led to the ground, Noelle did her best to keep her head high, her shoulders square—and her eyes front. The last thing she wanted to do was trip and make an even worse fool of herself by falling flat on her face.

She was shocked by a blast of cold air. After living in Texas for the last ten years, she'd forgotten how cold it could get in the Pacific Northwest. Her thin cashmere wrap was completely inadequate.

"One would think you'd know better than to wear a sweater here in December," Thom said, coming down the steps directly behind her.

"I forgot."

"If you came home more often, you'd have remembered."

"You keep track of my visits?" She scowled at him. A thick strand of curly hair slapped her in the face and she tossed it back with a jerk of her head. Unfortunately she nearly put out her neck in the process.

"No, I don't keep track of your visits. Frankly, I couldn't care less."

"That's fine by me." Having the last word was important, no matter how inane it was.

The luggage cart came around and she grabbed her briefcase from the top and made for the interior of the small airport. Her flight had landed early, which meant that her parents probably hadn't arrived yet. At least her luck was consistent—all bad. One thing was certain: the instant Thom caught sight of her mother and father, he'd make himself scarce.

He removed his own briefcase and started into the terminal less than two feet behind her. Because of his long legs, he quickly outdistanced her. Refusing to let him pass her, Noelle hurried ahead, practically trotting.

"Don't you think you're being a little silly?" he asked.

"About what?" She blinked, hoping to convey a look of innocence.

"Never mind." He smiled, which infuriated her further.

"No, I'm serious," she insisted. "What do you mean?"

He simply shook his head and turned toward the baggage claim area. They were the first passengers to get there. Noelle stood on one side of the conveyor belt and Thom on the other. He ignored her and she tried to pretend he'd never been born.

That proved to be impossible because ten years ago Thom Sutton had ripped her heart right out.

For most of their senior year of high school, Thom and Noelle had been in love; they'd also managed to hide that fact from their parents. Sneaking out of her room at night, meeting him after school and passing notes to each other had worked quite effectively.

Then they'd argued about their mothers and the ongoing feud between Sarah and Mary. They'd soon made up, however, realizing that what really mattered was their love. Because they were both eighteen and legally entitled to marry without parental consent, they'd decided to elope. It'd been Thom's suggestion. According to him, it was the only way they could get married, since the parents on both sides would oppose their wishes and try to put obstacles in their path. But once they were married, he said, they could bring their families together.

Noelle felt mortified now to remember how much she'd trusted Thom. But their whole "engagement" had turned out to be a ploy to humiliate and embarrass her. It seemed Thom was his mother's son, after all.

She'd been proud of her love for Thom, and before she left to meet him that fateful evening, she'd boldly announced her intentions to her family. Her stomach twisted at the memory. Her parents were shocked as well as appalled; she and Thom had kept their secret well. Her mother had burst into tears, her father had shouted and her two younger sisters had wailed in protest. Undeterred, Noelle had marched out the door, suitcase in hand, to meet the man she loved. The man she'd defied her family to marry. Except that he didn't show up.

At first she'd assumed it was a misunderstanding—that

she'd mistaken the agreed-upon time. Then, throwing caution to the wind, she'd phoned his house and asked to speak to him, only to learn that Thom had gone bowling.

He'd gone *bowling?* Apparently some friends from school had phoned and off he'd gone, leaving her to wait in doubt and misery. The parking lot at the bowling alley confirmed his father's words. There was Thom's car—and inside the Bowlerama was Thom, carousing with his friends. Noelle had peered through the window and seen the waitress sitting on his lap and the other guys gathered around, joking and teasing. Before she went home, Noelle had placed a nasty note on his windshield, in which she described him as a scum-of-the-earth bastard. Their supposed elopement, their so-called love had all been a fraud, a cruel joke. She figured it was revenge for what her mother had done, losing Thom's grandmother's precious tea service. Not *losing* it, actually. She'd borrowed it to display at an open house for another real estate agent—and someone had taken it. That was how the feud started and it had escalated steadily after that.

To make matters worse, she'd had to return home in humiliation and admit that Thom had stood her up. Like the heroine of an old-fashioned melodrama, she'd been jilted, abandoned and forsaken.

For days she'd moped around the house, weeping and miserable. Thom hadn't phoned or contacted her again. It was difficult to believe he could be so heartless, but she had all the evidence she needed. She hadn't seen or talked to him since. For ten years she'd avoided returning to the scene of her shame.

The grinding sound of the conveyor belt gearing up broke Noelle from her reverie. Luggage started to roll out from the black hole behind the rubber curtain. Thom stepped forward, in a hurry to claim his suitcase and leave, or so it seemed.

Noelle was no less eager to escape. She'd rather wait in the damp cold outside the terminal than stand five feet across from Thomas Sutton.

The very attractive Thomas Sutton. Even better-looking than he'd been ten years ago. Life just wasn't fair.

"I would've thought your wife would be here to pick you up," she said without looking at him. She shouldn't have spoken at all, but suddenly she had to know.

"Is that your unsubtle way of asking if I'm married?"

She ground her teeth. "Stood up any other girls in the last ten years?" she asked.

His eyes narrowed. "Don't do it, Noelle."

"You're the one who shouldn't have done it."

The man from the back of the plane waltzed past Noelle and reached for his suitcase. "Why don't you two just kiss and make up," he suggested, winking at Thom.

"I don't think so," Noelle said, sending Thom a contemptuous glare. She was astonished to see his anger, as though *he* had something to be angry about. *She* was the injured party here.

"On that I'll agree with you," Thom said. He caught hold of a suitcase and yanked it off the belt with enough force to topple a second suitcase. Without another word, he turned and walked out the door.

No sooner had he disappeared than the glass doors opened and in walked Noelle's parents.

At Christmas miracles do happen...

It's a month before Christmas and Jenna Campbell
is flying to Alaska to marry a man she met on the
internet—until her seatmate takes it upon himself
to change her plans. Which is how Jenna ends up
stranded in tiny Snowbound, Alaska, alone with
Reid Jamison (plus a bunch of eccentric old men
and a few grizzly bears). And then there's a
blizzard... Maybe she'll be a Christmas
bride after all!

Take a trip to
Cedar Cove

Make time for friends. Make time for

DEBBIE MACOMBER

Taking a chance on love would be worth the risk...

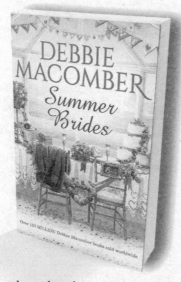

Chase Goodman has three weeks to find a bride, so he takes out an advert: Bride Wanted. Except when Chase ends up rescuing Lesley Campbell, he unexpectedly falls head over heels. Too bad Lesley is the only woman he's met who isn't looking for a husband...

Over 150 MILLION Debbie Macomber books sold worldwide